GUARDIANS OF TRUTH

Michelle Janene

STRONG TOWER
PRESS

Sacramento, CA

Strong Tower Press
PO Box 293632
Sacramento, CA 95829
http://strongtowerpress.com

Publishers Note: This is a work of fiction.
Names, characters, places, and incidents are either
products of the author's imagination or used factiously.
All characters are fictional, and any
Similarity to any person living or dead is entirely coincidental.

Cover Art by: Whetstone Designs
Editing by: Susan S. Sage
Images: Key - gilc Image ID : 34427385, 123RF Stock Photo
Swirl - seamartini Image ID : 11497604, 123RF Stock Photo
City - Jordan Rowland, Unsplash
Castle - vkovalcik, Image ID:12037604 Cardiff Castle, Depoit Photos
Backcover - leolintang, image ID: 125596342, Deposit Photo
ISBN: 978-1-942320-23-4

To Almighty God,
For the gift of stories.

To my Jon and Sharon Murray,
Whose unconditional love and support overwhelm me daily.

To Lori, Mary, and Pete,,
Writing tribe, who share our love for God, words, and laughter.
You inspire me.

And a special thank you to Susan
A writing sister who makes my words sensical, puts the
commas where they belong
And polishes my prose.
I couldn't do this with out you.

To Almighty God,
For the gift of stories.

To my Jon and Sharon Murray,
Whose unconditional love and support overwhelm me daily.

To Lori, Mary, and Pete,,
Writing tribe, who share our love for God, words, and laughter.
You inspire me.

And a special thank you to Susan
A writing sister who makes my words sensical, puts the
commas where they belong
And polishes my prose.
I couldn't do this with out you.

Chapter 1

Detective Drew Merritt sat in his unmarked, silver police sedan, staring across the street at his suspect's apartment building. His hands clenched the steering wheel and nearly wringing the leather from it. He imagined it was Alex Wright's neck in his grasp. No matter the cost, he would find out what she had done to his brother.

Six months. Didn't seem possible his irresponsible little brother had been missing that long. But Drew couldn't deny the truth. He slammed his fist against the wheel. As far as anyone could determine, Miss Wright had been the last person to see him.

His police radio alerted him to a burglary across town. Not near his location. Not his department. Not his problem. He whirled the knob silencing the radio and crumpled up the scrap of paper his partner had left on the seat. He hated when Andersen rode with him. Without his wife nearby, the man couldn't be called anything other than a slob.

His gaze returned to the fourth floor. A shadow passed by the window of the corner apartment. Drew smashed his fist down on the wheel again. The throbbing in the side of his palm didn't distract from his anger. He snatched his electronic tablet, rested his elbow on the door, and held the device so he could still keep an eye on the stairs in front of her building. Glancing at the screen, he saw it—a file marked: Merritt, Brendon. He'd pulled several strings to get access to it without the captain knowing. As a relative of the missing person, he wasn't authorized to investigate the case, but that didn't stop him from looking at the evidence they'd collected. He tapped the file open.

No new credit charges. When was the last time B went even a day without charging something? The man tore through money faster than he earned it. No activity in his meager bank account either. Drew slammed his fist on the steering wheel, his vocabulary laced with curses. "Where are you, B?"

A petite woman with long dark hair stepped from the apartment building and strolled down the steps. Alex. She didn't glance around. Her steps were steady and unhurried. "The broad acts like she doesn't have a care in the world." He hit the steering wheel another time as she headed east up Hampton Street past another slightly taller apartment building and then several single-story businesses.

Drew shoved his tablet under the seat while he watched her disappear around a corner a couple of blocks away. He stretched as he rose from the sedan, rolled his neck and shoulders, and smoothed his creased slacks. He missed his pickup. The new captain had said it was impractical for a detective. It wasn't like he transported perps in his vehicle, thus he resented giving up his ride.

Shaking off the irritation, he buttoned his suit jacket once; had it grown looser since B vanished? Drew now spent a lot of time in the precinct gym working off his frustrations. He and B usually had burgers and beers a couple nights a week. A quick glance at the two lanes separating him from his target didn't reveal too many city dwellers milling nearby who paid any attention to him. The traffic was light since the workday had already begun. As he jaywalked across and bounded up the steps, Drew unclipped his badge from his belt and dropped it into his slacks pocket. Ignoring the elevator, he climbed the deserted stairs two at a time to the top floor.

Drew waited and listened at the fourth-floor door to make sure no one was in the hall. Slipping out of the stairwell, he crossed to the second door on the left, 408, and pulled a bump key from his back pocket. He was in her apartment in less than fifteen seconds. He closed and locked the door behind him. "Okay, Miss Wright, what are you hiding?" His voice reverberated in the sparsely-furnished space.

His phone whistled in his pocket.

Andersen texted. "Where are you?"

He silenced the chime and shoved the device back in his slanks. Andersen's unspoken warning called out in his imagination. Drew could almost hear him reminding him of the lack of a warrant. Andersen would also tell him to get out of there before he got caught, and he couldn't use anything he found anyway." Drew knew all that, but he didn't care.

The living room was unremarkable with nothing more than a small TV, couch, coffee table, and chair. The exterior wall next to the door held a floor to ceiling bookshelf crammed with books. Drew scanned them. One full section held nothing but history books. Seemed like they covered many time periods in human existence. The rest were a hodge-podge of humanities, cultures, weapons, personal defense manuals, and other topics. "Wouldn't have taken her for the intellectual type. No Danielle Steele, or John Gresham for this girl." He noted a well-used Bible on a side table. "Wouldn't have figured her for a religious zealot either."

He moved to the narrow kitchen. His phone vibrated. Sure it was Andersen again, he ignored it.

On the counter sat the largest container of protein powder he had ever seen. He opened it and shook it a little to see if she had hidden anything inside. Just powder. One drawer was overflowing with protein bars and another with nuts of every kind. The freezer was packed with fish, beef, pork, chicken and several ice packs. The fridge held a mind-boggling array of cheeses, a gallon of soymilk, a few Greek yogurts, leftovers of some bean dish, a couple packages of turkey bacon and four-dozen eggs. "What kind of weird diet is this chick on? No sweets, no chips, nothing fun or bad for you—not even a drop of chocolate, everything in here is protein heavy."

He moved through the open door into her bedroom. A strange mix of menthol cream and baby powder assaulted his nose. He sneezed once. Two of the walls were floor to ceiling shelves filled with books too. Still no fiction and heavy on the history. Her bed was made. "Wonder how many times Brendon took a tumble in those sheets?" Drew tossed the thought aside with frustration. There was no evidence his brother had ever come here—that was what he was looking for now. Proof she knew him as more than a student.

He picked through her drawers, and closet—ordinary clothes— nothing to implicate her. Another Bible and a journal were on the bedside table. He snatched up the journal and sat on the side of the bed. He flipped to the entry for January thirteenth—the day his brother was last seen. There was nothing written.

He scanned back a few entries.

12-20 *He's becoming insistent about going. The Conclave hasn't responded to my query yet. I don't know what to do. It has happened before, but not usually of an A.J.*

12-30 *I had the dream he's been telling me about last night. Don't know if it's because of how many times I've heard it or it was from You. Lord, is this the right thing to do? Do You want him to go?*

He scanned to the first entry after Brendon disappeared.

1-16 *Lord, bless his decision. Give him peace and joy and fill him with Your presence as he carries You in this new life.*

New life? Did she mean Brendon?

1-17 *Give him peace and happiness in his choice. Help him to rely on You always.*

Well, if this was about his brother, he didn't sound dead. So where was he? And Brendon had never been much of a religious guy. He liked his women and drink too much. He would never be one to buckle down to the restrictive life of a Bible thumper. Maybe this wasn't about Brendon after all.

Bzzzz. The annoying phone again. He pulled it out.

"Where are you?"

"You better NOT be doing anything on your bro's case or Captain Cruz will have your hide this time. Text me. Now! We caught a case—dead body."

Drew replied with a groan his partner would never hear. "Text address. On my way."

He stuffed the phone back in his pocket and skimmed through the rest of the journal.

2-2 Oh Lord, he's so mad. He hates me. He can't possibly understand—and even if I could tell him, he would never believe it. Lord, comfort him.

2-28 He wants to charge me with murder. How did this get so messed up, Lord?

4-12 Lord, I'm tired. I can't fight anymore. Isn't there another way? Something else You can call me to do?

A large gap of days went by with no entries between her pleas for help.

5-18 I'm still here, Lord. Wrung out, used up, weary beyond what I can bear. He hates me. I see it in his eyes. He wants me dead because he believes I'm a killer. Lord, You promised You would never leave me to do Your work alone—but this is too much. If I can't quit, will You take me home?

The page was crinkled like water droplets had splashed on it and then dried. Tears? She sounded like she wanted to die.

Bzzzz. He glanced at his phone. The address. Close by, he had time to peek in the other two rooms.

The investigation so far revealed she only worked out of her studio part-time. How did she manage to pay for a three-bedroom apartment on the upper side?

A glance in the bathroom revealed an overflowing hamper—the only disorder in an otherwise organized living space. A piece of paper with fancy script was taped to the mirror: with words from a Bible verse his mother use to have on her mirror—Be still and know that I am God. Ps 46:10—Mother's sink counters were nowhere near this neat. Alex's medicine cabinet only held some industrial strength ibuprofen and muscle ointments, which could account for the menthol smell.

He pushed open the door to the next room. The entire interior was a walk-in closet. Clothes from every time period and style hung around the edge of the room and on movable racks down the middle. It was like a costume factory.

A glance in the last room revealed accessories. Belts, shoes, hats, with one wall dedicated to weapons. Swords, daggers, bows, arrows and several things he couldn't even identify. "What's this chick into?" She had to be involved in something weird. But for the life of him he couldn't put the evidence together. Defense trainer, martial arts specialist, hand weapons master, history buff, and costumes all equaled… what? Civil War actor? Renaissance fair participant? There was no evidence she took part in any theater troupe.

*B*ᴢᴢᴢᴢ.

"Oh, keep your shorts on, Andersen. I'm coming already."

He slipped out of the apartment and back to his car with more questions than when he'd begun.

Chapter 2

Drew yawned. He stretched listening to the pops he hoped would release the tension of the last several days. Allen City rarely had a murder, and the one they started investigating a few days ago had more suspects than seemed manageable for the handful of trained detectives. Mahoney and his partner Silas were narrowing down the leads tonight. He and Andersen would pick up the trail in the morning.

Tonight, he sat outside Alex Wright's studio. The lights were still on though her last class dismissed thirty minutes ago.

He scanned through the file on his tablet, which he wasn't supposed to have. No living family and no friends. Apartment and the studio owned outright—something nearly unheard of in this town. Modest balance in the bank, and income hovering steadily around $2,000 a month. No huge purchases. No debt. "Where'd you get the dough to pay for all this property?" Drew muttered.

The investigation revealed her phone records showed only calls from clients. None lasting more than a few minutes and few repeated for long periods of time. Only a smattering of calls had been recorded between her and Brendon—again none lasted more than three minutes. A search of her website held only description of the classes she offered. Nothing leading toward any hidden content.

Drew looked up from the screen, as the lights flicked off in the studio. "You live a dull life, Miss Wright. You're almost too squeaky clean." Drew brushed his hand over his head. She made no sense. As a detective, he excelled at putting the pieces together, but not one piece fit with another concerning her. He exhaled a sharp breath.

She exited and locked up before heading down the street in the direction of her apartment. Her steps were slow and heavy. Her hair hung in a loose ponytail with the end dangling over her shoulder.

Drew remembered her anguished pleas in her journal. Maybe she had more cares than he knew—and he figured he was one of them.

Once he couldn't see her anymore, he moved to the door and using the bump key again, let himself into her studio as easily as he had her apartment. He stopped in the foyer. Using a flashlight, he glanced at the posters lining the waiting area. Self-defense classes at all levels. She also offered a few different types of marital arts classes. Odd. Most people only specialized in one form. She didn't have any employees and didn't she share her space with any other trainers. He moved to the list of her prices. Her fees seemed fair if not a little low.

He stopped and glared at the last flyer. Weapons training. That's what had brought B here. Sword fighting.

"You're going to do what?" Drew sat in his brother's run-down place a couple days before B's birthday drinking horrible instant coffee.

Brendon nearly bounced out of his skin. He couldn't sit still for a moment. "I'm taking sword fighting lessons. It's my gift to myself."

"B, you have done some stupid things in your day—but sword fighting lessons has to top the list."

"Shut up, D. You think everything I do is stupid."

"An how will this new-found skill help you land a decent job?"

"I have a job."

"At a gas station. Seriously B, when are you going to stop playing and get a real job—start taking responsibility for your life?"

"I pay my bills and enjoy myself. It's more than I can say for you."

Even now, Drew curled his hands into a fist remembering the urge to pop his brother in the jaw.

Brendon smirked at him. "She's the best sword master west of the Rockies. And it's gonna to be sick. Won't the ladies think I'm something when I whisk in to save the day with my broadsword?" B took a wide stance and swished an imaginary sword through the air at some unseen villain.

Such a child. "Wonder how long before you get arrested for drawing a sword in some bar." Drew's mug clunked on the chipped countertop.

"Where is your sense of adventure?"

"Where is your thought of responsibility?"

Drew focused back on the present and moved from the class flyers into the main room. It was a huge open space with a couple of benches lining one wall and a thick mat covering the floor. The inside wall held racks of wooden practice weapons.

He moved to the wall opposite the entrance. Here the real blades and various lethal weapons hung locked behind thick glass and heavy mesh wire in a metal case anchored to the wall. Inside, swords of every kind dangled on pegs. Why the fascination with these antiquated weapons? His hand ran over the Glock in the holster at his hip. He'd take the ability to a fast and reload quickly any day.

He held the flashlight with his teeth and used his bump key again to gain access into Alex's office. Compared to her home, this was even more sparse. No photos on the desk—come to think of it, he didn't recall any in her apartment either. Who doesn't have any photos? Even he had a few shots of B and him and an old family photo from when mom and dad were alive.

The couple of desk drawers were empty other than a scant array of office supplies. He booted up the computer. "Okay, so what's your password?" No pets. No boyfriends to offer him clues. He rubbed his chin. The screen came right to the desktop with two icons: Appointments and Payments.

Who doesn't password protect at least their business computer? He should have checked her laptop at her apartment. Drew scanned the appointments. Brendon's name appeared on weekly appointments for private lessons from August through early December. The visits increased to twice a week. Then two weeks prior to his disappearance, they were meeting at least three times a week—the sessions scheduled for several hours.

He opened the payments file next and saw Brendon had paid for lessons once a week. The payments never changed. Maybe they weren't really training with the sword all that time. No evidence rose to show they met anywhere outside the studio though. Drew raised his head and glanced out the door to the matted floor of the studio. The streetlights outside the wall of windows bathed the room in dim light. He couldn't imagine them having sex out there in the open. Looking around the small office it didn't seem a likely spot either. So what were they doing?

He opened her web browser and scanned the history. Amazon was the only thing to come up. She'd been looking for books on life in a castle. Drew had found a couple books on that topic at B's place.

"Miss Alex?" a muffled call came from the street with a thump against one of the windows.

Drew's hand twitched, as he clicked off the computer. He shook off the notion of being caught, closed and locked the office door, and hoped this was the break he'd been looking for. Keeping to the shadows, he moved to the front of the studio to see where this led.

"Miss Alex? Where are you?" the voice choked with tears.

Chapter 3

Drew thought better of his location and tried to escape Alex's studio unseen, but in the entry he ran into a teen. The boy clung to his suit jacket. "Miss Alex. I need Miss Alex. Where is she?" Drew frowned. Would he have to pick this kid off the ground? His shaking would surely make him end up there. Hmmm, the trembling, red-rimmed eyes. A junkie coming down hard.

"She your drug dealer?"

"No," the kid cried. "She offered to help get off the stuff. Miss Alex!" His shouts echoed through the small space of the entryway.

Drew cringed. "It's late, kid. She's gone home. Come back in the morning." He tried to pry free and leave.

The kid shook him refusing to let go. "You don't understand. I have to see Miss Alex. I won't make it till morning without her."

What did this kid expect a self-defense trainer and sword master to do for him? This kid might be the key to figuring out what she was really up to. And what happened to B.

Drew freed one hand, pulled out his phone, found her number, and connected the call before handing the phone over.

"Hello?" he asked tentatively. "Miss Alex! Miss Alex is that you? It's Hack. I'm in trouble. I need you bad." Hack released Drew and wobbled back and forth across the narrow entrance raking his filthy fingers through his long stringy hair. "You have to come." Hack seemed to ignore Drew and looked up as if trying to figure out where he was. His head dropped, and he shoved his hand in his pocket, as he started pacing again. "Your place." Silence "No. Work. The dojo." Silence "K."

Hack spun a few times before spotting Drew near the door. "She's coming," he said handing back the phone. "She'll fix it. She has to." The kid went to pacing again—hands alternating from his pockets, to his hair, to biting his nails. He was beyond jittery.

Drew again slipped into the narrow foyer. Alex didn't have a car, and the walk usually took her about twenty minutes. He kept an eye on Hack but pulled back out of sight when Alex came running up in six minutes. He could hear her muffled voice through the windows.

She looked around outside. "Hack? Tyler? You here, Tyler?" She reached for the door and startled when it opened. "Could have sworn I locked that—I'm really losing it," she mumbled, as she pulled it all the way open. "Tyler, you in here?"

"Miss Alex?" The kid sobbed.

She moved into the center of the main room and Drew to a spot he could watch and learn.

Hack, or Tyler, ran to Alex and seized hold of her shirt and shook her.

Great! He was going to have to save the chick. Maybe he'd let the kid get in a couple of blows first. But he wouldn't get any answers from a corpse. Drew moved to another spot where he hoped he wouldn't be seen but could intervene if things went south.

Alex placed her hands gently on either side of Hack's face and pressed her forehead to his. She whispered for a few moments, but Drew couldn't hear what she said.

Hack let her go and crumpled into her arms in a puddle of tears. He gulped air with a loud slurping sound coming from his nose. Drew's stomach heaved. Blood, guts—no problem. Missing limbs, delivering babies—no problem. Snot—he shuddered.

She walked him toward a window and they sat on the floor. She put her arm around him as he continued to ooze all over her shoulder. "Tell me what happened."

Kid was about fifteen or sixteen. Alex was twice his age. Where did these two cross paths?

Through tears and shaking, Hack spilled the details. "She threw me out! My own mother doesn't want me no more." His voice rose, and he hit his fist against his thigh. "Doesn't she know how much I need her? Where am I supposed to go? And she threw my stash away. I'm hurting bad. Don't have no money neither. What kind of mother is she?"

"A smart one," Alex said calmly.

Hack gasped.

Drew raised a brow. *Doesn't pull any punches, does she?* A smirk of admiration lifed the corner of his mouth.

Hack tried to pull from her grasp, but Alex didn't let him wiggle free. "How can you say that? I thought we were friends."

She didn't answer his question. Didn't really even look at him. "I didn't know you hated your brother and sister so much." She said it as though talking to herself.

"I love Emma and Joey!"

"No," she shook her head staring across the dimly lit room, "you can't care anything about them."

Hack raised a fist and tried to twist his arm to grab a handful of her hair, but she held him fast.

"If you truly loved your family, you would never put them in such danger." Her voice was calm, matter-of-fact, and direct.

He liked that about her. Surprise. A harsh frown pulled at Drew's lips, he didn't want to like anything about the woman you had something to do with whatever had happened to B.

"They're not in danger. My dealer doesn't even know where I live."

"But you brought drugs into your home."

Hack didn't say anything.

Now she looked at him. Her gaze was hard and—though not angry

—Drew wouldn't have wanted that look turned on him. "Tyler, do you know what would happen if anyone found those drugs? Emma and Joey could find them and get sick… maybe even die." She allowed the last word to hang between them. "Even if your brother and sister never got their hands on your stash, if the cops found out you had dope in your house, and they believed your mother knew about it—but did nothing, she would lose Emma and Joey. CPS would take them away from her. Do you want them in foster care, Tyler?"

She returned his head to her shoulder and stroked his hair.

Drew shuddered again. The kid was grimy.

"Your mother has tried everything. She moved across town to get you out of that neighborhood and into a different school. She has tried four times to get you help—but you refuse to work with the doctors."

Her eyes closed and her head dropped back against the window. "If you were home right now, what would you be doing?"

Hack twitched in her arm, the streetlight shown off the drops of sweat covering his face. He started rubbing his head with a hand that shook like he had a nervous disorder. But he didn't answer. Withdrawal was hitting him bad.

"You'd be stealing from your mom's purse. Taking the money she needs to buy food and medicine for your family. You'd then be out on the street trying to find someone to sell you a quick high."

"I'm hurting," he groaned, as his hand moved to his stomach.

"I know. You're hurting your brother and sister. They need a role model and someone to keep them safe. What if your mom's next boyfriend has a taste for someone younger than your mother? Who's going to protect your sister? Who's going to walk your brother to school after your mother goes to work at the first of her many jobs each day? You're breaking your mother's heart. You can't see the pain you're causing. Stealing. Running around all hours of the night and day. Skipping school. She blames herself. She did the only thing she had left.

She told you—no more."

Hack made a sound like he was going to throw-up.

"If you have to vomit, do it on the mat. It will be easier for you to clean up."

Drew choked on a chuckle. He had a feeling she'd make the kid clean up his own puke without batting an eye.

"You have to help me. I'm sick."

She pushed him back and held him by the shoulders. "You know my terms, Tyler. You know how I'll help. You ready for that?"

He shook his head, doubling over his arms pressed against his belly. "I can't," he moaned. "I need something. I can't do this."

Her hand rested on his back where he now lay crumpled in a ball—forehead on the mat. "I will never give you drugs, Tyler, and I don't have any cash on me. It's my way or nothing."

After emptying his gut, Tyler spent the next three hours alternating between both dry heaving and resting his head on her thigh and begging her for help. She didn't answer his crying, but rubbed his back and head while her eyes remained closed, and her lips moved.

Was she praying? Drew shook his head—confusion making it hard for his tired brain to think. *The kid's a lost cause. Even his mother knows that.*

Deep in the shadows, Drew did some squats and shook out his legs over the next couple of hours, as Hack experienced violent tremors and groaned in pain. Drew hurt too. Stiff and sore. Surveillance was one thing in a car. He'd never done a whole night standing in a dark entryway. He moved slowly so she wouldn't hear, but every time he rolled his neck, the pops echoed throughout the narrow space. He dared a glance through the opening to the practice mats. The kid's shirt was soaked through with sweat, but Alex hadn't moved. She'd drawn her line in the sand, and she wouldn't relent.

The woman had a will of iron. Even he would have called the ambulance for the kid by now.

Chapter 4

Thankfully, the outer door wasn't in the line of sight from the opening into the studio. Drew slipped outside, twisted, then swung his arms through the air to release some of the stiffness. His legs burned, and his feet were on fire. He'd stood for hours watching Alex hold Hack, as he suffered through the beginnings of withdrawal. He held his watch to the light. Two in the morning. The kid had finally relented and agreed to her terms—whatever they were.

Drew walked to his car shaking out his aching legs. He'd missed a night's sleep for a lead on what Alex had done to his brother. Instead, he learned about Alex's deep, stubborn, uncompromising desire to help some junkie kid for no apparent reason other than it was the right thing to do. He used both hands rake over his crew cut.

He reached for his car door, as Alex helped walk Hack out of her business. The kid could barely put one foot in front of the other. One arm draped over her shoulders. She held onto his wrist locking his arm around her. Her other arm hugged tight at his waist. By the hitch in Hack's jeans, she must have had her thumb looped in his belt.

"I can't," Hack whined.

"If you can't walk four blocks to the clinic, then you aren't strong enough to get well. Well for you or your family."

Drew paused for a moment. Should he offer to give the kid a lift?

Alex pushed the kid up against the last window of her shop. Holding him upright with a hand planted in the middle of his chest, she used the other to slap his face. Not hard but enough to get his attention. "Tyler, do you want this? Do you want to be free of what this poison is doing to your body, your life, and your family?"

He gave her a single nod.

She slapped him again. The light sound echoed in the quiet street. "Say it! Tell me so I believe you. Are you done with drugs?"

Hack threw back his head with a *thunk* on the window. "What does it matter? I've messed up everything already anyway."

She slapped him again, as a gust of air exploded from her. "Lord, give me patience and give it to me now!" She straightened, trying to square her shoulders—but she didn't manage to stand straight. "Tyler, who fixed my computer when it crashed and I thought I lost all my records?"

"Me," he moaned.

"Who helped your mom create and set up her website to sell her jewelry online so she could quit one of her jobs to be home more with you and your brother and sister?"

"Me."

"Who will give you a job when you're clean?"

He lifted his head and looked at her this time. "You?"

"Of course. And who will help you get back on track at school?"

"You," he managed with a little more confidence.

"Batting a thousand so far, Tyler. Now, who will welcome you home with a rib crushing hug and all the love you can stomach once you have proven you're clean and want to stay that way?"

"Do you really think Mom—"

She slapped him again. "Tyler, I'm too tired for this bull."

He nodded.

"Now, tell me you want to be clean and sober."

"I wanna be clean and sober."

She raised a hand again but didn't let it fly. "I don't believe you."

Drew still stood on the far side of the street leaning against his car, arms crossed. The streetlight over his head was out so he didn't think she could see him. Bitterness bit the back of his tongue, and he stifled a growl. He hated how much he was beginning to admire this woman.

"I wanna be clean and sober." The words came out with a little more vibrato.

Alex shook her head. "Again. Convince me."

"I wanna be clean and sober."

"Again."

"I wanna be clean and sober!" Hack shouted.

Alex again slipped his arm over her shoulders and put her arm around his waist. "Then let's get you to those who can help. And know this, Tyler James Sims. I don't take kindly to being lied to."

A shiver skipped over Drew's shoulders.

The two disappeared down a cross street. Drew turned to his car, pulled the door open, and stared inside, indecision immobilizing him. Nearly 3:00 a.m. now. He yawned. He had lots to do in the morning, but the woman he desperately needed answers from was walking some drugged out kid through the streets—alone. She's a self-defense trainer; surely she can take care of herself. But what if… he cursed, slammed the door, and ran to follow the pair.

With the kid in such a condition, what should have taken them fifteen minutes took them nearly an hour before they came to the clinic on West Chester. From the shadows at the corner, Drew watched Alex prop Hack up and ring the bell. A man in white scrubs poked out the door, Alex said something, and he retreated without letting them in.

Drew stood on the sidewalk at a distance from the porch as the door opened again a couple of minutes later.

"Alex?" said a woman with short blond hair wearing a doctor's white coat.

"Hello, Dr. Wisse." Alex turned to Hack, "Tell her what you told me."

"I wanna be clean and sober," the kid was shaking badly again. "But I can't pay to be treated in this place." His chin bounced as he stared at his ratty shoes.

The doctor waved her hand and the man who'd come to the door first reappeared. "Please assist him inside." She again looked at Tyler. "Don't you worry about that now, young man. The clinic has an arrangement with Miss Wright. Your expenses are covered."

"I'll be checking up on you, Tyler," Alex called, as he disappeared inside.

"We'll take good care of him, Alex."

"Thank you, Jennifer." The door closed, and Alex walked down the stairs. She crossed the street and started toward home, but her steps slowed. The tips of her toes dragged as she moved each foot forward.

Drew followed half a block behind. Buttoning up his jacket, he noted she only wore a long-sleeved cotton shirt and bottoms. PJ's maybe.

Her hand went to the wall, probably using it for support, and her head drooped. She disappeared into an alley. When Drew caught up, all he saw was her silhouette leaning back against the wall, her face buried in her hands. Was she sobbing?

"Well, look who we have here, boys."

Chapter 5

Drew unbuttoned his jacket, released the snap on his holster, and gripped his Glock. Three large men ambled into the opposite end of the alley, and Alex turned to face them. She pushed off the wall and took a wide stance—though she swayed a little.

"Hound."

"That's Bloodhound, chicka. What'cha doin' in our casa? Come to join d' dog pile?" he chuckled. The tat-covered gang-bangers each sported a spiked dog collar and forearm guards.

The hairs rose on the back of Drew's neck as he held his gun tighter. Police reports buzzed in his head. Bloodhound and his pack had been rousted earlier. Weapons charges. Must have just been released from lockup. They *shouldn't* have any guns at the moment. Drew stayed in the shadows behind her.

"Came to deliver a message. Hack's off limits." Her voice was strong —unwavering as she faced three-to-one odds.

The woman's got guts, gotta give her that.

Her shoulders square. All evidence of tears and weakness gone.

Bloodhound laughed. "Hack's bueno. Few more hits, he'll be licking my boots."

"You or your pack comes within a hundred feet of him, or gives him another gram of poison, and you'll be answering to me."

No, not guts. Alex Wright has a death wish. Drew inched closer.

The two junior gang members stepped forward flicking open blades. Before Drew could step in, Alex spun from the blade of the closest one, passed him, and elbowed him in the back hard enough to knock him forward. Using his back as a platform, she leapt up and rolled over him bringing her feet down on the next guy. Her foot connected with his jaw, spinning him around, planting him face first into the dumpster with a resounding *bang*.

Drew cringed. *That's going to leave a mark*. Alex was a capable street fighter.

She spun back to the first guy, ducked a knife swipe, dodged one way, but the second time she took a fist to the jaw. It never slowed her as she switched to martial arts and roundhouse kicked him. The guy stumbled back and dropped his knife. She followed up with a dizzying array of kicks and hand chops until he fell. With the guy face down on the ground, she drove her foot in his back and twisted his arm behind him until it popped—either broken or dislocated.

She snatched up the lost blade and flung it at Bloodhound. It lodged in his hand disarming him of the gun he had been pointing at her. A quick pop of her foot, and the second guy, who was no at her feet, laid as unconscious as his friend. Alex moved to the leader who was still trying to draw the knife out of his hand.

She kicked between his legs, and he dropped to his knees, then she grabbed his throat and moved in close. Her one-handed hold didn't seem tight but with her fingers sunk deep around his windpipe, Bloodhound didn't move. "Now that the pups are asleep, let me make myself clear without all your posturing. You know who I am. You know what I can do. The Sickles—gone. El Norte—gone. Dragons—scattered. You and your pack is now on my radar—and you don't want that. Here's my deal. Hack's off limits. A hair on his head pulled, a threat or pain inflicted on him or any of his family or friends, a single gram of drugs found in his system, and *you* are mine."

Even in the dimly lit alley, Drew could see Bloodhound had no color in his face. His lips were turning blue. Whatever she was doing to him, he couldn't breathe.

"You get the word out. I don't care who does it. You'll pay the price. Do you understand me? Blink once for yes."

He must have blinked, because Alex tipped him back and released her hold. Bloodhound curled on his side coughing and gasping for air. Alex never looked back, as she walked from the alley. Passing the dumpster where Drew crouched, she didn't slow. "Thanks for the help, detective."

Drew stood, glanced at the fallen gang members, snapped his holster again, and followed. But how long did she know he was there?

Out on the sidewalk, Alex again braced herself on the building, as she struggled to put one foot in front of the other. She was a contradiction.

"It looked like you had everything under control," he said coming even with her.

"You can hunt me, investigate me, follow me all hours of the day and night, stalk me in my studio for hours, until your hair falls out and your teeth rot, but it won't get you any closer to your brother."

"What did you do to him?"

She stumbled. He caught her by the arm trying to steady her. Her whole body convulsed in a tremor. She pulled free of him only to fall back against the wall. "I didn't *DO* anything to him. I taught him sword craft. Nothing more. I did not date him, sleep with him, kidnap him, or murder him." With her back still braced, she put up both hands in surrender. "I can't do this anymore, detective. Shoot me now if you believe me capable of such horrible sins, and be done with it."

"I don't want you dead. I want answers. And I believe you have them."

Her hands dropped at her sides, and her head sagged back bumping the wall. "Nothing I can tell you will help."

"You're exhausted. Here, let me..." He moved closer intending to pick her up to carry her back to his car.

She planted her hands hard on his chest and pushed with more strength than he thought she possessed at the moment. "Let me be, detective." Her ice-blue eyes almost white in the growing light of dawn sent an eerie quiver through his belly. "We don't trust each other enough. I'll make it home on my own."

Drew pulled back and crossed his arms, "Stubborn, pig-headed—"

"Through and through," she offered him a weak smile, pushed off the wall, and trudged toward home.

Chapter 6

Two hours later, Alex finally made it back to her apartment. All the way home she sensed Detective Drew. He must like lurkin in the shadows and skulking in the dark corners because she never saw him. Only felt his presence. Did he intend to rescue her or hope to learn something new about her involvement with his brother? It didn't matter. She'd never see Brendon Merritt again. He'd made his choice, and the detective would never believe her if she tried to explain.

Alex dragged her feet to her couch and dropped face first onto it. *I don't think I've really slept in weeks?*

With Detective Drew screaming at her and waving his gun, Alex jerked awake so fast she fell off the couch. Her thigh banged on the corner of the chest she used as a coffee table and she smacked her elbow hard on the wood floor. *Typical. Why couldn't I have slipped cleanly between the two pieces of furniture and landed on the deep pile area rug? Since conceding to assist Brendon, my life has jumped its rails.*

Alex lay on her stomach on the cold floor and rested her head on the back of her hand. After a time, she pressed her fingers into her temple, as her breaths came in hitched gasps. Chill wrapped her like a blanket left on the line in a freezing rain. Her head spun. It hurt to think. "Lord, where is Your peace?" Tears burned her throat.

Turning her head, she noted the light pouring in at the edge of the blinds over the windows. Turning the other way, the clock near the TV read 10:18. Summoning her last ounce of strength, she stumbled to the kitchen, snagged a protein bar from the drawer, and munched it on the way to the bathroom.

Passing her room she noted the purple light flashing on the other modem—the one the Conclave used to give her assignments. "I don't care who's in trouble or needs my help today. Find someone else," her words barely distinguishable as she mumbled. But she knew she would have to deal with it soon. There were so few guradians now. There would be no one else to take care of it but her.

She peeled off her clothes and dropped them on the floor in a heap, as the protein started to kick in. She stood with her hands braced against the wall under the showerhead letting the hot water cascade over her head and down her body. Alex welcomed the torrent as it beat on her for a long time before she washed and stepped from the shower. Wrapped in a towel, she moved into her bedroom and slipped into her favorite baggy cotton pants and oversized long sleeve plum shirt. She tossed the wet towel on the dirty clothes pile.

"Later," she mumbled to the laundry left on the floor. The purple light beckoned her to attend to her duty. "Later for you too," she groaned and crawled into bed She'd take care of the soaked pillow when she woke later.

Alex tossed and turned, catching an hour of sleep here and there. Mostly, she lay curled in the fetal position and fought back tears. Head covered to keep out the light, she prayed this world—and all the others —would go away and leave her alone.

In the late afternoon, she ambled to the kitchen and made two pieces of bacon alone with one over-easy egg. She wasn't hungry, but she had to get her reserves back up if the Conclave was sending her somewhere again. With effort, she forced down each bite. After putting the dishes in the dishwasher, she scooped up the dirty laundry and dropped it all in the hamper in the corner of the bathroom.

The purple indicator continued to blink, and she dropped into the chair at her desk. Alex accessed the Conclave site, entered her lengthy login, and put her ring finger on the print scanner beside the mouse. Three messages popped up.

The first was from the Conclave's Administrator: "Return trip still under consideration. Not looking promising."

Alex sighed. She really didn't expect them to allow it. She couldn't believe they had condoned the transfer in the first place.

The second message was from the deployment officer: Pending: "Zatha, Departure: 14 days. Term: 1 week."

She clicked the decline button. Not that it would do any good, but she would try. She'd only ever refused one assignment. She'd suffered several injuries in a car accident including a broken arm and sprained ankle. She was barely mobile at the time. That was years ago. After the accident, the Conclave had moved her in town, and she never owned a car again. Due to her years of faithful service, she prayed they would give her the break she needed.

The final message came from Conner Justice. One of the few people from the Guardians she had grown up with: "Hey Ally-cat." He was the only one who ever called her that—and she hated it though it brought back sweet memories. "You're never going to believe it. I found myself a girl and the Conclave has approved our marriage. She's a guardian from the Zentith realm. You have to come. Will send all the details when we have a date picked."

Great! He was only guy he had any shot of being with. Now he was marrying someone else. It wasn't fair.

She logged out and slammed the laptop closed almost in the same moment. Knots twisted her stomach, and her head whirled. She moved toward the bathroom—the churn in her middle turned sour. She slid down the wall and rested on her back on the cool tile and lay her arm on her forehead. "Lord, I am trying to honor You in all I do. I attend my assignments with prayer and attention to detail. I care for everyone You have cross my path." Well, maybe with the exception of Detective Merritt—but she was working on that. "I spend time in Your Word and in prayer daily."

Alex whimpered. Sweat covered her face and started to slip back into her hair. *Please no*, she begged. Whether it was exhaustion and stress from the pressure of Detective Merritt's investigation, or the sickness that came with her missions for the Conclave, she hated being sick, but puking was the worst. The wave of nausea passed and she continued her petition before the Lord. "Father, I feel so lost and alone. I know You are always with me and will never leave me. I know You have good plans for my future. But Father, I need someone with skin on them to come along side me and walk this path. I'm tired and weary beyond what I can bare, Lord. Help me."

Her heart flooded with oceans of pain. She curled on her side unable to put words to her grief any longer, as she drowned in the torrent of anguish. The rivers of tears she'd held back for months burst from her all at once pooling on the floor beneath her.

Chapter 7

Her tears spent, Alex managed to make it to the bed from the bathroom floor. Calm stomach. No lingering pain. The tiny meal she'd forced down hadn't made an encore appearance. *Thank You, Lord.* She flopped on the bed and buried herself in a mountain of blankets. Sleep flirted, visiting for only a few hours.

Her fitful slumber was interrupted by nightmares of the detective hunting her. *Lord, help me.* Her body ached, her muscles clenched and relaxed in waves. *Sleep, where are you? I want to lose myself in your dark oblivion.*

Before the sun cleared the horizon, Alex kicked off the covers and sat on the edge of the bed. Would the throbbing in her head ever dull?

Passing her desk, she ignored the purple flashing light on her Conclave modem. She slipped into a simple sundress and ran a brush through her hair. Grabbing her Bible off the side table in the living room she ambled outside and trudged the seven blocks to church.

A silver sedan followed her. Merritt.

Does he think I have his brother stashed away somewhere? Does he think he'll follow me until I lead him to the hideout? Alex laughed out loud—the first such sound to escape her lips in months, though bitter with irony. *If I did have him hidden away somewhere, he'd be dead from starvation or dehydration by now.* She never went anywhere but church, her studio, and home. Where did Detective Merritt think she had stuffed Brendon? She tried to put the intimidating man out of her mind as she entered the sanctuary.

Church soothed her spirit but provided no answers. Scanning the surroundings as she strolled down the steps in the warm sunshine after the service, she spotted the sedan across the street. Though tempted to lead him on a wild goose chase—the nightmares she'd been suffering changed her mind. She didn't need to antagonize the man. She went straight home.

Alex flicked on some praise music. When the melodies didn't serve to distract her, she tried to lose herself in a book. Her heart wasn't in anything. She couldn't grasp more than a few words before her nightmares spilled over into her waking hours too. Food tasted like cotton. Unable to keep her eyes open or her head up, she staggered to bed early.

Detective Merritt now shadowed her early every morning and in the evening as she went to and from work. Didn't he have real crimes he should be investigating or something else to keep him busy? A girlfriend to distract him? Did he know that she knew he was there, or did he think he was being covert?

The third Sunday he followed her to church, she slipped out the back at the end of service and moved down and around the block. She came out of an alley and up to his passenger window and knocked twice. The window *whooshed* down. She bent over and leaned on his door.

Her gaze fixed on him for a moment. He didn't look much like his younger brother although their hair color was the same—like dark chocolate. But while Brendon wore his longer, Detective Merritt cropped his short to his head—military style. His face was round and fuller than his younger brother's narrow lean features. It was the detective's eyes that stole her attention most. In truth, their amber color, almost leaning toward red, made her breath catch in her throat. She had never seen any like them in all her travels. They haunted her dreams with the intense stare they held her with even now.

She swallowed past the tightness lodged in her chest. "You would get more out of the sermon each Sunday if you came inside, detective."

He opened his mouth but said nothing.

"I'll be going home now, without stopping, if you want to just meet me there...?" She moved down the street without glancing back—though she smirked at the surprise that had registered in those unforgettable eyes.

He didn't show up outside her place the rest of the day. Later, she opened the Conclave site—unable to ignore the blinking light any longer.

Two new messages. One from the administrator: Return: `"Approved."`

The second from deployment: Pending: `"Vilnund. Departure: 3 days. Term: 2 days. / Zatha, Departure: rescheduled 18 days. Term: 1 week."`

Alex sat up a little straighter. She scanned her appointments again. She'd only have to reschedule one class—they were pretty flaky with their attendance anyway. She shot her clients an email about the reschedule and walked to her supply closet—one of the two extra bedrooms in her house.

She yanked down a cloth bag with a drawstring. Certain things she would need hid well under the flap. "Please let this work, Lord. Let Detective Merritt get the answers he needs to be at peace with his brother's decision."

Chapter 8

Drew glanced at the calendar on his fridge. June 22. Drew rubbed both hands over his head for a moment before smashing his fists down on his kitchen table. His coffee danced at his violent disruption, and he grabbed for it—hot liquid sloshed out. He cursed, took the once-full cup to the sink and dumped it out. Standing there, braced on the sink, he fought the rage brewing in him like a vile concoction in a witch's caldron.

"Awwww," he howled, spun, and chucked the empty mug.

Bam, bam, bam. A fist pounded on the common wall with the apartment next door. "Keep it down," came the muffled order through the thin divider.

Drew glared at the shattered *I'm the responsible brother* mug. His birthday gift from Brendon. His brother had a mate to it with the words, *I'm the fun brother* painted in matching bold white letters. Brendon's cup was now in a storage cubby in the basement of Drew's apartment with the rest of Brendon's few belongings.

"Today would have been…" Drew swallowed hard and turned back to the sink. "Today *is* Brendon's twenty-fourth birthday."

Drew's pulse hammered in his skull. He hadn't seen Alex Wright in two days; not since she'd caught him trailing her.

He spun on his heel, snatched up his keys and gun—but not his badge—and slammed his front door as he stormed out of his apartment. "She will give me answers today or else."

Drew parked a couple blocks from Alex's apartment so she wouldn't see his car. As he walked toward her place, she came down the front steps. But she didn't head toward her studio. She walked the opposite direction and turned south at the first corner.

She'd never gone this way before. What was she wearing? Drew dashed across the street and quickened his steps to catch up. Laced-up high boots came over her knees, but the flat leather soles made no sound. Dark tights peeked out from them before disappearing under a bulk of teal and brown fabric bunched below shapely hips. Her white baggy blouse fluttered in the breeze. The sleeves were pushed up above slender elbows. Her dark hair lay in a dizzying array of braids that wound together atop her head and fell in one single rope swinging like a pendulum down her back. A cloth bag hung over one shoulder.

Clearly something from the costume room.

She crossed the street and continued east another block.

The street was empty of foot traffic, and many of the stores weren't open yet. Drew increased his speed closing the few feet between them. She moved to the outside edge of the sidewalk. As Drew came within a foot of her, she stepped between the slender metal pole of a parking sign driven into the cement and the side of a mobile newsstand. She had the whole sidewalk to herself, but she walked through this narrow gap. Did she think she could get away from him this way?

He seized her as she stepped through. "Alex Wright you wi—"

His words were stolen as a blast of frigid air hit him. Tears streamed from his eyes, and he couldn't tell if they were open or closed in the blackness. Air churned like a hurricane. He couldn't capture a breath. His lungs burned. While the gale-force winds battered him, another equally powerful force pulled him forward. It felt like he was being torn apart at the cellular level. Through the din a scream battered him. It was a woman, and her shriek of pain dug under his skin and inside his skull. *Alex.*

Chapter 9

In the next heartbeat, Drew stood in the middle of a bathed-sunshine field. He fought to draw breath. It rasped down his throat as Alex slipped from his grasp and dropped to her hands and knees. They both coughed trying to gulp down air, but Drew braced his hands on his knees and fought to stay upright.

Alex chugged air, her body trembling to the point she might collapse further.

"Where... are... we?" He inhaled between each word trying to gain control of his lungs and shake the cold that still left his teeth chattering.

She turned, dropping to her backside and sat looking up at him. All color had drained from her face; her skin sickly white—almost with the pallor of death. He couldn't see her irises, now so pale they merged with the surrounding white—only the large pupils remained. "What have you done?" Her voice was more air than sound.

Her hands shook violently as she pulled open the bag and searched it. Her breathing shallow as she drew out a small bundle wrapped in cloth. Alex flipped back the corners to reveal a protein bar—though it looked homemade. With both hands she brought it to her lips and took a small bite. Her mouth worked slowly. She swallowed with effort. As she ate, the tremors quieted.

His breaths came more easily, and his skin warmed under the sun, though a cool breeze tickled his skin. Drew straightened and assessed his surroundings. They were in the middle of a low depression about a mile wide. Modest, undulating hills surrounded them on all sides. Only a few large oak trees broke up the endless expanse of grass. Curses filled the quiet air. "Where are we? What just happened?" Drew glared at the woman sitting at his feet.

Alex still stared up at him as she ate a second bar. She shook less and a little of her color had returned.

Drew stepped forward, yanked her up, and shook her. Still not caring that his language may be offensive, he yelled at her. "Tell me what's going on!"

While he held one elbow, she took her free hand and popped the heel of her palm against his sternum.

Drew's heart fluttered uncomfortably. He coughed and gasped for a breath as he released her. He stared at her, and she glared back—the rim of her ice-blue irises finally visible. He rubbed his chest where she had struck him. He had the feeling, if she hit him a little harder, she could stop his heart entirely. He knew of cases where people died after being hit in exactly the right spot and at a perfect speed.

"You have no idea what you have done. You... you..." Alex muttered repeatedly. He figured a good church girl like her couldn't say the foul words that seemed to be clamoring at the back of her teeth.

"Where are we? Answer, Wright. Report. This instant!"

"You... You arrogant...Vile...Oh, you Yormorian troll!" She huffed out the last in exasperation. Alex spun away from him, her face now flaming like a pink rose. She snatched up the bag, and pulled out several things dropping them on the ground. Next came out some cloth. She threw it at him. "You want answers? The only way I will say another word, is if you put those on, disarm your weapon, and remove the clip. Put everything in this bag," she held it out to him. "You'll carry it and do everything I tell you—to the letter—without question."

Fisting the rough garments in his hand he stepped directly in front of her, hoping to intimidate her. "I'm not doing a thing until you explain yourself."

She stepped to him in response her forehead almost even with his chin. She was forced to look up at him, but it didn't make her look any less a formidable opponent. "Not another word until you do what I say." She thumped him in the chest with her finger. "You have no idea the dangerous mess you're in, detective. You want to get home—alive?" Thump. "You want answers?" Thump. "Comply!"

Drew reached for his gun, slid the safety off with his thumb, and raised it to her temple.

Alex shifted her weight back, arms crossed, head tilted to the side, and one slender brow arched high. She glared. They stood unblinking in the ultimate stand off.

Chapter 10

Still holding his gun to Alex's head, Drew glanced at his surroundings for a moment. He didn't know where he was or how they had gotten there. He had no idea how to get home or even what lay beyond the hills. He clenched the gun so tight it was a wonder it didn't fire. He worked his jaw to release the tension.

Taking a slow breath, he spoke with carefully enunciated words and his uncompromising cop tone. "You *will* tell me where we are, how we got here, and what you have done with my brother."

She crossed her ankles and plopped down. Like an ancient tree stump petrified into an unchanging form, she sat with her arms crossed and stared at him. He barely heard her breathing, and she rarely blinked.

Drew's pulse drummed in his ears and throbbed against his eyes. Her fight of wills with the junky kid, Hack, came to mind. "You stubborn, obstinate, disagreeable, pain in the——." He swallowed hard and shook until his teeth rattled. She continued to stare unmoving.

His arm lost its strength and dropped to his side. Air leaked from his lungs. "Why won't you tell me—something?"

She indicated the clothes in his other hand with a nod of her head.

He felt nothing but the breeze caressed his searing cheeks. His vision blurred and he closed his eyes. For now, it would be her way or not at all.

Holding the garments under his arm that she'd thrown at him, he released the magazine in his Glock and let it drop into his hand. He cleared the chamber by pulling back the slide. Then he dropped the weapon in the bottom of her now empty bag.

She rose silently to her feet, swayed, and closed her eyes for a moment. Alex turned away as he started to unbutton his dress shirt. She scooped up a leather vest from her pile on the ground, slipped it over her shoulders, and laced up the front.

As Drew pulled the rough homespun shirt over his head he caught a glimpse of her profile. The vest revealed her narrow waist, and accentuated her assets. The blouse under the vest came to her collarbone, keeping her modestly covered—though maybe not authentic if judged by the drunken maidens he'd arrested after too much fun at the annual renaissance fair. They all had more exposed cleavage than what they had covered. He tried to ignore the reaction humming over his skin.

Next, she retrieved a small black net studded with pearls. "Oh thank You, Lord." She picked a capsule from the inside, popped the brown-filled pill in her mouth, and tossed back her head.

"What was that?"

She glanced at him over her shoulder and pointed at the other garment still held in his hands.

With her back facing him, she wound her braid up to the nape of her neck. With ease, she slipped the net over the bundle she'd created and pulled it to the crown of her head. She secured a few pearls into the smaller braids at the back of her head before moving to her skirt.

She undid six or eight yellow ribbons spaced evenly around her waist and the skirt dropped from mid-thigh length to covering her boots. She worked at the ribbons again retying the teal skirt in swoops coming to her calf while revealing the deep brown skirt beneath. The double-layered skirts looked to be made of the same heavy coarse fabric now scraping against his skin, making him itchy and sweaty.

He laced up the pants she'd given him as she belted her blade to hang over her left hip. A flash of metal caught the sun at the small of her back before she turned. She slipped the binding from her sleeves, and they dropped the full length of her arms. The back part of each sleeve continued down to her knees.

"How do you swing a sword with that flapping in the breeze?"

"'Tis not easy, but can be done."

Drew folded his soft, refined clothes, and placed them in the bag on top of his gun.

Alex's gaze ran from the top of his head, passed his socks showing under the short pants, to his dress shoes, and back up again. Trussed up in medieval garb, the wash of her mere gaze warmed him.

She was a fine looking woman.

She scowled, and the amorous feeling fled like rats from the light.

"What?" he asked as she muttered something.

Her gaze met his again, but her brows were now drawn together, and she held her breath. "'Tis far from ideal. We are blessed I had anything— since I knew naught of yer coming." The last words were spoken as an oddly phrased jab. He cocked his head at her, and her critical gaze washed over him again.

She moved forward, dropped to her knees, and slid a small dagger from her back. Drew tried to step away, but she grabbed the back of the ankle upsetting his balance. "Be still. I merely attempt to adjust the ill-fitting garments to make them more believable. I shan't harm ye."

Not only her clothes marked her as a medieval maiden, but her speech slipped further and further into old English each time she spoke.

Using the blade with skill, she cut the hem out and made the bottom edge of both pant legs jagged and uneven. Now the garment looked old and tattered instead of made for someone much shorter. She carefully poked a hole in the shin of one of the legs and tore a gash in the thigh of the other distressing them further.

When she stood, she swayed.

Drew grabbed her by the arm before she toppled. "You all right?"

She glared, "Whether or not I be hale is of little import now."

Drew wasn't entirely clear what she had said but understood the dig in the tone.

She moved next to his sleeves that ended mid-forearm and were so tight his fingers tingled. Alex cut the cuffs away and frayed the edges like she'd done with the pants until the pieces dangled above his elbow. She stepped back and appraised him again.

Once more she knelt. Using her blade, she dug a small hole. She scooped up a fist-full of dark soil and smeared it on his pants— especially the tattered hem and then rubbed off her hands on the front and back of his shirt.

Wiping her hands and dagger blade clean on the underside of her lower skirt, she looked him over again. She walked all the way around him before replacing the dagger in the sheath at her back. She shrugged. "Not remotely ideal—but 'tis passable." Her scrutinizing dropped first to his wrist. "The watch too must go."

He choked on his irritation as he dropped it in the bag with all the rest.

Her inspection continued to his feet, and she frowned. "Ye may keep yer footwear for now, but they must be removed prior arriving in yonder village."

"I am not walking around barefoot—"

She stepped toward him and thumped on the sternum using three fingers this time to sharpen the pain. Color flushed her cheeks, and fire lit her eyes. And her medieval vocabulary vanished. "Now you listen here, you bulled-headed detective. If it is your shoes or your life, you'll give up the dang shoes! Forget your modern world, your controlled life, and mantle of authority. Here, I'm the only thing standing between you and an ugly demise. So quit ticking me off." She thumped him again. "Grab the bag, and do as you're told."

Chapter 11

Alex snatched up her cloak and whirled from the infuriating man who brought curses to the tip of her tongue. Securing the garment round her shoulders, she tried to get her bearings. He'd never let her forget it if she got them lost after that tirade. After a moment she found the lopsided oak tree. Keeping it to her right she headed toward the hill where it perched. Detective Drew came up beside her.

She walked a pace before she started. "I will explain who I am and how we got here first."

"Will you tell me what drug you popped back there?"

She stopped, fists perched on her hips, and grunted. "It was no drug. It was a capsule filled with protein powder. Considering all you saw with Tyler a few weeks ago, you think I'd have anything to do with drugs?"

A hint of color touched his cheeks. "I didn't realized you knew I was there the whole time," he muttered.

"Good thing you don't go undercover, detective." She started walking again. "You suck at sneaking around."

The detective didn't reply, and his head drooped a little. She hadn't intended to attack his ability to do his job. What was it about this man that made her so mad? She shook off the tension tightening her muscles and focused on calming her breathing. "Lord, help me," she whispered.

"You said you were going to explain."

"I am a Guardian of the Truth. Two thousand years ago, as Christ's disciples were starting churches thoughout the Roman Empire, a small group of His followers found they were different genetically—though they didn't have that word for it at the time. They saw things others couldn't and could go places no one else even saw doorways to.

"Perhaps you have heard the theory that there are many alternate realities that exist parallel to ours? Each time we make a decision, the universe splinters and reality continues down both."

Drew nodded.

"It's not quite like that, but there are other worlds alongside ours—hundreds of them. Some seem familiar to our history, and some are far beyond where we are now."

"That's where we are? In another world?" His voice was snarky, arms waving around but pointing at nothing specific.

"This reality is called Vilnund. It's a reality fairly near to ours." Alex stopped to catch her breath before they started up the first of what she knew would be three rises. She needed a hearty meal and a full night's sleep—not miles of walking across the dale and through the woods.

"You really don't look well, Alex."

"The cost of coming through the portal."

"There is a cost to walking between worlds?"

"Energy. Strength."

"The protein diet," Drew muttered as she started off again. "Do I need to have some too?"

"No, the gateway feeds on my DNA. It's how I can open it. You'll be fine."

They walked for a few feet in silence. "This group who can wander between worlds—the Guardians—what truth do they keep?"

"Yes, the Guardians. They go where God leads in order to strengthen, save, and help believers." She stopped halfway up the rise to catch her breath. "There are many different types among those with the gene. There are those who can see the unseeable. They search the worlds looking for where the help is needed. In the beginning, there were less than two hundred guardians. They grew in number as the church and Christianity became the dominant religion of most all the realities. At the height, we had several different types of guardians. Those who saw the need, teachers who educated the next generations on all they needed to travel between, the keys who were the only ones who could open the portals, and those who guarded them as they completed their mission." Another rest at the top of the first rise. Thankfully, the next two were much smaller, and they could make better time over them.

"You're a key." It was a statement, not a question.

"Aye, the portals are opened by my DNA, but there are so few of us now. We are even smaller in number than the original group. Now we have a few who see the need, they report to the Conclave—our elders or governing body. They decide which of the needs is most viable and are most likely to succeed with the least amount of collateral damage. Then they send out a key—alone."

"So why are you—we—here? What's your current mission?"

"A personal one. I requested it. I hoped to collect... something to help me. Something to provide peace and end my haunting dreams."

His brow rose as he considered her.

They walked silently. Alex struggled to fill her lungs with enough oxygen. Limbs quaking and energy failing, she grabbed a tree to steady herself.

The detective stopped and considered her. Before he could offer help she started off again. They continued walking.

Finally, she moved in front of him as they descended the final hill. "'Tis time to lose yer fanciful shoes, servant Andrew."

A line of trees stood before them. "I don't think so."

With speed she'd trained all her life to master, Alex drew her sword, struck, and watched him drop to her feet.

Chapter 12

The dull ache came first, radiating out from his temple like rays of sun from behind a cloud. Musty dirt filled his nostrils and something poked him in the back. He rolled to his side with a groan and squinted as he cracked open his eyes.

Alex sat with a tree at her back a few feet away, arms crossed, staring at him.

Drew sat and rubbed his head. He remembered the flash of metal before everything went black. "What'd you do?"

A cool breeze brought his gaze to his feet—bare feet.

"Where are they?" His hand flipped out at his naked toes. "What'd you do with my shoes?"

"They're gone."

He stood. So did she, though she struggled. "Listen here, wench…" He stepped on something sharp and yelped.

Her hand rested on the hilt of her weapon. "No, ye heed me warning. 'Tis not yer world. Things carried between the realities leads to misfortune in all the realms. It may seem familiar to ye from some scholar's lessons, but ye know naught of the truth of this place." She pushed off the tree she'd been using as support and swayed before turning away. "Until our return, ye are me servant, Andrew—"

"Servant? No!"

With a gust of wind, her foot slammed into his stomach. He flew back a foot and landed on his back. He groaned and coughed until he could capture a steady breath and sit up again. This little lady was kicking his well-trained behind.

Alex looked down at him, but stayed out of his reach. She crouched, her forearms resting on her knees. Did her hands tremble? "Let us attempt to come to an understanding." The old English was gone. "My *servant*, Andrew, either walks in on his own power, or I drag in an unconscious, battered—peasant I found in the field." With a noble air she rose, chin high as she straightened her skirts. The older verbiage also resumed. "The choice lays with ye."

Drew brushed himself off and glared.

"I invited ye not on this quest. Had I warning, mayhaps I could have prepared a better role for ye to play. Will be hard enough to convince the local laird ye are capable of serving me. But yer mystifying foot coverings, and no grasp of the King's English, would mean yer certain death. Ye have no authority here." She rubbed her neck as she rolled her head around. "Mayhaps even my death." The last words were muttered.

Drew pushed to his feet, his pulse pounding in his aching head. He clenched his fists so tight his short nails dug into the skin. "A little over dramatic, me thinks."

She looked over her shoulder, stepped out of his path, and waved him forward with a sweep of her arm as she bowed. "By all means, blunder forth on thy own." A smug smile soured her lips. "See how far ye make it before someone challenges ye. Surely, ye know the words to say to keep yer head upon yer shoulders. Mayhaps Laird Eldridge will find yer poor manners and thy arrogant demands of yer ill-educated tongue humorous enough to make ye his court jester." Her arms crossed, and she waited for him to proceed.

"I hate this!"

"Then you shouldn't have intruded!" Even in the shadows of the surrounding trees, fire flashed in her eyes.

Drew's teeth grated together. "What must I do, *master*?"

"M'lady, is how ye are to addressed me here—"

"Well, of course." He shot her a glare he used to make suspects talk. Well, the weaker ones anyway.

But Alex Wright was nothing close to weak. The woman met him toe-to-toe and never backed down.

Drew nearly gagged in his attempt to swallow his pride. "M'lady." He bowed at the waist.

"Worry not, ye shan't be expected to taste the words ye find so sour, for it would be best for ye to say not one utterance. Most servants are never heard."

He snorted.

"Ye are to walk a half pace behind me—"

"How big's a pace?"

He was sure a growl rumbled in her throat. "Close to three feet. So, a half a pace would put ye a little over a foot behind me and to me left in case I've need of ye."

"Yes, m'lady. Is there anything more?"

"Aye. Ye are not to look anyone above your station in the eye. 'Tis disrespectful. Those here strictly adhere to the ardent observance of station."

Drew's arms swung out at his sides and he cursed again. "And how am I supposed to know who is, and who is not, above my station?"

"Curb yer tongue. Only drunkards in disreputable taverns speak so coarsely."

They frowned at one another.

"Assume everyone is above ye. Ye're a common servant." She turned and started walking though not as fast as before. "Though there's nothing common about ye, detective," she muttered.

Chapter 13

Servant Andrew. He still gagged on the lump in his throat at the absurdity. His feet hurt. He noticed fresh splats of blood on the cold flagstones as they approached a huge wooden gate in a massive stonewall. Splinters protruding through the rough wood of the drawbridge before them. The bricks of the area around the walls felt better, but he had to be mindful of the horse droppings and splashes of what reeked like urine.

He dared to raise his head and look around. Mud huts with thatch roofs crowded together. Some were two-stories tall but most were only one. He recognized a blacksmith's place with its glowing forge outside and the clanking of a hammer on anvil. The mug on the swinging sign over one door marked it as a tavern. The majority looked to be homes.

After winding through the town for nearing half an hour, they came to another gate. Two guards stood in full chain mail, swords on their hips, and spears held in their hands. The weapons were at rest with the shaft on the cobblestone. The tip gleamed in the sun over their heads.

"Halt. State thy business."

Alex, gave a small curtsy so Drew bowed. "The Lady Alexandria come to call on Lady Selby and Laird Eldridge of the Clan MacDougan."

"Ye are expected?"

"Nay, sir. I happened to be journeying hereabouts and thought to once again share a cup of friendship and a visit."

One guard nodded and turned. He shouted, and a boy came

running. He wore a long shirt with the same emblem on his chest as those on the flags snapping in the breeze over head. The guard spoke to him in hushed words, and the boy ran off. Alex and Drew remained standing in front of the gate. He wanted to sit and get off his damaged feet. He didn't dare move since Alex would likely kill him herself.

They didn't wait long before a man with thinning hair trotted their way. A plaid sash draped across his chest fluttering in the wind. It covered most of the embroidered vest and linen shirt beneath. He wore short pants that ended in cuffs below the knees and tall socks of the same plaid showed above his calf-high boots. Maybe Drew was happy he was dressed as a servant.

The man bowed to Alex, "My Lady Alexandria, 'tis so good to see ye again."

She curtsied a little. "Afton, if I recall correctly."

"Aye, good memory, my lady."

She inclined her head, and Drew fought to stifle the groan rumbling in his gut. *Let's get on with it already.* His feet were bleeding as these two danced around the formalities of greetings. He already missed the uncomplicated, "Hey," of his own world.

"We did not expect ye, Lady Alexandria."

"Business brought me close to the MacDougans. I could not be so near and not be blessed by the company of good friends."

Afton nodded with a soft smile as he looked passed them. "No horses, my lady?"

"Oh, 'twas not far, and the beauty of the day called for a walk."

Afton bowed again and waved his arm out. "Laird Eldridge bids ye welcome, and a meal is being prepared in yer honor. Please come."

Thank you! A man could die out here in the time it takes people to say hello. Drew limped along behind them though everyone acted as though he wasn't even there.

They were led across the walled enclosure to a huge multi-storied stone building. The center resembled a square tower and stood over the rest of the building by several floors. Inside, Drew waited for his eyes to adjust to the dim light let in by the narrow-slit windows high on the walls.

The room was long and filled with wooden tables and benches. Tapestries hung between torches that burned in metal holders. Two fireplaces took up most of the area at either end of the room. They were large enough to park his car inside. A small fire burned in each, but they did nothing to ward off the chill. Drew shivered. He'd hate to live here in the winter.

Afton bowed, took the sword Alex offered him, and left them standing a little way inside the room. She didn't move. Her hands were clasped loosely in front of her. So many places to sit, and yet Drew was forced to stand on his wounded feet. "Be still, and say not a sound," she warned again in a harsh whisper.

The clomp of heavy footsteps grew, and a man appeared from an archway near the fireplace at the far side of the room. "Lady Alexandria!" His voice boomed and echoed in the cavernous space. Tall with long red tinted hair pulled back in a ponytail, his full beard parted in a generous smile as he threw out his arms. He wore a kilt and plaid sash the same color and pattern as Afton.

"Laird Eldridge." She curtsied all the way to the floor, and Drew took a knee behind her. It felt appropriate, but mostly it took the weight off his feet.

Eldridge crossed the room in quick strides muffled by the straw thrown over the stones. He took Alex's hand and pulled her up. He kissed her hand and laughed. "Oh, ye are very nearly family, my lady." He pulled her close and kissed her on both cheeks.

Drew's hands fisted, and his stomach knotted. Why'd he care that this man graced her fine cheeks with affections?

"Ye favor me over much, m'laird," she sighed. "Ye look well."

"As do ye, my lady."

The laird's words didn't sound convincing. Alex didn't look well. She hadn't for some time—but today she was every bit a ghost of herself. Oh she still managed to summon her strength to challenge and bully him, but it vanished again when Drew complied.

"Has been over a year since ye last graced us with yer presence, has it not?"

A year? Then Brendon wasn't here. He'd only been gone six months. Drew's heart clinched.

Drew continued to steal glances from his place on one knee. Eldridge took a silver goblet covered in decoration from a silent servant who bowed and disappeared. "To the return of good friends," he raised it to her in toast. He took a sip, and passed it to her, and she drank for a few moments.

She brought the cup down to hold it before her chest in both hands. "Oh, m'laird, yer are ever kind. Ye have remembered."

"Aye, ye loved our berry mead last ye were here. I saved a keg for yer visits."

She curtsied, careful not to spill the liquid. "Thank ye, m'laird."

More boot steps came toward them. "Laird Eldridge, I heard we have a visitor."

That voice!

Drew leapt to his feet. "Brendon!"

Alex gasped and whirled in the same instant. Her palm slammed against his cheek with a resounding *smack* that drove him back to his knee.

She dropped to the floor beside him, her face nearly in the straw. Her voice trembled. "M'laird, please forgive me. I have poorly trained me servant. He is new, but the fault is mine for the dishonor visited upon yer house."

Chapter 14

Alex's stomach was knotted so tightly she wasn't sure she could stand straight, as Laird Eldridge took her hand and raised her to her feet. "I blame ye not at all, my lady." His hard gaze fell on Detective Merritt where he knelt in the rushes. Air fled her lungs at the set of the laird's jaw. "Servants can be difficult when learning their place, but I am sure thirty lashes would make the matter clear."

Alex choked on a gasp.

"My laird," Laird Brendon, the detective's brother, spoke—his voice harsh. "As the offence was directed at me, I claim the right of punishment. He thought to address me as equals—and friends."

Laird Eldridge looked between the men. "The right is yers, Laird Brendon. I leave his penance to ye."

Alex bowed low again. "M'lairds, if I have found any favor in yer eyes, I beg a boon."

"Speak freely, my lady. If it be in my power to grant, 'tis yers," Laird Eldridge said.

"M'laird, me servant has committed a grievous affront to be true, but he is me servant, and I have need of him. I will only tarry two days before me responsibilities will call me back." She swallowed the terror making her words crack and squeak. "My servant would need many days abed from thirty lashes, m'laird."

Laird Eldridge looked to Brendon, "What say ye? The punishment is yers to give."

Brendon glared down on his brother, but fear flickered. "What think ye of fifteen lashes, my laird?"

With a glance at her, Eldridge put his hand on Brendon's shoulder. "Mayhaps ten would be more fitting. Ye owe the Lady a far larger boon, do ye not?"

"Aye, to be true, I owe her all. As ye wish, my lady. Yer unruly servant will receive no more than ten lashes."

She bowed to them both. "Thank ye, m'lairds. Ye are ever kind and merciful."

Laird Eldridge picked up the cup of friendship Alex had left on the floor at the detective's outburst. Thankfully, the detective stayed silent and on his knees during their exchange. "My lady," the laird inclined his head toward her as she took the cup in quaking hands. "I have another matter to see to, if ye will pardon me absence? Afton has prepared your room."

"Thank ye again, m'laird."

As he strolled away, he spoke to Brendon, "The servant is yers to deal with."

"Aye, my laird. The matter shall be handled at once." Brendon nodded to her with a grave glance at his brother.

Brendon smiled at her sadly, "'Tis good to see ye, my lady. Shall we deal with this unpleasantness before we share what has transpired in our separation?"

She nodded, and he moved toward a side door not far from them. As he held it open for them, she grabbed hold of the detective's ear—though not as hard as she wanted to. "In all the humbleness ye have ever possessed, follow him—eyes down and without a word. I cannot save ye further from what is to come. And for that, I am sorry, but I beg ye—make it no worse."

She pulled him up, and he slunk behind them as they walked down a long brick hallway.

Brendon looked up and down the passage and then ushered them into a storage room, snatched a torch, and secured the door behind them.

The detective whirled on his brother. "What's going on?"

Brendon slammed both hands into Drew's chest driving him back a step. The detective lost his balance and dropped on a pile of burlap bags full of grain.

"What are you doing here?" Brendon kept his voice low.

Matching his volume, Alex looked between the two brothers. "I came to get something from you to ease your brother. He has tried to charge me with involvement in your disappearance."

"Which you were," the detective interjected.

"Shut up, Drew!" Turning, Brendon nodded for her to continue. "Why'd you bring him?"

"It was not my plan nor intention. He has been stalking me for weeks and grabbed me as I entered the portal. Then he fought the transport through."

"What!" Brendon's volume rose. "Sit, my lady. I know now why you look so poorly." He yanked his brother off the bags and threw him against the shelves on the opposite side. The stoneware jars rattled.

He pinned his brother to the shelves with his arm across his chest. "Fye, Drew! By all that is holy, what is the matter with you?"

"You were missing. I had to know what happened. It's my job. And you're my brother." The detective's voice was flat and without remorse.

Brendon snorted. The brothers had that in common. "You care not as much for my welfare, as you care about keeping me under your thumb. You have never accepted my choices. You wanted to make sure what I was doing met with your approval. But, by all that is holy, Drew, you could have killed her."

"Killed her?"

"Aye, it costs her greatly to traverse the hidden pathways. You cost her double to bring you through. But to fight her? That is nearly unforgivable. She could have died, and you would have been lost in the void. You have always been thick headed."

Brendon pulled back and raked his hand through his long hair, loosening much of it from the warriors knot. "And now you have gone and insulted a laird and his son-in-law in his own home."

"Son-in-law?"

Brendon threw up his hand for silence. "Aye, I am blissfully wed, brother. But even I cannot stay your lashing." He paced a few steps back and forth in the tiny room.

Drew crossed his arms and smirked. "Surely you have to be kidding. You are going to whip me for talking to you?"

"I will do what I can to make it bearable, but 'tis a whip." He glared at his brother again. "Your own dictatorial, unbinding actions, have caused you to leap into this without considering the consequences. Such warrants some penalty. Act first, ask questions later—that is your way."

He moved back to the door, "You have to know, Drew, I will take no pleasure in this. It makes me sick to lay a whip to anyone—let alone my own blood." Brendon peeked outside, waved the two of them to follow, and replaced the torch before leading the way to another door. He glanced one last time at his brother. "Let us be done with this horrible business."

Chapter 15

Drew smirked as he shadowed Brendon. His lazy brother now sported a massive amount of muscles, and he did have an air of authority—even Drew almost believed. But there was no way his brother was going to whip him. They were blood, the only family they had left in the world—or worlds. He was putting on a really good show though.

Drew followed his brother outside and toward what looked—and smelled—like a stable. In the glaring light Brendon's muscles rippled and bulged all the more under his long sleeved shirt, leather vest, and tight pants. A sword hung at his waist, and it looked as though it had always belonged there. But the biggest difference was Brendon's hair. It reached past his shoulders and was bound at the nape of his neck in a ponytail, and his face sported a short beard.

Brendon picked up a whip and snapped it once.

He was really going all out.

"Will you submit to your punishment, or will you require binding?"

Two men waited with ropes to tie Drew's hands. He glanced between the ropes, B, and the top rail of the corral. Drew narrowed his gaze. Was he serious? He was really going to punish him for calling out his name when he'd finally found him after all these months? Drew dared a glance at Alex behind him. She worried her lip and wrung her hands. When he didn't move she mouthed, *Please.*

Drew yanked off his shirt, tearing it in places with his roughness, and tossed it on a hay bail. Turning his back to his brother, Drew placed his hands on the top rail. The other two men moved away at Brendon's nod. Drew was going to kill his brother for taking this so far. But he knew B. He couldn't do this.

The whip snapped across his bare back. Drew hadn't expected it to be so hard—or even to touch his flesh at all. Clenching the rough wood, he bit down on his tongue to keep from yelling out. A metallic taste filled his mouth. His own brother!

It snapped again, though the pain was not as searing as the first.

Pain seeped into his back muscles while rage radiated through every other cell. How dare he do this. They were family.

Snap.

His legs trembled beneath him. Drew had looked after him when mom and dad passed. He kept B out of trouble. Made sure—

Snap.

Drew really was going to kill him.

Drew held tighter, air trapped in his lungs to prevent him yelping out at the next strike. He looked at Alex standing not far to his right in front of him. She cringed and startled at each blow as though she felt it in her own flesh. A blond joined her. They hugged. She was a little taller than Alex—though most everyone was. And even more shapely.

"Stop leering at my lady wife!"

Snap.

One of Drew's knees gave way, and he staggered to keep both feet under him and remain upright. He panted for breath. Pain overrode most all thought. He compared the two women.

Snap.

His head hung between his arms as the last three blows came in rapid succession.

Brendon moved beside him. The whip touched the ground as it hung from his brother's hand. Blood shone on its twined length. "See to it ye mind yer place in the future. Ye'll not find me so merciful next time."

Merciful? Drew trembled in pain, which kept him from seizing his brother by the throat. He knew if he released the railing he would drop to his knees. He turned his head and glared hatefully at him.

Brendon spoke to the two men. "Help him to Lady Alexandria's outer chamber."

One arm over each man's shoulder, they supported him back inside and up four flights of narrow stairs. He wouldn't have made it without the help.

They sat Drew down on a long backless couch. It had no sides, but one end that was high and curved out away from the rest of the piece. Drew leaned one elbow on that side as pain rattled any other thought than to stay conscious and not vomit.

Alex entered as the two men exited, Brendon on her heels. She held a blue glass jar and sat beside him. She glared at Brendon as he sat at a small table opposite them.

"Oh, do not look at me so, my lady. I did what I could," Brendon said.

"He's bleeding." The fear in her voice chased away the medieval façade.

Brendon crossed his arms. "Had Laird Eldridge or one of his men done it, there would be little flesh remaining on his back. As it is, only half the lashes broke the skin, and they will leave no lasting scars." He put his hands up in surrender as if warding off an attack from her. "There had to be blood. It had to be done. You know this."

She harrumphed and handed Drew a twig. "Chew on this."

He eyed it. "Why?"

"'Tis willow bark." When he didn't respond, she added under her breath. "The main ingredient in aspirin."

"Do I eat it?"

"Chew," his brother said dryly as Alex's finger stroked across one of the whip's lashes with something cool and gooey on her fingers. Her touch was feather light and warm compared to the ointment.

"So what happens now?" Drew asked.

"Ye attend yer lady at meals. Stand behind her, fill her cup when t'is empty—or before. If there is anything she requires provide it." Brendon recited his duty as it talking to a forgetful child. "And whatever ye do, don't speak."

"At the end of the main meal, the servants will gather at boards. They sit further back in the hall and ye may take time to eat," Alex added.

"Boards?"

"Long picnic style tables were everyone eats," Brendon said.

She finished the first-aid to his back and sat on the floor in front of Drew. She picked one of his feet and grimaced. "The water basin, m'laird." While she waited, she looked up at Drew. Heavy lids covered her eye,s and her lips turned in a frown. She couldn't hold his gaze. "I am sorry."

"Do not offer contrition to the man who badgered you for months, joined you without asking, and nearly killed you. He reaps his own harvest." Brendon set the large bowl beside her and filled it from the matching pitcher in his other hand. "I shall call a servant to do this, my lady. Ye should not be sittin' on the floor tendin' him."

She put out her hand—palm up, and after a moment he dropped a cloth in it.

Where her hands held his foot, a rush of warmth started and crept up his body, until it filled his face. Here this woman he'd chased and wrongly accused sat on the floor and washed his feet. He couldn't say if the tables were turned, he'd willingly do the same for her—or even his own mother, had she still been alive.

"Forgive me," she mumbled.

Drew nodded unable to form words on his stone tongue.

She dipped her fingers in the jar and rubbed ointment on his feet. When each was done, she put on his socks, which she pulled from the top of her bag.

From where he sat motionless, Drew considered the lumps in the bag and knew his shoes weren't hidden in there as well. They were probably buried in the forest somewhere.

"Where are your foot-coverings?" Brendon asked.

Alex answered before he could. "I removed them. They were out of place here. I didn't think the remaining walk would have caused such damage."

"It wasn't the only damage you caused." Drew rubbed is temple noting the tenderness of a bruised knot.

"I gave opportunity for ye to remove them yerself."

Brendon chuckled. "Sword hilt?"

Alex nodded, a small corner of her mouth turning in a mischievous grin.

Rubbing his own head, Brendon's laugh grew, and his medieval accent slipped. "I feel your pain, bro. Got conked in the noggin a few times myself."

Alex took a playful swipe at his shin. "Can ye provide anything for him, m'laird?"

"Aye, I can give him an old pair of house boots which no longer fit. I shall collect new garments as well. He cannot serve in the hall looking so disheveled."

When she completed tending to both Drew's feet, Brendon squatted beside her. He brushed a loose strand of hair from her check. "My lady, ye have done all ye might—and beyond. Now ye need rest. Go lie down until the meal. 'tll help ye replenish some of what was lost. I'll have a maid toss the dirty water and refill the pitcher. And a maid will be provided for yer private needs later."

She opened her mouth as if to protest, but Brendon put his finger up to quiet her. "For once, my lady, don't fight me. Ye have done us both a service in bringing us together one last time. I'm ever grateful. Now let us address our matters alone while ye take yer ease."

"As ye wish, m'laird."

Brendon helped her stand as he rose. She gave a small curtsy, and he bowed deeply, before she disappeared through another door deeper within the room.

Chapter 16

"So one last time? I guess you're not coming home." Drew carefully leaned against the end of the couch thing while still chewing on the stick.

Brendon stood looking out the window with his back to him. "This is my home now, D."

"Explain that to me. How can you abandon everything and live in this place—they don't even have running water."

"But 'tis here I fit."

"You're no Guardian of the Truth, B. What are you doing here?"

Brendon turned and a smile filled his face. "No, not by the makeup of my cells, I shall never be a true guardian. But here, I accomplish God's work."

"God's work. B, you forget I know you. I know the kind of man you are. Bars. Women. Cussing. Need I say more?"

As he lost his smile, he sat beside Drew, forearms resting on his thighs. The more he talked the less he sounded like the old world. "That is who I once was to be sure, and sore I regret every moment of that life. I've changed, brother." He sighed. "Let me see if I can explain.

"I saw the sign for the sword fighting classes a week before my birthday—but I couldn't stop thinking about them. I was obsessed like some junkie on the corner looking for his next high. I have never wanted anything so badly in my life, and I didn't know why. I worked all the overtime I could to pay for it." He turned his head to look at Drew for a moment. "Remember, I bailed on our traditional Thanksgiving football fest to work? I even took a second job to save the money for the full course. A year long.

"But when I met Alex, I knew I was there for more than swinging a sword. We started talking about God—not in the *hey do you believe there is a God?* kind of way. It was… different. Deeper. Real." Brendon glanced at him again. "I always liked going to church as a kid. I know you hated it."

"I didn't *hate* it." Drew protested. "But seeing how those good church-going people acted Monday through Saturday soured me on believing there was anything real going on when Sunday came and they were singing their pretty music."

His brother chuckled with a nod. "Imperfect sinners make up the body, that's for darn sure. But there are those—like Alex—who take the truth of Scripture seriously. They live what they believe, and it's powerful. I wanted that too.

"Not long after I gave my life to Christ, I started having weird dreams. At first they were only of a beautiful blond. She'd smile, tilt her head, giggle. Then they changed, and I kept seeing her on a run-away horse—gown flowing behind her, blond hair loose and catching in her face." His head sagged between his arms. "D, I can't tell you how many times I watched her, or held her in my arms, as she died from being thrown. In my gut I knew I needed to save her—but I didn't even know who she was or where to find her. We'd never said a word, but I knew I loved her." Brendon's voice broke, choked by tears.

"So Alex brought you here to save her?"

Brendon shook his head and offered him a smirk. "Not a first. I explained my dreams, each time with a little more detail regarding the place I saw her. It took weeks before she told me about the different realms and where she thought my ladylove might be found. Once she cleared my transfer from our world to this one, which apparently was a pretty rare thing for the Conclave to do, we trained hard. She crammed me full of history, how to talk and fight, and what would be expected of me, including three weeks of a crash course of cultural emersion into medieval life. The day came. I dressed as a laird with boots and breeches, tunic and doublet." His hand ran over his head with a chuckle. "Hair wasn't long enough for a warrior's knot yet, but the beard was coming in nicely."

"I was wondering about why you were growing a beard. You always hated them. Wish I'd asked."

Brendon's arm returned to rest on his leg. "I should have told you, but the Conclave gave very strict orders.

"Alex and I hadn't been here more than fifteen minutes when my dream came to life right before my eyes. We were walking across a grassy depression, and the woman of my dreams came screaming over the hill. I ran and stood in the horse's path. He reared. I grabbed his reigns, and a moment later she was cradled in my arms." His words turned breathy and filled with awe.

"When we walked the Lady Kolena back to her home, her father, Laird Eldridge, insisted I stay. We were married within a few months. That was a year ago."

"How can it be over a year for you when you have only been missing for six months?" Drew said.

He shrugged. "The time between realities is wonky. Alex tried to explain, but I didn't get it."

"Do you know what day it is back home?"

Brendon shook his head.

"June twenty-second."

"My birthday."

"I had to know. I had to find out what happened to you. And here you sit married and happy without a word."

"Well, like I said, I couldn't tell you much, but I left the note."

"There was no note."

"Sure there was." Brendon straightened. "I donated most of my stuff or trashed it. Put the personal things I couldn't bare to throw out in a box on the coffee table with the note beside it. Told old Jamerson I was moving out and to have you come get my stuff."

"That wily old man didn't call me for at least three weeks. Then he had me pay the rent for the next four months as I tried to figure out what happened to you. It wasn't until he got a new renter who paid him more that he gave me a box with your belongings tossed into it. But no note."

"That old—" Brendon stopped short of the curse word he used to favor.

"I can't convince you to come back?"

He shook his head. "I have floundered all my life trying to fit in, do the right thing, be responsible, as you love telling me. That's who I am here. I'm a husband, a protector of the kingdom, and I am bringing back the old ways by teaching them about God and faith in Christ again. I have never felt so… so right. So at peace. I belong here."

Drew hated the churning in his stomach, and the tightness in his throat. "And did you decide to forget about your family—your own brother?" Brendon was all the family he had left. But he couldn't live here. He liked his car, a toilet, and fast food—the kind he didn't have to chase down and kill. This was it, the day Alex took him home, would be the last time he'd ever see his brother.

Brendon stood, "You have all your cop buddies and lots of friends. You never needed me. I was an embarrassment to you." He glanced out the window and put a hand on Drew's shoulder—gently. "I need to get you those things I promised and find Alex a maid. I am deeply grieved I caused you cause you such pain." He smirked. "A bit of advice, brother to brother? When she tells you to do something," he tipped his head toward the room Alex had disappeared into, "'tis best to do it—to the letter."

Chapter 17

Drew stood with the other servants at the back of the raised platform as everyone gathered in the hall for the evening meal. Eldridge pulled Alex to the center of the room. "Friends, we welcome our guest and friend Lady Alexandria to our boards this night."

The men and women seated for the meal thumped the top of the long wood tables, filling the room with a thunderous noise.

Eldridge raised his hand to quiet them. "Laird Brendon has asked that the honor of saying the blessing for us be bestowed upon our lady."

Every head bowed, and the room fell as silent as an abandoned building.

Were women allowed to lead prayer in medieval times? Drew scoured his mind for any of his history lessons and came up lacking. But this wasn't their world. Maybe things were different for women here.

"Our gracious and loving heavenly Father," Alex's voice rang out strong and sure. "We come to Thee with grateful hearts, thanking Thee for the provision of Thy hand to nourish our bodies and cherished friendship to minister to our souls. May Thy hand always be upon this land, and its people. Amen."

"Amen!" everyone echoed as one booming voice.

Eldridge smiled at her and motioned for her to take her place.

Drew stood against the wall with a few other servants behind the long wood table. He wore a long tan shirt that hung past his hips and belted with a length of rope. The long sleeves kept the chill at bay—as did the two roaring fires. His brown pants reached inside the ankle high boots Brendon had provided him. He now looked the part of a proper servant. As long as he didn't look or act out of place, he went unnoticed altogether.

He scanned those gathered with a sharp eye. He would normally look for possible weapons and threats, but as both men and women carried daggers to eat with, it might be easier to spot someone who wasn't armed. Eldridge and Brendon were the only ones with swords on their hips but enough lined the room to warrant most the men had brought them. It was hard to judge their movements as threats or not. They didn't move like people from his world.

He tried to focus on Alex sitting directly in front of him. She was at one end of the table with Laird Eldridge sat to her right. Then his daughter, Kolena, Drew's sister-in-law, and Brendon sat beside her at the other end.

Drew would never know his brother's wife. They were not of the same station in this world, and she would never be in his.

Stamping down his thoughts and locking them away, Drew grew numb. The atmosphere in the hall rang out with merry laughter. But it could have been as far away as one of the other worlds Alex told him about, because it never touched him.

He stepped forward and filled Alex's goblet from a pitcher as she laughed. It was not the tittering bells of Kolena's giggles but a hearty chortle. When she covered her mouth, Drew wondered if she hid a dainty snort at the end.

"Where is yer Lady Selby. I have not seen her since I arrived."

"She is lying-in."

Lying-in what? Drew turned to move back to his position.

Alex gasped with a wide smile. "Oh, m'laird. The blessing of another bairn—what a joy for ye."

Eldridge looked to his daughter before answering Alex. "Aye, it has been a year of many marvelous blessings. My precious daughter found her love; I have found love again after suffering so long following her mother's death. And now I am soon to welcome another child. I could not be happier."

"Mayhaps I can slip in and pray blessings over them both before I leave."

"I am sure my lady would welcome such a visit."

Taking his place back against the wall, Drew realized he'd never heard Alex laugh and barely ever seen her smile. Here she behaved so differently. She was open, free, and happy as she bantered with the laird and his family. But when she'd faced Drew, her smile faded, and her gaze lower. Drew held her responsible for breaking up his family. Brendon was all he had left.

Drew shook himself, stamping down the thoughts again. It wasn't Alex's fault. Brendon made the decision, and Drew had hunted her for it. He'd made Alex wither under his suspicion.

He glanced to his brother again. He looked and sounded the part of a knight of old. And Drew had to admit, when Brendon looked at Kolena a true and deep love showered down on the woman. This was not his normal love-struck puppy dog stare. This was real—like the way Dad once looked at Mom.

Kolena looked to Brendon, and Drew saw the feeling was mutual. She smiled at Brendon impishly and turned back to her father. She rested her hand on his arm. "Ask her, father. Please."

Eldridge cleared his throat and turned toward Alex. "My lady, Brendon tells us he learned the sword from ye. 'Tis true?"

Doubt painted Eldridge's face and voice. Perhaps the role of women wasn't so different in this time as in his own.

She dared a glance at the other end of the table where Brendon nodded and smiled. "'Tis true, m'laird." Alex looked better—stronger. The sun-kissed color had returned to her skin, and the tremor of weakness their journey had caused was gone.

"And how is it, such a fine lady as yerself, learned the sword?" Eldridge sounded more curious than offended. If Drew remembered his history, genteel women did not handle weapons for any reason—let alone train with them.

"My father had but one child. He thought it prudent to train me to care for meself and our lands for the time he would no longer be there to watch over me."

"Did he not have men to guard ye?"

"He did, but he favored me and wanted me to be prepared in all ways."

"And what of a husband, my lady. Did he not find a proper match for ye?"

Drew saw her head dip and she sighed.

"Father died before such matters seemed prudent to discuss. I favored one boy I grew up with and hoped for a match, but he has found another to love."

The sadness of her words was real and deep. Drew had interviewed enough people in his life to know when someone was telling the truth. She had loved someone, but they were now married, leaving her alone. Her loss brought his own feelings to the surface with such force; it stung his eyes and burned his throat. They were both alone. Again he forced down his own hurt, refusing to acknowledge it, feed it, or wallow in it.

"I am sorry, my lady," Eldridge patted her hand making Drew's muscles contract and his back ached once more. He really shouldn't care of another touched Alex.

"Father. Will you not ask?" Kolena probed again—her voice pleaded and her hand gripped his arm.

Eldridge's brows furrowed as he looked at Alex again. "Forgive me, Lady Alexandria, but my daughter wishes to know if you would perform a demonstration with your sword on the morrow?"

Alex chuckled and looked past both father and daughter to Brendon. "What say ye, m'laird? Shall we spar like in days past?"

Before he could answer, the room erupted with the banging on the tables again, making Drew want to cover his ears.

Brendon laughed, "It would seem everyone is in agreement, my lady."

Alex nodded. "On the morrow then." Her smile was radiant with joy and a hint of mischief. They talked on as Alex ate heartily of the meat and cheeses provided—the protein her unique DNA demanded. She shied away from the breads and vegetables favoring those things that would most quickly restore her strength.

Chapter 18

As her meal ended, Alex motioned for Drew to approach on her left. He stepped forward and bent so his ear was near her face for her to whisper—though the stretching of his back made him wince. "Andrew, ye may take yer rest and eat. I know it has been a trying day." He followed her gaze to a table at the back of the hall. Several men dressed similar to him, sat eating at one table, and a group of simply dressed women at another. He nodded and turned to the stairs leading from where the lairds and ladies ate.

"Do ye require something, my lady?" Eldridge asked when he had only taken a step.

"I admit me shortcomings, m'laird. For I fret over me servant. I have sent him to sit and eat."

"Ye are a kind soul, my lady."

"Thank ye, m'laird, and," she hesitated, "if I may ask another boon?"

"Ask, my lady."

"Might I have two matching bound volumes?"

"Of course. Tell my scribe what ye require, and it will be made for ye at once."

Their words faded as Drew moved across the room and sat at the end of a bench with the other male servants. The cop in him assured he sat with his back to the wall and as many entrances as possible in his line of sight. A hard loaf of bread, that had been hollowed out like the bread-bowls filled with chowder at home, was offered to him. Drew noted that the others each had one, and it served as a plate for the thick stew they ate. Drew shrugged. Bread bowls weren't a new or original of an idea.

He wasn't hungry, but a glance back at the high table brought his gaze to Alex. They would be leaving soon, and he needed to be prepared this time to help lessen the cost to her. Something niggled inside him, like a stray bullet. Her welfare mattered to him. How had his feelings altered toward her so fast? *What was it about this woman? Why am I feeling this way?*

He took the make-shift bowl and raised a shallow wood spoon to his lips. Unfamiliar seasonings and gamey meat washed over his tongue. He wanted to spit it out. His gaze flickered to her again, and he swallowed it —and finished all he'd been given.

Before he forced down the last of his meal, a small group of musicians started playing in the middle of the room. Had Drew been at home—in his own world—he would have left. A party was the last thing on his list of activities he wanted to occupy his time. He could find nothing even remotely happy in this day—well, Brendon was alive. There was that.

But this was not his world. And he couldn't do as he wished.

Brendon led his wife down to the floor, and they danced with several of the other couples gathered to eat with the lairds and ladies. Drew didn't watch them, but he kept eyes on Alex. She clapped in time with the music, and laughed—oh the sheer joy on the woman's face.

Then Brendon invited Alex down to dance. No, it wasn't the bump and grind of home—in fact, other than linking elbows to turn or pressing their raised palms together like some lengthy high-five—they didn't even touch. But Drew's heart drummed in his chest out of sync with the music. The opposing rhythms added chaos to the things swirling inside him. Thoughts and ideas he wouldn't let spring from the dark holes where he banished them.

When Eldridge claimed Alex as partner, Drew stood. He moved into the shadows against the wall, pressing his sore back onto the rough stone until the pain drove out all other thoughts. Even so, his hands fisted at his side so tight his arms shuddered under the strain.

After only a few dances—far more than Drew thought he could tolerate—Alex curtsied to both lairds and moved toward the doorway they had entered through hours ago. Brendon looked toward him, but Drew was already on the move. He followed Alex through the corridors and up the stairs. He opened her door, and they went inside.

Alex stopped in the middle of the room and turned to him—the smile gone, her eyes filled with an emotion he couldn't read. Regret? Shame? Hatred? Worry? "How are you feeling? Do you require more ointment or willow bark?"

Drew bowed to her, "I am well, m'lady."

A smile toyed on her lips, and his heart did an odd jig in his chest. "The servant's spot has been prepared for you." She pointed to a box like structure in the corner with a curtain drawn across it. "Though with your injuries, the divan might be more comfortable."

"Di—what?"

He was rewarded with a small chuckle for that. She pointed to the odd one-armed couch thing he'd sat on earlier. "Divan." She looked at him, her eyes holding a small twinkle deep within them. "It must be challenging—so many familiar things with odd names, strange conversations, and customs. I should be doing more to help—"

He raised a hand to stop her, "Worry not, m'lady." Her smile returned larger this time. "I shall manage." He leaned forward and whispered. "This old dog can learn a few tricks too."

Her hand came to rest on his forearm, and the jig of his heart turned to a full-on mambo. "Are things well with you and Laird Brendon?"

He kept his voice low. "Don't know much of this Laird Brendon," he shrugged with a wince. "But I know my brother has found his niche. He is more peaceful and assured of himself than I have ever seen. I can't fault him for choosing to stay."

She gave his arm a gentle squeeze and nodded. "Sleep well, detective." She whispered the last word.

"And you do the same, m'lady."

She showed him a slim smile before she turned toward her private inner chamber, but a tiny knock sounded on their outer door before she made it two steps.

Drew opened the door a crack.

"I am here to attend the Lady Alexandria," a young girl said.

Drew shot a look over his shoulder. Alex nodded, and he admitted the maid.

The girl approached Alex and curtsied low, "Maci, at yer service, m'lady."

"This way, Maci. Mayhaps ye can help me manage these troublesome plaits. They are giving me quite a headache."

"Yes, m'lady."

The two women disappeared beyond the inner door leaving Drew alone in the outer room. It really was more of a sitting room than a bedroom. He moved to the servant's cubby to investigate. Basically, it was a narrow bed in a wood box built against the wall. Small and cramped, and the way the bed sat, he would either have his back pressed to the rough wall or dangling out over the edge. He certainly couldn't lie flat—neither because of the pain or the short mattress. He snatched up the pillow to move it to what Alex had called the divan. Working slowly and with great care, he removed his boots and tried to get comfortable. He thought he'd found a position when another tiny knock sounded on the outer door.

Chapter 19

Drew opened the door and admitted Lady Kolena. Her curvaceous form slipped into the room like a breeze through a meadow. The yellow of her gown added more light to her golden hair.

"M'lady has retired. I shall see if she might speak with ye," Drew said in his best medieval speech, gazing to the floor. As he took a step, he realized too late that he'd forgotten to bow. He stopped, bowed, and straightened again.

"No. Please."

He turned toward her again and dared raise his head a little. A demure blush kissed her cheeks, and her long lashes batted sweetly. "I would speak to ye, sir."

The inner door creaked open, and Alex stepped out alone. She closed the door behind her. She now wore a long white gown almost entirely covered by a dark blue cape or robe. Her black hair tumbled over her shoulders in bumpy waves.

"The Lady Kolena, wishes to speak to me." He hoped he didn't sound as petrified to them as he did to himself.

Alex nodded. "'Tis still proper for a married woman to be chaperoned when meeting with a single man. It protects her honor."

Kolena nodded but seemed unsure if she should speak.

"Speak, m'lady. I am only here as honor demands. Whatever ye say will never pass me lips to another soul."

"Thank ye, my friend." She turned to Drew as Alex sat with her back to them near the fire and pulled a brush over her hair. Drew glimpsed Kolena's pretty smiled before he lowered his gaze once more. "I know who ye are, sir." She whispered so low, Drew wasn't sure he'd heard her clearly.

She placed a finger under his chin and raised his face until their eyes met. "Ye are me Brendon's brother."

Drew didn't know what to say, and with his face propped upon her delicate appendage, he couldn't look to Alex for help.

"Oh, do not fret so, I reasoned it out of me own. Though the knowledge is there for any who take the time to see it. There, in yer eyes is the same intensity, and upon thy face the same straight nose." Her gaze to run down the length of his nose. "And the sweet little half smile I love so much." Her gaze now brushed of his mouth. 'Tis so plain to see the shadow of the one in the other."

"M'lady…" Drew truly didn't know what to say.

She took a couple steps, twirled causing her skirt to whoosh and plopped—very un-ladylike—on the divan. She sighed motioning for him to sit in a chair opposite her. "Ugh, formalities can be bothersome."

Drew sat and stared at her. She was attractive. B. was a lucky man.

"I know me Brendon has come from some far off land. He says the oddest things sometimes." She shook her head. "But he has oft spoken of his older brother."

Drew cringed.

"Oh, fear not, Brendon holds ye up with great respect. He confesses he was quite a—how does he say it?—Aw yes, quite a *hot mess* in his youth." She giggled at the odd words, and Drew coughed to clear a snarky laugh. "He says 'twas only yer guidance that kept him from horrible ruin." She leaned forward and her fingertips lighted on his knee for a moment. "Thank ye, for takin' care of him until he came to me."

Drew nodded.

"I know things are quite different where ye both hail from so that there are no social barriers between peoples as there are here. As things are now, he cannot claim ye as brother as he so dearly desires. And such means that I may not know ye as my brother by marriage. I find it all very displeasing and… and, well, frustrating."

Drew couldn't contain a small laugh. "I whole-heartedly agree, m'lady. 'Tis most frustrating indeed."

The tinkling bells of her giggle filled the air. She rose, and Drew did likewise. "I must go before yer brother sends out the entire household staff in search of me. He does not long allow me out of his sight."

"Nor would I allow such a beauty as ye to be far from me side." Drew's head ached from being mindful of how he formed each word and sentence.

Kolena giggled again. "Oh, true brothers, there is no doubt." She considered him for another moment, her eyes batting again. "I am so glad ye have come, brother of my marriage. Ye are always welcome here. And ye must know that whether we may speak of it in the company of others or nay—we hold ye close in our hearts."

"And ye in mine," Drew bowed.

She bit the corner of her lip. "Might I be allowed—?"

"M'lady?"

"A brotherly kiss to ye me kin?"

He blinked and nodded. She brushed each of his cheeks with a quick kiss and moved to the door all in near the same moment. "Brother," she curtsied. "My lady," she said to Alex and slipped out the door.

Drew jerked from his musing when the movement of Alex standing wavered in the corner of his eye. He fumbled for words.

Flickering light from the lamps and fireplace danced in moist pools in her eyes. Her voice was unsteady when she spoke. "Sleep well."

Before he could ask, she'd disappeared behind the door again.

Chapter 20

Alex rubbed dried tears from her eyes as Maci stirred outside the curtained bed. Rising without a word, she donned her short chemise and layered skirts. This is what she hated most about being on mission—the same clothes. Day after day she wore only what she'd brought. One outfit. By the time she returned home, most garments smelled as if they could walk on the strength of their own stench. Once removed, she would spend over an hour scrubbing her flesh in the hottest showers.

"Does something trouble ye, m'lady?" the servant girl asked as she plaited her hair.

She glanced at the reflection of the door in the mirror. She couldn't put words to the fears strangling her. On the other side of the door, he waited. Detective Drew Merritt. The man who would be the end of her. Oh, true, he no longer wanted her blood—to kill her for the disappearance of his brother. No, he knew the truth now. The two men had made peace with Brendon's decision yesterday.

Detective Merritt no longer posed a threat to her life. His investigation over, now her emotions were on the line. He would rip out her still-beating heart and tear it to shreds. She couldn't believe she had let him get to her emotions. Why did it matter what the detective thought about her anyway? It had always mattered. More than not wanting to be thought of as a criminal—his opinion mattered. And she hated that.

Her skin warmed. He had been quite charming last night. The quintessential gentleman—with his cheeky "m'lady." In those moments hope bloomed, only to die a mere handful of minutes later under the beauty of Lady Kolena. The hardened detective became besotted by her perfection. The hole left in Alex now was a festering wound that she feared would never heal.

"M'lady?" Maci's call pulled her from the pain.

"'Tis naught, Maci. I am well." She moved to the door. *Steel yourself, Al. Steel yourself well.* She inhaled one last deep breath and pulled the door open.

"Good morning, m'lady," Drew bowed, and his face didn't snarl with pain.

"Good morn, Andrew. We go to the breaking of the fast?"

He hurried to open the door, his brows knit tight together. "Breaking of the fast?" he muttered as she passed. "Breaking—oh! Breakfast." He chuckled to himself, and her resolve weakened. *Protect yourself. Banish the hope. Don't let him in, woman!*

Maci disappeared, and the detective followed close on Alex's heels—too close. "You're wearing the same gown."

"I travel light." Did he mutter something about a "costume closet?" She couldn't be sure because he fell behind and his steps grew softer. Leather slapped stone as he caught up with her on the stairs. "Maybe Lady Kolena would let you borrow a gown. She is taller and shaped—well differently. But her gowns should surely fit you well enough."

Tears burned. She stumbled. His arm encircled her waist, and he pulled her back against his chest to steady her. His muscles were hard. His heart fast. No, she certainly did not look anything like the shapely Kolena, but the gowns would fit her *well enough* as he had said.

"M'lady?" The concern in his voice almost sounded genuine.

She wiggled from his grasp. "Ye mustn't let anyone see ye being so familiar."

"Yes, it would dishonor ye to have yer slave's filthy hands on ye—even to save ye from a nasty fall down hundreds of stone steps." His words bit and tore the wound open a little more.

She turned and looked up at him. "I could not bear to see ye punished again. I would sooner the whip be laid across me own back than be witness to it again on ye." She whirled and fled down the remaining stairs before he could see her tears. She hated to cry, and she swore he'd never see her pain.

Chapter 21

Drew struggled to keep pace with Alex as she careened down the twisting stairs. Narrow corkscrew stairwells weren't part of his beat in Allen City. It made him dizzy and want to hurl. By the time he shook the nausea off and found the hall through the maze of passageways again, the meal was well underway and another servant stood in his place seeing to her needs.

Alex did not acknowledge his entrance, but Brendon did. His brother scowled and raised a brow in question. Drew could only shrug. *What the heck was going on?*

He plopped down on the bench with the other servants and shoved the food in his mouth, trying not to choke as he went over the events of the last several hours.

He had elicited a smile and even a small laugh from her. He thought she might have finally forgiven him for all he'd done. But when Kolena left, he thought she was crying. He'd hoped she'd been happy for the connection they made, but maybe not.

This morning she'd been brusque. Greeting him with the efficiency of a drill sergeant, not sparing him a glance, she'd nearly stormed from the room. He tried to be helpful when she stumbled, but she'd jerked free as if she couldn't bear his touch.

He scrubbed his scalp. His head ached. In the very next moment, she voiced concern for him with teary eyes. He tossed his head to clear it. What an irrational, confounding woman. She'd give a profiler a run for their money.

Following the meal, those gathered, moved en masse to the open space near the stables. Drew followed. Afton returned her sword, and Brendon offered her another. Brendon shot her a roguish grin, which she, of course, returned—bright and shining. Drew's gut wrenched. She was perfect—with everyone but him.

Drew shouldered his way between two servants as the crowd formed a ring around the two combatants. How did one go about crowd-control in a foreign realm and alone?

"Two blades, my lady?" Eldridge said from the opposite side of the crowd.

"Aye, my laird," Brendon answered with a laugh. "Our lady is possesses unmatched skill and favors the offensive of two blades and not the—how do ye say it, m'lady?"

"The hindrance of a weighty shield restricting me arm." One hand held her short sword something like the Romans in movies. The other held a shorter weapon the length of a long dagger. She swung them— individually and then in coordination. She did the same thing Drew did when he held a new gun, testing its weight and balance. She never took her eyes off Brendon. His sword—near twice the length and width of her larger one, rose high in the air, the sun glinting off the polished metal.

As she nodded, Drew noticed the front hem of her skirts where tied up with the yellow ribbons and he could see her boots at the ankles. Also, the long flowing sleeves were wrapped around her forearms and secured, he assumed to allow her freedom of movement.

The two circled, blades clinking together, testing, probing, trying to draw the other in close. The crowd hushed. Drew's heart stuttered, and his lungs refused to work.

Brendon attacked first, his wide swing caught on the longer right blade. As she raised it and pushed it away, she twisted until her back nearly touched his chest, his arm useless and high above them. She elbowed him in the ribs, and a puff of air burst from Brendon as the crowd cheered.

She twisted the opposite direction, under his arm, and elbowed him in the back. Brendon stumbled forward to more cheers.

Drew lost track of the next several moments as their swords clashed together in a wild flurry. All he saw was Alex. The grace and speed of her body as she attacked, defended, or more often dodged away from Brendon's strike. She reminded him of the pure perfection of a tigress on the hunt.

While Brendon used his larger weapon, to hack at her with his longer reach and superior strength, she floated around him like a watercolor of smooth, quick, agile movements. Drew's breaths came in quick pants as his heart thundered. Instinct told him to watch the crowd, be alert for trouble, but he could only watch her.

Brendon anticipated one of her turns and caught her in the shoulder with the hilt of his weapon. Alex stumbled. Drew took a single step forward and froze—willing his body to stay with the cheering crowd. Alex laughed—joyous and full.

"Well met, m'laird. You have learned some new tricks."

Brendon panted for breath, nodding at her compliment. Their blades crossed in a new dizzying array of singing metal, each taking and giving harmless strikes—though Drew knew there would be bruises.

Movement opposite him caught his eye, and Drew almost swallowed his tongue as he watched Eldridge draw his sword and step toward Alex. Drew's hand went to his hip for the gun that wasn't there.

While expertly keeping Brendon occupied, Alex deflected the first of Eldridge's blows with her shorter blade. All three combatants smiled broadly.

The yelling crowd drowned out the thunderous beat of Drew's heart. Alex's skill was a marvel to behold. She fought two as easily as one.

The fluidity of her movements never faltered. As elegant as any dancer on a ballroom floor, she wielded the deadly blades fending off the men's attack.

Eldridge moved behind her as Brendon engaged her.

Drew was sure he was going to suffer a heart attack as the two pinned her between them.

Brendon and Eldridge lunged as though on cue, but Alex somersaulted away. The men drew up short to keep from impaling one another. Alex tried to stand but stepped on her skirt as she rose.

The crowd gasped.

Still not fully standing, her left arm swung out blocking Eldridge's next blow. She planted her sword tip in the dirt and using it like a cane attempted to get her weight off the fabric to free herself. She stumbled back into Brendon, blocking his downward swing with her shoulder in his armpit. With a wild warrior cry, she jerked her body spun behind Brendon, sunk her knees into the back of his, and forced him to the ground. In the blink of a single terrifying moment, she went from near failure, to standing behind a kneeling Brendon, her right blade flat against his chest and her left blade outstretched with Eldridge's neck at its tip.

Not a sound remained in the sudden stillness.

Drew could see the quick rise and fall of Alex's chest and the sweat that glistened on her face as she raised her head to consider Eldridge. The hardened look of a warrior ready to kill, slipped into a gorgeous smile as her arms dropped and blades crossed behind her. She inclined her head to the lairds as her smile grew.

Drew about jumped out of his skin, again reaching for his phantom gun, as the crowd exploded with a strange chant that sounded like 'Huzha' to him.

"Brendon, me lad, I fear I did not believe yer tales of the wonders of yer master." Eldridge bowed deep at the waist with a sweep of his arm—sword still in his hand. "My lady, I have never met yer equal."

As she slipped into a deep curtsy, Drew dared approach her. He held out his hands and she relinquished her blades. His mouth dry and throat tight, he took them—his skin tingled as their hands brushed.

She smiled with a nod before looking back to Eldridge. "I was blessed to have a teacher of unsurpassed skill, m'laird."

Drew lost her in the push of people wanting to congratulate her, and it was as if the sun lay hidden by storm clouds. He shivered. This was not safe. All these men crushing in on her. He could not protect her from the perimeter. He needed to be at her side. He belonged at her side.

The need rattled him. He swayed and staggered away. Afton approached holding up the sheaths to her blades. Drew handed him the weapons. Once enclosed, Afton handed her own sword back.

"Ye may keep this in the lady's chambers. She relinquished it when she entered to laird's hall out of respect, but I need not see to its care."

The crowd began to thin, and Drew strained to catch a glimpse of her. Before he could get a peek, a hand slapped down on his shoulder.

"Now, do ye see why I had to train with her?" Brendon moved on before he could answer, but Drew did see the appeal of—well everything about Alex Wright.

Chapter 22

Drew stood near the hall as the hunting party prepared to set out. Brendon had offered to allow Drew to accompany Alex, but he also knew Drew hated horses. As a simple attending servant, Drew wasn't needed on the outing. There were *plenty* of men to protect her. Finely armored knights and mighty lairds would guard her—though Alex had proven she could take care of herself. All those men and Alex. Drew dreaded leaving her with them.

Drew ground the toe of his brother's hand-me-down boot into the dust. His fists clenched and unclenched. He should have gone. Insisted on it. But he wasn't a guard, or knight, or even a cop here. Here he was nothing more than an errand boy. His vision lost its focus as he tried to watch their preparations. His stomach twisted and jaw ached.

Brendon handed Alex a quiver and bow as Drew fought to stay on the sidelines. The thought of tackling his brother into the dust filled his hazy vision. If the others weren't around, it would feel good to release his building frustration on his little brother. They had their own way of sparing with one another.

Alex slipped the quiver over her head, the wide strap going from her shoulder, between her perfect breasts, and onto her exquisite hip— opposite her sword. Drew's heart convulsed.

A growl strangled him as Brendon helped lace a wrist guard on her arm. She smiled and laughed. He should at least be assisting her. She tested the draw of the bow before slipping it over her shoulder.

Squires led horses to each rider—huge powerful beasts that snorted and pawed the dirt. They reminded Drew of draft horses—but these were for riding. He shuddered.

The lad leading the black monstrosity Alex would be riding, braced his open palms on his knee and, and after she rested her foot in his hands, boosted her into the saddle. As she vaulted onto the creature's back, Drew noticed she'd changed. The pale blue blouse she now wore had cuffs at the wrist and not the long dangling sleeves. The dark skirt was not a skirt at all, but wide-legged flowing pants. "What is she wearing?" he muttered.

A giggle tinkled beside him. "She wears me riding skirt," Kolena said. "'Twill be more comfortable for her astride her mount and since it is the only one I own…" She whispered an impish grin. "Father does not like that I have it at all." She leaned back and her gaze returned to the mounted hunting party. "But as 'tis me only one, I offered to show ye our home while the rest hunt."

He really should have gone with them and Drew did not that there were a few women included in their number. Alex rode off without even a glance in his direction.

"This way, *brother*," Kolena giggled through a whisper.

Drew sighed, shaking off his irritation with the twittering maiden, and followed where she led, a maid close behind. Riding a horse couldn't be any worse than this.

The hunters returned triumphantly in time for the evening meal. Alex's cheeks were kissed with sunlight. Here with Brendon and his friends, she looked better than Drew had ever seen her. Healthy and at peace, she laughed and smiled most of the time. His heart ached at the distress he'd caused her over the months of his investigation. He needed to apologize.

Thankfully there was no dancing following the evening meal, and Alex retired early. Drew followed obediently and opened the door for her. She spared him a smile, and his heart skipped a beat.

"Sounds like the hunt went well." He wanted to keep her in the room—to share a few minutes of friendship like she did with the others.

"Aye, the men were very successful."

"And you were not?"

She stopped and flashed a slanted smile at him. Her nose crinkled. "Not a big fan of killing Bambi," she whispered.

"I can see that about you."

"I did help take down a boar. Those are nasty, mean creatures. They charge the horses and the hunters with their sharp tusks which can tear a leg off. And they're hard to kill. Takes a team effort."

"I'm glad you are uninjured, m'lady. Huz-ha," he tried with a fist pump.

"Huz-ha?" Her brows drew together.

Drew shrugged, his back still twinged in places. "I thought that is what everyone was cheering after the sword fight."

"Oh," she laughed. "Ye mean Huzzah! 'Tis an old cheer."

"Huzzah to killing the boar then." He earned a bright smile for his attempts to stay in character. He was doing better than her at the moment.

"So how did ye pass yer afternoon?"

He sighed, "Lady Kolena gave me an extensive tour of the town."

The smile vanished. The light from her eyes disappeared. Her words were choked, and the medieval vanished. "Then you had a grand afternoon, to be sure." She bobbed her head and disappeared into the other chamber.

Drew wanted to throw something. Alex Wright was maddening.

Chapter 23

Back in her own blouse with the dangling sleeves and her layered skirts the following morning, Alex Wright didn't even afford him a glance as they went to the meal. She spent her morning with Lady Kolena and his brother as they visited the merchant stalls in town. He been told to remain behind and rest. His feet still ached and his back was tight this morning, but surely he could follow them around the dusty streets. It was clear Alex didn't want him around.

Drew sat on a bench outside the inner gate and waited for their return. Again she didn't even look at him as they passed on the way to the midday meal. Drew fell into line behind them and they went in for lunch.

Later, when she rose to leave the laird's hall, a man approached her with two large leather bound books. The woman collected books wherever she went.

Alex nodded for the man to hand them to Drew to carry, then turned with a small wave to catch Brendon's attention. The three of them returned to Alex's outer chamber. Drew placed the volumes, that reminded him of old family Bibles, on the table, and Alex sat beside them. She flipped one onto its front and set the books against one another—raw edges to raw edges.

Brendon took a seat on the other side of the table, and Drew flopped on the divan. Both watched her silently for several minutes.

Alex opened the book on her left to the back cover and the one on her right to the front cover as it lay upside down. She pulled the two closer together until the covers rested over one another. Then with slow, careful precision she began to intertwine the pages. Back and forth, page on page, she wove the two blank books together.

Brendon tilted his head at her. "What do ye, my lady?"

"Binding them together."

"Nay can they be used—" Brendon said.

"I'll explain in a minute. First there is something I need you to do."

Brendon nodded. "Of course, my lady."

"Detective, where is the bag I brought?"

Drew frowned at her aloof manner. "Here," he offered holding it up.

"In the bottom, there is a hidden flap. Pull out the items below it."

Drew did as she requested and withdrew a ballpoint pen and three postcards.

She turned to Brendon, "Can you fill those out?"

Brendon took them and laughed. "A postcard from Dublin, one from Paris, and one from London. Look here," he showed them to Drew. "Each bears a stamp and postmark by the appropriate post offices as having been sent." Turning back to Alex, he prepared his pen and asked, "What missive would ye like, my lady?"

"This is why you came," Drew words struggled through his aching chest.

Brendon looked between the two of them.

"You intended to use these as poof B was still alive. This was your way of getting out from under the investigation?" Drew wanted to be mad at her. The deception, the lies she was willing to tell to keep her secret. But then he also couldn't fault her for wanting to clear her name.

"I hoped to ease your pain," she said quietly unable, or unwilling, to look at him.

"Oh, geez, I... I didn't... I'm sorry," Brendon muttered to both of them and his medieval verbiage vanished. "D, how would it be best to word these? It has to be logical and feasible for your fellow officers to believe, right?"

Drew nodded. "Be your normal irreverent self. Talk about the *fun* irresponsible things you're doing—things you're seeing—how much I'd hate it." His voice was dry.

Brendon sat with his pen poised over the first card. "Why haven't I called?"

"You have a cra—" He cleared his throat and dared a glimpse at Alex as she continued to weave the pages of the two books together. "You have a junk phone. It can't make international calls. You can't afford a new one. Or you're playing too much to call me."

"Sorry, bro." Brendon considered him for a long moment. Drew nodded, and Brendon started filling out the cards. They batted ideas and phrases back and forth as Alex continued with her books.

"You know it's too bad we can't get a video message recorded," Brendon said.

Alex looked up at Drew. "Your cell have any battery left?"

"It should." Drew pulled his slacks from her bag and fished his phone out of the pocket, powering it on. "But it will be recorded on my phone. How's that going to help?"

"Tyler."

"Tyler?"

"You know the kid I took to rehab the night you started following me?"

"Hack?"

"You were following her?" Brendon broke in.

"That was the night it started to be a regular occurrence," Alex answered Brendon, her lips drawn in a harsh line, and her words bitter. Turning back to Drew she scowled. "Tyler is his name, only the thugs on the street who got him hooked call him Hack."

"Right. Sorry." He hoped apologizing would soften her. "So what can Tyler do with a video of Brendon recorded on my cell?"

"If it involves technology, Tyler can work it. He can get it off your phone so that it was never there and then send it to you like you received it from the outside."

"Sweet." Brendon reached for the phone and opened the video app.

"Be careful what you include in the picture. You know the CSI techs will pull it apart and try to figure out were you are and what you're doing." Alex warned.

Brendon changed his angle so an open window looking out on a cloud filled sky was framed behind him. He held the phone up a little higher to cut out most of his medieval shirt. Setting the phone down for a moment, he adjusted his hair so it didn't look so long and checked his look in the cell once more.

"Okay, I think I have the scene set. I think you should giggle, and tell me to hurry up and come along, Alex. That will help me keep the message short. Make it sound like Kolena."

For the first time, Alex frowned at Brendon. Not that he noticed.

"All right, quiet on the set," Brendon was like a big kid with a new toy. "Action," he poked the record and said his lines, Alex added her Kolena impression—though she didn't look happy about it.

When Brendon was done, handed the phone back to Drew who powered it off and returned it to the bag as Alex finally closed the covers on the two books. Now completely woven inside of each other, she stood them up on their bottom edges. A few gentle taps on the outside spines of one book and the pages sat nestled completely inside other.

Alex pulled the small dagger from her back. "Laird Brendon, your left hand please." Brendon's brow rose, but he stood and offered her his hand. Using the dagger, she pricked one of his fingertips and drizzled a narrow zigzag line of blood on the top page edges. She flipped the books over and did the same across the bottom page edges.

"Thank you." She smiled at him. "Detective, your hand." No smile, only a cold order for him. She repeated the prick and the thin coating of the top and bottom edges. He didn't even get a thank you.

Next, she poked her own finger and overlaid their blood trails with her own. She reached for the chain around her neck and pulled it until an amulet lay in her palm. The old fashioned skeleton key at the end was about as long as her hand was wide. The top was a heart-shape blue stone. She dripped a couple of drops of her blood on the heart and set the key on the front cover of the joined books.

Her words were breathy and almost too quiet to hear.

"One to One,
Side by Side,
Blood of Blood,
Words to Bind.

Span the Distance,
Cross the Divide,
Share each Life,
Words will Bind.

Lord, I seek Your favor to join those torn apart. Mend the broken, restore that which was lost. Because of Your great love, allow this bond to remain. Amen."

When Alex fell silent, brilliant light burst from the top and bottom pages of the books. Drew looked away. The brightness lasted only a moment.

Chapter 24

Alex pulled the two books apart when the light vanished.

"Magic?" Brendon took the word from Drew's lips.

"No, technology our realm doesn't yet possess, and the blessing of God." She handed one volume to Brendon as she spoke to both of them. "These books are now bound together. You can use them to communicate with each other. What is written in one will appear in the other. Think of it as texting between the realms."

She started to hand Drew his book. It hung in the air between them —gripped in one of her small hands. "You will need to get a quill or old style pen and liquid ink. No ballpoint or crayon." Still holding Drew's book she again spoke to them both. "Don't write in specifics to your world. No old English," she nodded to Brendon. "No Super Bowl results," she said to Drew.

They both nodded, "Understood," they said at the same time.

As Drew reached for his book, he asked, "Is this how you communicate with the Conclave? Through your journal?"

The book was snatched from his grasp. She narrowed her gaze on him. His book was gripped in both of her hands. Her nails dug in the leather and her knuckles turned white. "What. Did. You. Say?"

Drew swallowed his guilt.

"The protein diet," she repeated his muttered words from when they had first arrived. She stood and took a step toward him. The fire burning in her eyes scorched his skin. "The costume closet," another thing he'd let slip on the second day. Another step closer, and Drew backed away from her fury "My. Journal!" she slammed his book into his chest driving the air from his lungs and slamming him into the wall behind him. "You broke into my home!"

He couldn't deny it. He couldn't breathe.

"You read my private thoughts." Her fist slammed into his jaw.

Pain radiated through his skull.

"You... you arse!"

If his face hadn't hurt so bad, Drew might of laughed at her old English cussing, when she'd never dream of saying the modern version.

"I hate you!"

The thought of laughter died as her words plunged into his heart more deadly than her blade.

Tears soaked her face. "I hate you," she sobbed and fled the room.

"Alex," Drew called as the door slammed behind her. He clutched the book to his chest where she'd left it.

Brendon grabbed his arm, and held him still. "Let her go. She needs time to cool off. In her current state, she is likely to take your head off." Brendon released him with a long stare. "And I can't blame her. Seriously D? Breaking and entering? Dude, what were you thinking?"

"That my only brother had disappeared without a trace, and she knew something."

"Even if you found evidence, you couldn't have used it against her."

"I'm aware of that." Drew looked at his brother. "You're my only family. What was I supposed to do?" He turned toward the door. "I need to apologize."

Brendon stopped him again. "Let me try first. I'll smooth the way for you." He sighed. "After all I am partly to blame."

"Partly?"

A fist slugged Drew in the arm. "Shut up."

Chapter 25

Alex stood in the torchlight on the roof of the keep far above her room. She didn't attend the evening meal—she had no appetite. She would pay the price if they left soon, but she couldn't sit in the hall with Detective Merritt glaring at her back and waiting on her like a common slave. Tears distorted her vision, and her pulse pounded in her head like a tribal drum. She fought for an even breath through her crying hiccups. She wrestled for one clear thought.

"There you are."

She startled at Brendon's quiet words. Alex turned to hide her face—sure she looked frightful with swollen red eyes and tear soaked face. "Did Laird Eldridge notice my absence at boards?"

"Aye, I told him ye were deep in prayer as ye prepared to leave his enjoyable hospitality and return to yer duties. He said Andrew could bring yer meal to yer chambers if ye wished it later."

"Thank ye, m'laird."

The shuffle of another pair of footsteps joined them on the roof.

"Tell me, he did not accompany ye, m'laird." She couldn't face the detective now. She was a hot mess—as Brendon liked to say. She'd said things she didn't even know she was capable of uttering.

"No, 'tis only Maci." He leaned in to whisper, "I shall guard yer honor as ye did me Kolena's."

"Honor?" she croaked. "I called him a—you know—and told him I hated him. Not so honorable, me thinks?"

Brendon chuckled as he crossed his arms and leaned back against the tall merlon next to her. "Mayhaps a fair bit un-lady-like…"

She raised her head, "It is unkind to make sport of me, sir."

"Ow, nay am I making sport of ye, my lady. Merely saying 'tis not as terrible as ye might think. He blames himself and seeks yer forgiveness. He knows full well and good he was every bit a—"

She put up her hand so he wouldn't say the word yet again. "I understand why he did it. Part of me cannot fault his behavior."

Brendon's laughter grew. "Yet at the same time ye wish to run him through for what he did. His actions were uncalled for, my lady. He stands in error according to the law he is to uphold, and he tarnished his own honor by his reprehensible behavior. I would not fault ye if ye chose to leave him behind when ye returned."

Now she released a strangled laugh. "If all this happened at the disappearance of a *brother* of the law man, what would become of me if he himself vanished? I shudder at the mere thought, m'laird." She rested her forearms on the crenel and looked down on the bailey below. A few servants and men-at-arms still went about their duties in the late hour. "I would never consider leaving him. He knows the truth. Mayhaps there can be a peace in him now. I have done all that I might to appease him."

"You can also forgive him, my lady. And me."

She turned to consider Brendon in the flickering firelight.

"I sore regret placing ye in his path. I was a coward in not telling him of me departure as ye advised. Had I been an honorable man, I would've told him face to face and not in a written missive left for another to hide from him."

"Hide?"

Brendon leaned close so the servant couldn't hear. "Yes, I left a note for Drew along with some personal belongings—mementos, family treasures—and told my landlord to give them to my brother. He didn't. He hid both, lied when Drew came to investigate, and milked him out of four months rent before he handed over the box—with several items missing. Drew is going to use the video recording to confront him."

"That's terrible."

Brendon straightened. "Aye, but would nay have happened had I not played the coward. So, my lady, I seek your absolution for my sins against him and by extension ye. Will ye forgive me?"

"Of course."

"Thank ye." He paused and held her in a long stare. "Will ye forgive him?"

She looked back at the bailey. Thoughts and feelings jumbled inside her like clothes in a out of control dryer.

"If ye do not forgive, than neither shall the Father in heaven forgive ye."

"Aye, I know well this verse. I believe I taught it to ye. Pray for me, m'laird, for my spirit is willing, but my flesh is weak. I know I should, but I rebel at the very idea."

He pushed off the wall, placed both hands on her shoulders, bowed his head and began praying instantly. She didn't hear much of what he said, for even in seeking God, she rebelled. God could—and would—change her heart. But she really didn't want Him to—not yet anyway.

She thanked him for the intercession when he finished and stepped toward the doorway with a yawn. "Long passed time to—" Warm air caught in her lungs. Her skin buzzed like she stood too near high-power lines.

"Your way home."

She spun to look directly at him. A brow arched high as her mouth hung open.

"I know that look well." He rubbed his arm and whispered, "And my skin tickles like ants are crawling over it. That has only ever happened three times."

She continued to stare until he explained.

"The day before we left to come here. When you returned home. And two days ago."

She nodded and moved to the edge of the keep walking around each side until she could see it. In front of a recessed doorway in the north side of the hall, the familiar shimmer of a portal doorway drew her attention. Like heat off the pavement on a hot day, it opened there for only her eyes to see. She told Brendon where it was. Together, planned for how she and Detective Merritt would slip through without being seen.

As she turned to leave, she paused and asked, "Will ye instruct him on the preparations needed and the process?"

Brendon sighed, "Aye, my lady. As well as plan for yer departure."

She curtsied quickly, "Thank ye."

Chapter 26

Drew could not serve an empty seat. When Alex didn't come to the evening meal, neither could he find an appetite. He returned to her chambers and waited. He paced. He worried. Worried and paced. After what he'd done, he couldn't blame her for hating the sight of him.

His hands ached to smash into something. His hands fisted and opened repeatedly.

The door inched inward without a sound. She jerked rigid. Her wide gaze skipping between the still lit lamps and him as he stood behind the chair she'd used earlier. His knuckles white as he gripped the wood.

Drew straightened. "M'lady,—" He tried to fit into her world.

She raised a hand and positioned the young serving girl in front of her. Using her like a shield between them, Alex moved to the inner chamber. "I know what ye wish. Later," she whispered as she passed. "I am shattered—tired," she quickly clarified.

"I'm sorry," his hand brushed her arm, but she didn't stop. She nodded and disappeared beyond the other door. Drew dropped to the chair. He sat unmoving, his stomach clenched in a fierce knot—grateful that he hadn't eaten. The mere thought of food made him want to hurl.

Resting his elbows on the table, he buried his face in his hands. What an idiot. Look what he'd done. She'd never forgive him—and she shouldn't. He broke the law he swore he upheld, and tore her life apart.

Drew paced, his hands returning to their worthless movements in rhythm with his stomped steps. This inaction was intolerable. While locked in this other realm, he couldn't go to the gun range, or take down a perp, or even punch out his frustration in the gym with a woman who justly hated him.

After an hour, a couple of the lamps sputtered and went out. He didn't relight them. He staggered to the divan and he lay there drumming his fingers on the high side, his foot wiggling in an erratic twitch.

Tap, tap, tap.

Without a minute of sleep, Drew glanced at the new glow of the eastern sky and opened the outer door.

"Good, ye're up," Brendon said slipping through the opening.

"Couldn't sleep."

Brendon nodded. "She say anything last night?"

"Only to tell me—later."

"I've never seen her like this. You really did a number on her."

"Thanks, B. I needed that right now."

Brendon's hand fell heavy on Drew's shoulder. "She is a godly woman. Give her time. She'll come around."

Drew sat, his head hung limp as his arms braced on his thighs.

"I came on another matter… Dis she tell ye the portal is open for ye to return home?"

Drew nodded. He could get out of this backwards-medieval world. Go back to normal. Work. Hunting criminals. But he'd be leaving B. He would have to travel with Alex, but at least he would clear her name.

He stuffed the feuding notions aside. Action. What action should he do? "How do I prepare?"

"Each door is only open for forty-eight hours. That leaves less than forty before this one closes. Problem is, 'tis in one of the busiest parts of the bailey. Ye're sure to be noticed vanishing if ye go through during the day. We came up with a plan for ye to go through well past dark tonight."

The inner door opened. Alex and her maid crossed the room to the outer door. He and Brendon both stood. "Good morrow, m'lady," Drew said, his words raw in his tight throat.

Dark circles shadowed under her red-stained eyes. She inclined her head but kept moving.

Brendon's hand gripped Drew's arm preventing him from following her. His brother's brogue vanished as he instructed Drew in all he needed to do to prepare for the trip. "When you enter the portal, there is a rush of air that pushes against you. Don't let it push you back. Lean into it, tackle it head on as if it were a two-hundred-pound perp trying to take you down."

Drew nodded. "I won't fight her. I won't hurt her again."

With his hand on Drew's shoulder, Brendon spoke with sober words. "Even with perfect preparation and dogged determination to move forward through the portal, taking you along will cost her something. It is the nature of the transport. Such awesome ability does not come without a price. But your efforts will make it more manageable for her."

Drew nodded.

At the breaking of the fast, Maci served Alex at the high table. Drew moved to a spot among the servants and crammed in as many protein rich foods as he could stomach.

After the meal, Drew made to follow her, but Brendon stopped him. "She goes to Lady Selby to pray for her while she is lying-in."

"Lying-in?"

Brendon smiled as he steered Drew to the kitchens. "She is heavy with child and will deliver any day. They don't allow women in her condition out of their chambers until almost a month past the birth," Brendon whispered.

In the kitchen, Drew collected a few items for the journey. Eldridge wished to send them off with food as they walked back to whatever business Lady Alexandria claimed she was doing. However, Drew shook his head at the pointlessness of wrapping hard biscuits and jerky in cloth and filling water skins from the well. It would be a single step from this world to his own—but he did as instructed and then returned to Alex's outer chamber.

It took him a while to arrange Alex's now bulging bag. His book filled the bottom—Brendon's postcards tucked inside the cover. His gun and then his modern clothes were stuffed in next—now so wrinkled they'd need a week of ironing to straighten out. The food items were on top causing the drawstring difficulty in keeping the bag closed. He sat the water skins beside it with Alex's sword.

He made a quick sweep of the rooms to make sure they left nothing behind. For the first time, he stepped through the inner door into her chamber. While he'd been forced to sleep on the hard divan, or in the cramped box bed, Alex slept on a huge downy bed with curtains surrounding it and tons of covers to keep the chill that filled the stone structure at bay.

"Pampered much?" Drew groaned. But his stomach lurched at his own coldness. After what he'd put her through, didn't she deserve at least a comfortable bed?

The bells called everyone to lunch. Drew collected their items and sat them against the wall where he stood and served Alex for one last meal. Later, he ate as she said her goodbyes.

Eldridge said a blessing over her and kissed her on both cheeks.

Drew envisioned his fists in the man's face.

Brendon and Kolena led them to the outer gate so they could make a good show of leaving the laird's castle. They planned was to head down the road, swing back through the surrounding forest, and sneak in the rear of the castle to get to the portal when no one would see them. The two couples were a short distance outside the wall away from anyone who could see when Brendon gave him a quick hug. After his brother released him with a nod, Kolena took his place.

Drew didn't know what to do with the blonde hugging him tight. This was a break in protocol. Ladies didn't hug servants. This was his sister-in-law, but here her contact was surely inappropriate. Did he hug her back?

"May God guide yer journey home, and may it be in His will for ye to return to us one day, my brother."

Drew stared at her as she moved to Brendon's side. He couldn't find the words to tell her he could never come back. She wouldn't understand, and it would tear his already aching heart to pieces to put voice to his pain. Drew turned to join Alex, but she was already a short distance down the road, stomping off on quick steps.

This was going to be a long afternoon.

Chapter 27

Blisters bit at his toes and heels as Drew tried to keep pace with Alex's stomping charge away from Eldridge's stronghold. "Alex?" Air rushed through his lungs as if chasing down some criminal fleeing the scene. Only here, he was the criminal, and his victim fled from him. He almost came even with her, "Alex?" he tried again.

She made an abrupt right turn and charged off between two fields of low-cut stalks.

Drew paused, gulped down cold air, and swiped at his sweat-drenched skin. He quaked, gulped once more, and raced after her. He bit back a curse that was sure to offend "Freeze. Blast it all, woman." His words came in gasps. "Slow down. We have all day before we can reach the back of the castle so we can sneak in to reach the portal."

The muffle of her heavy strides changed to the crunch and snap of twigs as they moved into the forest. Drew stumbled on roots and caught his pants on bushes as he struggled to catch up with her. A bright ray of sunlight through the dense canopy slapped him in the face. Shadows chilled him.

A thorn bush caught her cape. A choking noise followed her grunt as she yanked it free.

Drew lunged in front of her and stood in her path gasping for air.

Her whole body heaved with effort to take in enough air.

Drew held up his hands in surrender. "A break? Please?"

Her fists went to her hips. Then she turned to the side, leaned back against a tree, and folded her arms under her cape.

Drew braced his hands on his knees and welcomed air into his lungs. The bag dropped from his shoulder and landed near his foot with a thud. As his breathing calmed and his heart slowed from its frantic rhythm, he straightened. He cleared his throat and opened his mouth to speak.

She turned and glared at him at the same moment.

"I know you hate me and want to be rid of me at once—"

"I know you'd rather be going home with Kolena—"

Their words had burst into the air at the same moment—harsh and accusing.

They both recoiled and stared at the other. Birds chirped overhead. Something scurried through the leaf litter.

"What?"

"What?"

Again their query entered the peace at the same moment.

"Kolena?" Drew started first. "You think I like Kolena?" He searched his memories for some reason Alex would accuse him.

"She is a beautiful woman."

"I suppose," Drew offered.

"Suppose? You become speechless anytime she comes near. All puppy dog eyes and drooling lips. And you *suppose* she's beautiful?"

A tickle fluttered in his chest. It bubbled and rumbled to his throat until it burst from his lips. He roared with laughter, fueled by her accusation and his pent-up anxiety. He couldn't stop it. "Kolena?" His laughter grew until his sides ached. He quieted for a moment, but the laughter continued to gurgle out of him in random bursts. "She is everything my brother ever dreamed of in *his perfect woman*." He fanned his face with an effeminate hand and mimicked Kolena's voice.

"Laird Brendon, I doest have broken mine nail. I think I shall swoon over the brutality of it all." He put the back of his hand against his forehead continuing to sound like his brother's wife. "Oh, the horror of it shall send me to my bed for weeks."

A soft chuckle danced in his ears. He turned toward it as Alex covered her mouth with her hand. "She isn't *that* bad."

She laughed. That beautiful rich sound that made his heart do an odd dance in his ribs. "Not that bad? She is the quintessential dumb-blond—who also happens to make for a great damsel in distress. And her insufferable giggle. Hee—hee, hee, hee, hee—hee—hee. I spent an entire afternoon listening to her titter away. I wanted to go back to your chamber and put my gun to my head."

Alex's laughter grew.

"Don't get me wrong, I would love to spend time at the holidays with them, but there is the tiniest part of me that is doing a Super Bowl touchdown dance knowing I won't have to spend days trapped in the same house with her."

Alex's laughter was punctuated by a small snort—which made her laugh harder. Even the birds above did not sound as sweet.

"But she is everything B needs," he said more seriously. "I've looked after him most of our lives. He needed someone to care for too. I didn't notice that before. Her meekness and damsel charm has been good for him."

Her laughter calmed, replaced by a roguish grin, "You're bad, detective."

Flashes of the truly despicable things he had done overwhelmed him, and his chest seized again. "I am. Terrible in fact. Alex, I'm sorry. I never should have—"

"I don't hate you," she blurted, turning to the side. Her beautiful profile was outlined in a ray of sunlight and glistened in pools in her eyes. "I know I said those vile words. I never should have. It's not the person I want to be to lash out at another."

"You had cause."

"It still wasn't right. I'm sorry I said it—or even thought it. And I'm not mad." She swallowed hard. "I was hurt and embarrassed."

"Embarrassed?"

"You read of my weakness, my failing, my—"

Drew stepped closer to her and lowered his voice. "I read of a woman at her breaking point—who never broke. A woman badgered by a thug trying to wreck her life—who never retaliated. That woman has carried too much on her own for far too long. You're strong, Alex Wright. I regret that I added to your trouble. I hope you can forgive me."

"I do, detective."

He side stepped in front of her and reached out his hand. "Mayhaps," he started with a flip of his heart and flutter in his stomach, "we could start again, m'lady. I am Drew Merritt. 'Tis a pleasure to meet ye."

As she extended her right hand and slid it into his, she swiped away a tear trickling down her cheek with her left. "Hello. Alex Wright. Pleasure's mine, good sir."

Her soft hand molded with his as if they were two puzzle pieces that fit only with each other. But the warmth flooding his heart at her smile was enough to chase off an entire winter of snow-blanketed cold.

"Shall we continue?" she asked, her head tilting away shyly.

He didn't want to relinquish her hand. "Might we proceed at a more sane speed?"

She laughed and nodded. "Yes, please."

Chapter 28

A breeze snaked through the trees brushing Alex's face, while playing with a few loose strands of her hair. Dried leaves crunched softly under their footsteps. The last visible rays of sunlight filtering through the forest turned some spots orange as the shadows grew long and deep. During their slow stroll Alex caught the detective stealing glances of her.

Her movements were purposeful but no longer frantic. The relaxed swing of her arms and dangling fingers mirrored his. The silence between them now didn't carry the tension it did before. Somehow, Alex believed it wouldn't matter what world she was in, as long as Drew Merritt walked beside her. But that could never be. The Conclave would never stand for it. He was not one of them. She also imagined he couldn't wait to get home and away from her and all this weirdness.

A wave of nausea washed over her. In a few hours, they would step back in their own realm. He knew the truth and would see her exonerated. There would be no need for any further contact. No investigation. No reports. No dinners. No friendship. No—she swallowed her tears. In fact, there couldn't be a reason. His involvement wasn't sanctioned. He'd suffer consequences if they remained friends. She shuddered at the thought of Drew banished to the Home of the Unredeemed. She couldn't bear the thought of him abandoned in some foreign realm with no friends and not way to provide for himself.

She straightened. Steeled her determination. She'd go back to training strangers for short periods of time. Detective Merritt would return to protecting the good citizens of Allen City. There'd be no place where their lives intersected.

The hole these thoughts left in Alex's heart nearly doubled her over. She placed her hand on the next couple of tree trunks to steady herself. The rough bark scraped against her palm.

She pushed the pain aside and walked closer to the detective. It would end soon, but she could pretend they were something more than cop and former suspect. For this moment at least.

The bells tolling the call to supper danced over Eldridge's high walls. They'd walked south away from Eldridge's stronghold earlier in the afternoon, turned west into the forested area bordering his village, and then moved back north. They ambled the entire length of his fortified home toward the rear wall through dense forest.

"There you are!" Brendon hissed when they stepped from the tree line. After going about his normal day, he'd slipped into the hidden passage and opened it for them. "I thought you two might have gotten lost—or worse." His gaze darted from Drew to Alex and back again.

"We stopped to…" Drew glanced at Alex. "…to clear the air."

"Everything okay?"

Alex nodded with a willing smile. "We're fine, m'laird."

After a few more glances from Alex to Drew and back again, Brendon turned and waved them to follow. In the shadow of the tall crenelated wall, Brendon searched. "Where is it? I came through the door only a moment ago?" He moved some dried, knotted brush aside revealing a wooden door. "Ah-ha. Here we are." Unlocking it, pulled the door open with a nerve-grating creak, and ushered them inside.

They stood in a narrow tunnel, rank with the stench of decay, chiseled from the rock holding up the thick stonewalls. Brendon used a torch to lead them down a small incline and back under the compound. Their feet waded through stagnant water sloshing over their feet which added to the air's rotten smell.

They wound around a couple of tight bends in the path where they had to turn sideways to shimmy through. There were several other places where both men had to duck beneath the low ceiling. They covered about a hundred feet before they came to a short staircase.

Brendon turned back and stepped past Alex. He took hold of Drew's forearm in a warrior-style handshake, then pulled him into an embrace and thumped him on the back. "Brother—" His words choked. "I shall never forget the lessons you have shared with me. I promise to be an honorable man and make you proud."

Drew tried to clear the sadness from his throat. "I will miss you every day, B."

"And I you." Brendon sniffed and whirled back to Alex. "Thank you. Again it doesn't seem like enough." He hugged her tight.

"God bless you, my friend," she said.

Brendon stood tall and cleared his throat. "You can't leave the torch lit. There is a frequently used larder on the other side." He pointed to the door at the top of the steps. "I hate to leave you in the dark, but it would be worse if you were caught down here."

Alex shrugged. "It'll only be for a few hours."

"Right, just until all in the keep take to their beds, then you can slip out. The portal is about twelve feet to the left of the outer door."

"We'll be fine," Drew said.

Brendon nodded. He climbed the stairs and put his ear to the door. A few moments later, he unlocked it and poked his head inside. "Take the key and lock the door behind me. Leave it under the flour bag," he pointed to something beside him inside the room. "I'll get it in the morning." He handed Alex the key and torch. With one last glance at Drew he said, "Love you D," and disappeared.

Alex locked the door and descended the stairs. She found a dry spot on a small island of rock out of the stagnate water and snuffed the torch. The inky darkness encased them like a shroud.

Chapter 29

"Alex?"

There was a little gasp in the darkness. "Yeah?"

"I don't want you to freak out, but I am going to hold you."

"Why?" she squeaked.

Drew stepped toward her voice, her soft cape brushing his fingers. "Because you're cold."

"Aren't you?"

He tried to suppress his laugh, "Freezing! But my teeth aren't chattering to the point the sound is echoing off the walls—yet." His hands slipped around her waist. He turned her and pulled her until her back rested against his chest. "Let's share some heat. There're still a couple of hours left."

She stood rigid in his hold for a few moments. "This isn't doing anything to warm you."

Alex Wright had no idea how her mere presence—her smile—her laughter—warmed him deep in his soul. He'd never been so attracted to any woman. She was perfect and completely out of his reach. He could loose his job if he got involved with a suspect. And she belonged to a secret society and had powers to travel through invisible opening to other realms. Talk about not moving in the same circles; they didn't even exist in the same world much of the time. If he could even convince her to date him, they'd have one heck of a long-distance relationship. He groaned inwardly.

She pulled his hands away. He felt the fabric of her cape brush his arms as she moved, but he couldn't figure out what she was doing in the utter darkness. Her gentle fingers guided his hands back to her waist. But he couldn't feel the fuzzy fabric of her wrap. His hands were on her belt. Then her fingers trailed up his arms, like angel's walking up them. When her wrists rested on his shoulders, she closed her cape around them both, and Drew realized she'd turned to face him.

Alex sunk into him. Her head tucked under his chin. Her warm breath slipped between the laces of his shirt setting fire to his skin. After a few moments, her shivering slowed and finally stopped as she melted into him. Her curves pressed against him, and he tightened his grip on her waist.

He would stay here in the dark until he took his last breath—if he could always hold her like this.

He shifted the weight to draw her even closer. The aligned perfectly with each other.

"You all right?" The vibration of her words hummed through his chest. He prayed she didn't notice the uptick of his heartbeat.

"Let me—" He cleared his throat as his voice cracked. He pulled her as he stepped back carefully. "I wanted to lean on the wall, so I can support us both."

"If I'm too much…" She tried to pull away, but Drew held her tight.

"Never. With your warmth I was feeling a little sleepy," he lied. "I didn't want to drift off, fall, and hurt you; I think I've done quite enough of that." He muttered the last few words. Lifting the bag strap off his shoulder and dangling it at his elbow, he found the wall. Drew brushed his fingers in circles up from the small of her back, as he leaned into the bumpy surface.

He felt the rumble from her more than heard it. It was like a purr rolling through her as he massaged her tight back muscles. Her head dropped under his chin again. Soon her breathing grew slow and even, and her weight against him increased.

While she slept in his arms he dared press a tender kiss to the top of her head.

Truly, he could stay like this forever. Too bad, she'd never see him as anything but the man who hunted her relentlessly without cause and broke into her home, violating her trust. He would take it all back—if only he could.

Alex's arm slid off his shoulder, and she startled in his grasp. She wiggled, stretched, and yawned. "I think I fell asleep."

"You must be tired. I don't think either of us got much sleep last night," Drew muttered with a yawn of his own.

She groaned as she pulled back from him. The chill left by her absence made his heart shiver.

"Is something the matter?"

"My arms are completely asleep. I can't even feel them."

His hands still on her hips, he let his fingertips trail up her back to her shoulders. With gentle massaging, he worked the blood back into her biceps, down over her elbows, through her forearms. He took one of her hands in both of his, and using his thumbs to rub and his fingers for added pressure, worked out to the end of each finger. He finished and moved to her other hand. "Better?"

Her voice whispered through the darkness, in a breathy gasp. "Yes. Thank you."

They were quiet for a few minutes. One of her hands still held tight in his.

"How long did I sleep?"

Not nearly long enough. He couldn't tell her how much he wanted his arms around her again. "I'm not sure. I think I dozed a little too. Maybe an hour or a little more."

"I think we should head out."

"Right." Time to head back to where he was utterly alone.

Her fingers still linked with his, she pulled him along. She stumbled, but his hold kept her from falling. "You okay?"

She laughed. "Yeah, on the training mat, or with a sword in my hand I don't have a problem. But walking down the sidewalk, I'm most likely to trip over my own feet."

Thunk!

"What was that?" Drew asked.

"Found the stairs."

"Was that your foot?"

"No, my shin. I'll have a bruise in the morning." Her laughter increased as she rose higher. Drew found the first step with a tentative probing of his toe. He followed her up until she yelped, quietly. "Found the door—and jammed my finger. I think I broke a couple nails too." She tried to make her voice sound pathetic, but her bubbling giggle betrayed her.

"Oh, no, m'lady. Whatever shall we do?" Drew teased.

She didn't respond. In the stillness she squeezed his hand a little tighter, and it felt like she shuddered. "I fear it is a hopeless cause," she muttered at last.

Scraping and a clicking followed. "I can't seem to get the key in the hole." Alex wiggled her hand free of his. The action, combined with her odd words about being a hopeless cause, left his heart flopping in the pit of his stomach like a dying fish. She pressed fabric into his palm. "Don't let go," she whispered.

Metal slid over metal, and the lock clanked. She pulled the door open toward them, and her weight shifted. She gasped, and Drew grabbed for her to keep her from falling back into him. As she tried to regain her balance and right herself, he became aware of the fact that his hands were cupped over her rump. Heat roared up his arms clear to his cheeks. He was grateful they stood in the dark. Drew wanted to release her—he didn't wish to give her another reason to hate him—but too much of her weight rested in his hands yet.

"Sorry for my hands," he mumbled.

"Better than letting me take you down with me. We would be wet in that disgusting water and might have broken something too." She shifted and came off his awkward hold. Alex reached for his hand, and they stumbled their way through the messy storage room until she found the other door. Pulling it open, the torchlight from high on the wall lit the room enough for her to return to the hidden door, lock it, and hide the key under the flour bag for Brendon. She returned to him and, after a quick scan of the space between them and the archway a dozen feet away, they slipped toward it.

Stopping in front of it, Drew only saw a curved top wood door, but he felt a tiny buzz tickling his skin. Alex glanced at him for a moment, her right brow raised high. He nodded and offered her his hand. She laced her fingers into his and stepped forward.

Freezing cold wind stole his breath—driving him back and rejecting his presence.

He pushed against it.

Light blinded him. Warm sun heated his back. A car horn honked in the distance, and a helicopter flew overhead.

Chapter 30

Drew squinted and opened his eyes slowly. His mind fumbled to comprehend the jolt to his system as he stepped from the middle of the night in late fall, to the blazing sun in the heat of early summer late afternoon in a single moment. A few tentative blinks and he realized he stood on a sidewalk in the middle of the block. No cars travelled the street at the moment.

Alex had already shed her cape. It lay spread out on the cement beside her. She unlaced her vest and dropped it on the cloth. Unbuckling her belt, she slid off the sword and dagger, adding them to the collection at her feet. Holding the belt in her teeth, she untied the cord securing her skirts. They fell to her ankles revealing that her shirt was long enough to touch the tops of her high boots. She secured the belt around her again, snatched up the skirts, folded them twice and dropped them with the rest. Next, she took the dangling ends of her sleeves and worked them up inside the full length of the arm until the tips appeared at her shoulders. She tucked the ends under her bra straps. Finally, Alex pulled the net accessory from her hair, removed the braid, and pulled her hair up into a high ponytail.

Drew stood mesmerized. In less than three minutes, Alex Wright went from medieval Lady Alexandria to hot chick ready for some clubbing—not that Alex would be caught dead in a nightclub. But when she turned to him, her eyes were watery. Her lower lip trembled, and she barely looked at him. *I made her cry again. What did I do now? I want to keep her here, to never let her leave, but in the eyes of everyone at the station, she's a suspect. I'd loose my badge. But I can't let her go—could I?*

"There is a bathroom in the park." She pointed behind him. "You can change there before heading on your way."

Drew glanced over his shoulder. Hope Park took up an entire block. They stood on the east side of it, so Alex lived seven blocks further east and two north. He was close to the same distance to the south, but he'd left his car near her apartment. When he turned back to ask how they were each going to get home, Alex wasn't there.

She'd gathered up her belongings inside her cape, slung it over her shoulder and was already a couple of feet down the block. "The Lord bless you and keep you safe, detective," she called without looking back. Her words were unsteady.

Drew's stomach pitched and rolled. His heart thudded out a labored rhythm as if trying to beat while buried in sand. The tightening of his chest like a python held him, made it hard to breathe. "Alex?" The word burst from his lips in a desperate cry.

She stopped. Then turned slowly, but only enough to reveal her profile, not face him. Even at this small distance, the pools hovering on her lids sparkled in the sun.

He looked around him—for something—anything—to keep her here. *Don't go. Don't leave.* The words burned in his throat, but he could not release them. The bag started to slide off his shoulder. He held it up. "Don't forget your bag." *Lame. Stupid. Pathetic.*

She continued on her way. "Don't worry about it." Her words sounded like they were choked—lifeless.

"Alex!" He couldn't catch a full breath. His whole body shook. Dizziness kissed his awareness, and his vision narrowed. *Keep her here. Don't let her go.* His thoughts railed at him, but he didn't know how.

She stopped at the corner, and waited, but didn't turn more than her head.

Which would be worse, to tell Alex how he felt and suffer her rejection, or to let her disappear? He held onto a parking sign, trying to steady himself. Both ideas were equally intolerable. But he had to say something. She stood there waiting. *Get a grip man!* He swallowed the fear strangling him. "What about the phone message?" He hoped she would meet him somewhere and they could go visit Hack, or rather Tyler, together.

Her entire body seemed to sag, like a deflated balloon she went limp. Her words were barely audible as they croaked from her throat. A tear sparkled in the sun as it slid down her cheek. "Tyler is in a six week program at the clinic. You can find him there. Tell him I sent you and to fight the good fight."

She was gone. Vanished around the corner. Out of sight, and out of his life. She couldn't leave him behind fast enough.

Drew staggered to the wall and fell back against it. The pain of all his losses crushed him.

Chapter 31

Numb, Drew stuffed away his pain like he would cram a receipt into his pocket. He slipped into the park—head down and eyes on his toes. A few minutes later, he emerged from the restroom dressed in wrinkled slacks and shirt. Alex's bag bore into his shoulder as he lumbered in the direction of his car. He barely pulled his phone from his pocket and powered it up before it blew up with incoming text messages and voice mails. The whistles and dings nearly vibrating the device out of his hand. Planting one foot in front of the other, he waited for the continuous racket to die before he started going through them.

All the texts were from his partner Andersen.

Drew texted back. "I'm here. Found brother, kind of. Will explain in the morning."

"Merritt! Where are you!"

"Heading home."

Drew's phone battery hovered at eight percent. How did a battery die when the phone hadn't even been on? He stuffed it in his pocket and kept walking.

Which were heavier, his legs, his eyelids, or his heart? It had been too long since he slept. He couldn't think.

Honk!

"Get in!" Andersen called through the passenger window.

"I said I'd see you in the morning. I want to get my car—"

"It's been impounded. Get in. I'll give you a lift."

Drew didn't have the energy to walk to the impound yard. He couldn't make it there on foot before they closed anyway. He pulled open the door and flopped into the seat.

Andersen pulled away from the curb with a squeal of tires. "So where have you been?" Curses littered his question.

Coming from the gentile world where course language was shunned, these familiar phrases grated against Drew. Odd how quickly his attitude had changed.

"You going to say anything or what?"

"Brendon's alive."

"You said as much in your text. So… spill."

Drew had spent some of the hours with Alex wrapped in his arms, coming up with a story for his coworkers. He planned to say he'd found the postcards in his mail and gone and gotten stupid drunk. He knew a bartender who owed him a favor. The guy would say that he slept it off in a back room.

"Merritt, you gonna talk or do I have to take you to an interrogation room and put the screws to you."

The contrived tale didn't feel right. "I went to my P.O. box for the first time in weeks. Found three postcards from B."

"Postcards? So where is he? Why hasn't he called?"

"He is flitting around Europe with some chick."

"Europe? How'd he get there?"

"I don't know. She must have paid for it. I didn't even know he had a passport."

"So we know where he is—sort of. What happened to you? You've been gone for a day and a half."

Only a day and a half had passed here while he and Alex spent three days in Brendon's world. B'd mentioned something about the time being weird between worlds. "I went to apologize to Alex."

"So it's *Alex* now?"

Drew ignored the dig. "I caught up with her as she was leaving town. I got sucked into her travel, and we finally returned home a few minutes ago."

"So… you spent the night together?" Andersen flashed a wink his way.

"She hates me. There is nothing between us—will never be anything after what I did."

The car stopped in front of the impound yard, and his partner turned to look at him. "We have wrongly accused hundreds of suspects over the years, none of them has affected you like this woman."

"This case was personal. And I made it personal with her."

"You broke into her place, didn't you?"

Drew reached for the door.

Andersen hit the electronic locks preventing his escape. "That day we caught the Smitherly case—you were in her apartment. I know you were."

Drew nodded.

Andersen slugged him in the arm. "You're an idiot. You could be suspended for breaking into her place. What were you thinking? What if she presses charges?"

Drew flipped the lock and pushed open the door. "She won't. Miss Wright doesn't want anything more to do with me. It's over." He stepped out and walked toward the booth where the attendant would give him his car—for a large fee.

"So why's this woman's rejection getting under your skin?" Andersen called out the window.

Drew kept walking without looking back.

Parking his car outside the clinic an hour later, Drew moped to the door. He was admitted and directed to the common room while the attendant went to get Tyler. Drew dropped into a hard metal chair and set his phone on the table. He'd charged it on the drive over, it was now at twenty-seven percent. Hopefully that would be enough for the kid to work his magic.

A clean boy with light brown hair appeared on the other side of the table. His hands were stuffed in his pockets. His face crinkled in confusion. "I know you, mister?"

"I'm a friend of Alex Wright's." His heart ached at the lie. "She thought you might be able to help me."

Tyler kept standing. His gaze narrowed on Drew.

"She said to keep fighting the good fight."

The kid pulled out the chair and slid into the seat. "Yeah, she's always telling me that. What'cha need?"

Drew slid the phone across the table. "There's a video on here I need to not be on here but it needs to look like it was sent to me." He pointed out the file.

Tyler cradled the device in his hands his thumbs tapping away at high speed. "That's easy enough." He jabbered on about a cloud, sending, wiping and a lot of computer jargon that was gibberish in Drew's tired brain. In truth, it probably still wouldn't have made much sense if he was fully awake and coffee-fueled.

"You're the cop who's hunting Miss Alex, right?" His voice was flat and accusing.

"I *was*." Drew emphasized the last word. "I now know my brother ran off. I've apologized to her. We're good now." Not as good as he wanted but definitely better.

After only a few minutes of silence, Tyler handed the phone back to him. "Done."

"Thanks. I really appreciate this."

Tyler stood with a shrug. "No, problem."

"Tyler." The kid turned. "Miss Alex is a friend. She's important to me. I care about her. If you don't do right by her—you'll answer to me. Understood?"

Tyler nodded.

"But that also means that her friends are my friends. You need anything—I'll do what I can to help." He passed the kid his business card. "Call me—anytime, day or night. I'll be there."

Tyler took it. "K." He disappeared down the hall, and Drew headed home. But he really wanted to swing by and check on Alex. What would she do if he showed up on her doorstep?

"Merritt!"

Drew halted from heading to his desk and moved to Captain Cruz's office. "Sir?"

"Close the door."

Well, this wasn't good. Anytime the captain pulled a detective into his office—alone—and close the door, that person was in for an earful.

"What on God's green earth were you thinking, Merritt?"

"Sir?"

Captain's finger speared out at him. "Don't play stupid with me, detective. You know you can't investigate your brother's disappearance. And you certainly can't go off on a romantic getaway with the suspect! I have to take your gun and badge."

"Captain! It wasn't like that at all."

"You weren't following Miss Wright?"

"I did on occasion," Drew admitted quietly.

"You didn't spend the last two days alone with her?"

"We weren't alone. She was—working. I accidently got sucked into tagging along."

Captain Cruz sat back and crossed his arms. "Accidently?"

Drew stifled the urge to answer with a medieval "Aye." He nodded instead. "My brother's made contact. He's alive." Drew pulled the postcards from his suit pocket and handed them to Cruz.

The captain scanned them quickly and passed them back. "That doesn't get you off the hook. It looks bad on the department if you are fraternizing with a suspect."

"Miss Wright is obviously cleared now, sir."

"Merritt, you're on desk duty until an investigation can be made. If you have any contact with Miss Wright—accidently or otherwise—you will be fired. Have I made myself clear?"

"Yes, sir." Drew left the office after a nod dismissed him. He knew the rules. He believed in them too. He'd even enforced them on street cops a couple of times. He dropped into his chair with a groan. But how was he going to stay away from Alex Wright? He held his head as his elbows propped on the desk.

"You got to stay away from her, partner. At least for now."

Chapter 32

Alex pulled her key from its hidden spot. Mr. Thomas, whose door sat kitty-corner from hers, poked his head out. She turned away to hide her face. She'd cried all the way home and knew her face told the tale.

"Well hello, Alex dear."

"Mr. Thomas." She moved to her door and fought to push the key in the slot with her quaking hand.

"Are you all right, child?" He closed his door and moved to the elevator. Mr. Thomas checked in regularly. He was the only one who cared for her.

"Yes, I'm well. It has been a long few days, though."

"You take care of yourself, dear." The elevator doors whooshed open, and the soft tick of his cane marked his movement into it. "You have to come over for tea soon, and tell me all about it."

"I will," she promised. As soon as the elevator was on its way down, she left her open door, returned the key, then disappeared inside her apartment. Alex tossed her medieval belongings in one room. She unlaced her boots adding them to the pile along with the belt. She yanked off her top and threw it in the laundry basket before dropping down on the comforter. Curled on her side, she again reviewed her journey.

The appearance of the detective had been unexpected and unwanted. She was sure to hear about it from the Conclave. She would get the full rundown of taking an Average Joe on missions and the consequences Drew would face if he ever breathed a word or joined her again. A tremor raced through her at the thought of him abandoned on some world to be forgotten with all the other AJs.

Thoughts of her legalistic, uncompromising overseers evaporated into notions of Drew. She'd misunderstood his feelings for the Lady Kolena. Her heart ached, her eyes were sticky from the drying tears, and her throat stung like it had been attacked by bees. But Detective Merritt wasn't into the lady—or her for that matter. It was for the best. There could never be anything between a guardian and an AJ. Though Drew was the least *average* anything she'd ever met. Alex couldn't get him out of her thoughts.

She'd acted like such a child. She'd stopped talking to him, tried to run away, said she hated him, but then he held her in the dark. The memory of his embrace ignited the tears again. Great sobs ripped from her body. How long had it been since someone held her? Touched her? Alex couldn't remember.

When they returned, Drew had called out to her. Hope sprang up like a fountain. Though she knew she couldn't have anything to do with him, she wanted to be asked. For once in her life she wanted someone to think her worthy of spending time with. But her momentary hope had dried up like mist in a wasteland, as he didn't want her—only what she could do for him.

Alex woke in the middle of the night. Her entire middle ached. But as consciousness dawned so did the unbearable pain in her soul.

After a couple days of wallowing, Alex needed to return to work, but there was no life in her. She pulled on her grey T-shirt and loosest leggings. She slipped her hair into a sloppy ponytail and headed out. As she left, she waved at Mr. Thomas as new tears choked her throat closed.

The grey sky, heavy with storm clouds, mirrored her soul. Her feet dragged along the sidewalk as though slogging through wet cement.

The clients who came to her studio blurred into a muted Picasso painting—disjointed and disfigured. Between sessions, Alex stared out the windows at the happy people going about their business and scanned the street for his car. But he never came. It was for the best—for him.

But not for her.

Chapter 33

"Merritt?"

Drew looked up as he hung up the phone. The desk sergeant from downstairs stood in the detectives' office doorway.

"You know this kid?"

Drew looked past the officer and noticed who stood behind him. "Yeah, he's all right." Drew stood and led the boy into a room at the end of the hall. Hair hanging over his eyes and hands shoved in his pockets, the kid slowly moved toward the table to join him. Drew motioned to the chair. "Hey, Tyler. How ya doing? You all right?"

His face hidden behind straight brown skater hair, the kid shrugged. "Yeah."

Drew leaned back in his chair and gripped the arms. Coddling a teenager was never in his wheelhouse—but the kid was important to Alex. He bit his tongue and waited to see what he wanted. "Can I do something for you?"

Tyler nodded.

Pinching the inside of his cheek between his teeth, Drew fought the urge to pin the kid to the table and take scissors to his hair. "Can you tell me what you need?"

"Yeah." Tyler shifted in his seat like one of the perps who more often used the chair. "I got sprung from rehab."

No? Really? Drew gripped the arms on his chair a little harder—and waited.

"I'm bunking at Boys Post."

"Good place." Drew had arrested youth who hadn't followed up with the rules at the home for boy's.

Tyler raised his head enough for Drew to get a glimpse of his smirk. "Yeah, Miss Alex fix me up. Nothin' but primo for her."

The mere mention of her name squeezed his heart until Drew squirmed in his own chair. "How's she doing?"

"Miss Alex?"

"Yeah." *Who else could he mean? Come on kid, keep up.*

Tyler raised his head and gave a small toss to clear the hair so he could look Drew in the eyes. His brows crinkled together. Then his face vanished behind the curtain of hair again, and the kid shrugged. "Okay, She seems… I don't know. Bummed, maybe. She's pitchin' in to get me squared in school again. History's her jam. She knows more than all my lame teachers rolled up."

Drew nodded, remembering all the history books in her apartment.

"English is fine, science too." Tyler chuckled and glanced up at Drew again. "But she sucks at math."

Drew laughed with him. "So Miss Alex has a flaw?"

Tyler's face disappeared, and his head sunk lower. "Ya didn't hear it from me. Miss Alex's lit. She's done right by me. Don't want her bailing like everyone else."

"I'll never breathe a word, kid." Drew looked at him for a moment as the silence hung between them like a wool blanket. "What about your mom?"

"Says I have to produce—no more dope—before she'll let me crash with her. Says she loves me—but…"

"But she's got your siblings to consider too."

"Yeah." Tyler shrugged again. The action was beginning to get on Drew's nerves.

"You want to stay clean?"

For the first time, the kid sat up straight and looked him square in the eyes. "I *will* kick it. I don't ever wanna be jonessing again. That was the worst. I won't let down Miss Alex either, and I'll never be a faker on my mom again."

"Good. Don't ever forget that determination."

Tyler's head dropped again, shoulders sagging as he slouched back in the chair. "Here's the 411."

Finally. Get to the point, kid. Drew'd gotten confessions faster.

"I'm applyin' for a part time gig. Chip in at home and keep busy." He laughed softly again. "Like Miss Alex is always sayin'. 'Idol hands are the devil's toys' or somethin'."

"Where are you applying?"

"Office Mart. IT department working on people's broken computers."

"Sounds like a perfect fit."

"Then you'll write me a rec?"

Drew stared at the kid, his fingers drumming on the table.

Tyler shifted to the edge of his seat. "Don't sweat it, Dude."

"Cool your jets, kid. I've heard that you're clean and want to stay that way, and I believe you. And you know that if I do this, I'm putting my reputation on the line, right?"

Tyler nodded.

"Alex trusts you and believes in you, so I will too. Meet me at the Cheesy Fry on the next block tomorrow afternoon around 5:15, and I'll have it for you."

Tyler stood and pulled his right hand out of his pocket, but it remained at his side. "Then were G2G?"

Drew stood and reached out his hand. Tyler shook it, but Drew didn't let go when they finished. "Yes, good to go. I'm trusting you, Tyler. Don't let your mom, Miss Alex, or me down."

"I won't get beat."

"And if you really want the job, keep your hair out of your eyes for the interview." He mussed Tyler's hair with his other hand. "Look the manager in the eye, don't slouch in the chair. I'll put you through a dry run tomorrow before I give you the letter."

"Thanks. That'll help." He eased from Drew's grasp and turned toward the door.

"Oh and Tyler, bring your math homework. I was pretty good with numbers in high school."

Tyler nodded and disappeared.

Chapter 34

"Hey, Tyler." Alex looked up from her desk. "Nice tie. Going someplace fancy?"

Tyler flashed a rare smile. "Detective D hooked me up for an interview. He scribbled a dope rec and prepped me too. See why ya think he's A-1."

Alex's emotions did the Jitterbug. "Detective *Drew* helped you?"

"Yeah," Tyler's head tilted and he stared. "Says he's got my back 'cause of you."

"Me?"

"Yeah. You chill, Miss Alex? When Double D first dropped in on me in rehab, he said you sent him to me for help. Then he rattled my cage."

"The detective threatened you?" Alex's breath caught in her throat.

Tyler laughed. "Yep. Said you mattered. And if I didn't do you right —I'd be answering to him."

"He said that?"

"Yep. Don't you two jabber?"

Alex shook her head, trying to loosen the bewilderment. Had she heard him correctly? Or had she stepped into an alternate version of her own world? "Haven't heard from him in weeks."

Tyler shrugged, "Well, that's the 411. He got me the job."

"Great." The word snagged in her befuddlement and came out with less enthusiasm than she wanted.

"It'll jack up our cram-sections and add my work with Double D.

Won't have time left to sleep."

Words fled her lips.

Tyler tucked his head; his hands snuck into his pockets and shifted the weight between his feet. "He's coverin' math. You ain't ticked?"

She smiled. "No. He can have all the annoying variables and equations. We can work on the rest."

He looked up, and the smile returned. "Thanks, Miss Alex. I'll be trainin' for a few days, but I'll drop a call when I get squared." He bounded out of the studio and disappeared down the street.

Alex didn't have long to ponder his words or the confusion that whipped her insides. The members of her next class started to show up, stretching and waiting for her to begin.

Drew parked near Alex's studio. He'd been cleared of any wrongdoing in their involvement two months ago. He'd keep the flag on his file though. Still, Alex monopolized his thoughts. He should have cleared his intentions, but he didn't want to be told he couldn't see her.

Drew reached for the car door handle five times before he finally opened it. Another ten minutes of raking his hands over his head, starting across the street, only to turn back to the car. He reopened his door twice. The worst she could do was throw him out. Or he'd get fired for being here. The thoughts only served to twist his guts into knots and caused him to stop in the middle of the street.

Honk! He jogged for the sidewalk to get out of traffic.

Three women in skin-tight workout clothes exited laughing as they passed.

Drew stood paralyzed outside the door. Surely, being with SWAT on a raid against fully armed combatants wouldn't be this terrifying. He'd met women before. Dated many times. Yet, Alex was different. And it was more than her being part of some secret supernatural organization.

Oh, for heaven's sake. He was a grown man not a high schooler asking a girl on his first date. One deep breath, then he yanked the door open and took two quick steps inside. He moved across the tiny foyer, his frazzled nerves soothed by the sounds of a Christian melody. Drew moved to the inner doorway.

Alex was in the middle of the room. She preformed Tai Chi with her eyes closed. Her fluid movements reminded him of a ribbon of water. No harsh edges or stark jerks, she slid from one form to the next.

The breath he had gulped down to get in the door eased out of him, and he leaned against the doorframe. He couldn't disturb her. It would be like a train horn blaring during a perfect pink and orange sunset over a calm lake. Alex embodied perfection in every way, and he could watch her for—well, forever.

Awk. Alex let out a small squeak as her hand flew to her chest. She took one step back. "Detective?"

Drew jerked upright, and his heart flew into his throat. He coughed and sputtered for a moment. *Doing great so far, D.*

"How long have you been standing there?"

"A while. I didn't want to disturb your—" *Your what? Perfection? Beauty? Workout?*

"Detective, did you need something?" Her hand still lay protectively on her collarbone, and her brows drew together. Did she tremble?

His thoughts rattled like a ricocheting bullet. But who would it kill when it finally hit a target? He shoved his hands in his pockets to give them something to do—and like lightning, he saw Tyler in a whole new light. Hiding your hands in your pockets gave them something to do.

A thought sparked in his brain, and he removed one hand offering her a deep bow. "I come seeking a boon, m'lady."

One corner of her mouth pulled up in a small smirk. Her hand slid to her side.

Chapter 35

Alex offered the detective a slim smile.

Drew stared unable to move or think.

"Detective?" Her head tipped to the side. "Your boon, sir?"

"Right. Boon. I was hoping. I mean, if you aren't busy. It's late notice and all, so I'll understand." Drew clamped his mouth shut and turned away from her. What an idiot. What was he, thirteen? *Come on cop—man up.*

He turned slowly to see a grin spread across her face. *Did she laugh at him? Hands out of the pockets. Breathe, man. Speak. Whole sentences.* "It's my birthday."

"Happy birthday."

"Thanks." Sweet, but not what he was looking for. "I always go out with B—Brendon. And I wanted to know if you…"

Her smile took on a sad edge, but she nodded. "I would be honored. Can you wait a few minutes while I change?" She waved her hand over her baggy, long-sleeved tee and running pants.

"Sure. Yeah, of course."

She turned, and her ponytail swished across her back. "I'll be quick, detective."

"Oh, one more favor?"

She turned, glancing over her shoulder with a nod.

"Drew."

She tipped her head, brows pulled together.

"Will you call me Drew?"

"Be back in a minute, Drew." She disappeared around a corner in the back of the studio.

He stifled the urge to whoop and holler, jump, or fist pump the air —but the effort made him feel like he would explode. She'd agreed. *Take the win. Be a grown up.*

For several moments Drew looked out the windows at the busy street, a goofy grin reflected back at him off the glass. Soft steps crossing the mat made him turn. Alex stood in a white dress, fitted at the top and flared at her waist. All thoughts vanished.

She smoothed her hand over the fabric, "Is it wrong? Did you have something else in mind?"

"Un-uh." *Seriously. What had happened to his brain?* He swallowed. "Ah, no. Nothing wrong. It's a… I mean you look… I didn't expect you to be done so…" He clamped mouth shut again. This was a disaster.

She shut off the light in her office before pulling the door closed. She moved toward him. "I thought it would be rude to keep the birthday gentleman waiting."

He smiled but didn't dare open his mouth.

She looked at him for a moment. "Did you have a place in mind?"

He shook his head, and she giggled softly.

"How about Daly's?"

"Daly's?"

"Yeah." She moved toward the doorway out to the foyer, clicking off the lights as she went. "Daly's Diner."

"Never heard of it."

Her head tipped again as she locked the door. She shivered.

Drew yanked his suit jacket off and draped it over her shoulders.

"Thank you." She smiled. "I guess it's time to bring some winter clothes down to the studio."

"My car is this way," he waved his hand and pointed across the street.

She walked in front of her studio, down the sidewalk, away from the car. "Daly's is only half a block down. We can walk."

He fell into step beside her. "So what do they serve? Steak? Seafood? Doesn't sound ethnic."

"It's more about how the food is prepared than a theme on the menu. You can get a wide variety; steak, Chinese, vegan and a whole bunch more. Their deal is fresh and local. With the exception of the seafood, everything comes from within fifty miles of Allen City. They have gluten free options and things for people allergic to dairy or eggs or whatever."

They crossed an alley and stepped back onto the sidewalk. She stopped at the first door, waited a moment, then reached for the handle.

"Oh," Drew leapt forward and pulled it open. He looked up scanning the storefront. "I didn't realize we were here."

She stepped inside the dimly lit room.

"Miss Alex, welcome. We haven't seen you in a while. Your usual... oh, you have company tonight." The tone the middle-aged woman behind the counter used was a cross between surprised and suggestive.

Alex turned toward him. "I use a little out of the way table in the back, but we can sit—"

"Sounds perfect."

"The usual table, Betty. Thank you."

They followed the woman, through a smattering of other diners engrossed in conversation, to a café table that literally sat in the corner. He pulled out a chair for her and took the one against the wall with the best view of the entire restaurant.

Betty handed Drew a menu but spoke to Alex, "Your usual, Miss Alex?"

"Umm, I think the number three plate."

"Of course, I'll send Natalie right over with your tea and to get the *gentleman's* order." She winked and disappeared.

"Number three?" Drew asked trying to decipher the menu in the dark.

"Orange chicken, fried rice—made with brown rice, chow mein—all gluten free, and some cheese wantons. My favorite."

He set down the menu. "Sounds perfect."

Chapter 36

Their conversation staggered like a drunk trying to find his way home, until the food arrived. Drew wound a few noodles around his fork and stuffed them in his mouth to occupy it with something other than his foot. He was surprised by the flavors dancing on his tongue. He speared a hunk of chicken next.

"Okay, I confess, I didn't have much hope for this place. Most alternatives claiming to be healthy taste like cardboard. But this is good."

Alex laughed. "Then why did you say you'd come?"

He put down his fork and wrung the life out of his napkin. He didn't dare look at her. But he had to say it. "It wasn't about the meal, it was the company."

"Oh."

He raised one tentative brow and snucked a peek at her.

"Thank you. I think that is the nicest thing anyone has ever said to me." Her voice was quiet, breathy. Were there tears in her eyes, or was it only a reflection of the flickering candlelight?

His shoulders slid down, back muscles relaxed. "I mean it. Thanks for agreeing to come."

She nodded and reached for her glass.

Drew returned to eating.

"Tyler said you threatened him."

He almost choked on his rice. It sprayed across the table as he coughed and sputtered. She handed him her tea, and he filled his mouth.

"Ugh, what is that?"

"Sweet tea." Her laughter danced across the table.

"That is like drinking a glass of cotton candy." He stuck his tongue out several times hoping to get the taste out of his mouth.

The waitress passed by. "Everything okay?"

"He'd like more water, please, Natalie."

Drew coughed once more dislodging the last of the rice. "Now, what is this about threatening Tyler? I didn't—"

Alex put up her hand cutting him off as water cascaded into his glass. He motioned for the waitress to stay as he downed almost half of it in one swallow. The waitress refilled it and slipped away.

"He said you told him to do right by me, or he'd answer to you."

"Oh, that. Yeah, I told him that."

"He also said you helped him get a job, and you're tutoring him in math."

"He's a good kid."

Alex's warm, soft hand covered his like the caress of a breeze on a hot day. "He is. Thank you."

Thoughts turned to mush. He nodded.

She lowered her gaze, and her hand slipped away. Drew stopped himself from snatching it back. Their atmosphere eased, and the conversation, at last, flowed smoothly.

Drew leaned back and rubbed his stomach. "I'm stuffed. I'll have to remember this place."

"Too stuffed for dessert?" Alex turned to approaching wait-staff.

A gang of employees filled their corner. A humongous brownie smothered in melting ice cream and drizzled with chocolate fudge appeared before him. The candle in the top was lit, and they broke out into a silly birthday jig. Those around clapped along, and Drew wondered if he could fit under their table.

When the singers dispersed, he looked at her, "How on earth did you let them know? You haven't left my side since we sat down."

The cheeky grin she flashed him made his heart flip. "I have my ways, sir."

"Well, you are going to have to help me finish this, if you don't want to see me crawl out of this place."

She looked at him for a long moment, "Hmmmm, that could be—"

He handed her a fork, "Help me please, m'lady."

The warm brownie, drowning in vanilla and fudge, tasted like a slice of heaven. "This is amazing."

"Best thing here. Hard to believe it is gluten and dairy free."

"You're kidding?" he mumbled around a mouthful. He was making such a wonderful impression.

She shook her head. "I have tried to sneak the recipe from the baker, but he won't give it up."

"Maybe I should arrest him and seize it as evidence."

Her hand flew to her mouth to cover her sudden chuckle. "On what grounds? Crimes in favor of taste buds?"

"I was thinking of concealing irresistible concoctions."

She laughed harder and snorted.

This was the perfect evening.

Chapter 37

"Thank you for a lovely evening, Drew."

"No, thank you, Alex. This was—well it was the best birthday ever."
He rubbed his stomach again. "Well, other than I ate entirely too much."
He looked at her to-go carton. "You were smart. Next time we come,
I'm taking half mine home too."

"Next time?" Her brow arched high and she searched his face.

"Well, I hope there will be a next time," he muttered quietly. "I'll
drive you home."

"Oh, you don't have to go to the trouble. It's not that far—"

"I am either driving you home or walking you home, m'lady. It's late,
dark, and cold."

"Then we better take the car so you don't have to walk all the way
back."

He waved out his hand with a flourish and a bow. "After you,
m'lady."

She chuckled.

In a matter of minutes, the evening was over. He pulled up in front
of her building. His chest tightened as he dashed around the car to open
her door. Taking her hand, he pulled her to the curb, but he didn't step
back. She stood almost toe-to-toe with him. Her hand still held in his.
She looked up. He lowered his head. She smelled like flowers. The puffs
of her breath washed over his face in waves. A little lower. Another half
inch. Her eyes searched his. Would she allow him? Just a little—

Honk!

Both of them startled and stepped away.

"Get out of the road, jerk," came the shout from the driver.

Alex pulled from his hand. His jacket slipped off her shoulders, and she handed it to him. "Better not stay there too long in a red zone. I'd feel terrible if you got a ticket." She didn't look directly at him. Her voice was low, quiet.

Had he gone too far?

"Happy birthday again, Drew." A brief smile, and she hurried across the sidewalk and up the stairs. Rubbing her bare arms as she went, she disappeared into the building and out of sight.

Another horn blared as he made his way back to the driver's side. He had the urge to flip off the driver, but Alex left him feeling too good. Sliding behind the wheel, he inhaled deeply of her smell on his jacket before pulling out into traffic. He caught sight of his goofy grin in the rearview mirror. Yep, this had been a good day.

"All right, what gives? What did you do on your birthday that has you in such a good mood this early in the morning?" Andersen stared at him as they crossed under police tape into the busy crime scene.

"Just dinner."

"Bull!"

"I went to dinner at a place I'd never tried. Daly's Diner. It was really good."

"I know you aren't into that health food crap, so what gives?"

"I was surprised how good it was. We should try lunch there some time."

His partner pulled him to a stop before they got swept up in the details of the case. "Okay, so *who* did you have dinner with?"

Drew turned to the uniformed officer approaching them. "Caleb, what do we have here?"

"It was Wright wasn't it?" Andersen said.

Caleb pointed to the broken glass. "Looks like a smash and grab. Clerk has been taken to the hospital. Till's empty."

"They have cameras?" Drew ignored Andersen's stare and stepped past him.

Caleb pointed. "Roberts is in the back checking it out."

Andersen fell into step beside Drew as they moved to the backroom. "I thought Captain Cruz told you the broad was off limits."

"She was cleared of any involvement with Brendon's disappearance. IA found I'd done nothing out of line."

"Do they know you searched her place? Does she?"

"They don't. She does. Can we get to work now?"

"What is it about this chick that has you crossing the line?"

Drew stopped and looked him square in the face. "I have absolutely no idea." He smiled. "But I'm looking forward to figuring it out."

"Careful brother. That's how I ended up married with three boys."

"I could be so blessed."

They joined the other detective at the black and white monitors.

Andersen's head jerked around as a confused gaze narrowed on him. "Blessed?"

Drew still had a spring in his step and a smile on his face three days after his birthday dinner with Alex. Not even the overtime and a tough case could dampen his mood, though he'd wished there'd been time to call Alex. He'd driven by her studio a couple of nights, but she had already gone home. Or maybe she was not even in *this* world. He laughed at the thought as he opened his apartment door.

The keys clinked in the glass bowl by the door, and he tossed his badge next to it as his phone rang.

"Hel—"

"Double D, it's tore up. The windows are smashed. She's jacked up bad."

"Tyler?" Drew had his keys and badge and was out the door before he had an answer. "Who's hurt?"

"Miss Alex."

Drew gripped the stair rail to stop his free-fall down the cement steps. "Call 911. I'm on the way."

"On their way. But D., she's really bad. There's heck-a blood."

"Where are you?" The car engine roared to life and the tires squealed as he threw it into reverse.

"The dojo."

"I'm on my way. Be there in five." Drew heard the sirens through the phone.

"Step on it."

Why hadn't he driven by her place tonight? Maybe if he had… he couldn't go there. It wouldn't do him any good. The flashing emergency lights from the grill of his car glared through the dark streets, and his siren screamed. He laid on the horn a couple of times, though he could hardly hear it over the pounding of his heart. One more block.

Chapter 38

Drew's car skidded to a stop in the middle of the street alongside three patrol cars. He exited at a run nearly leaving before the engine died. A blood-covered figure lay strapped to a stretcher being loaded in the back of an ambulance. His breath lodged in his throat. Alex's face was so swollen he almost didn't recognize her. One eye so puffy it couldn't open. And the blood...

"Alex!"

"Sorry detective, transport is urgent." The paramedic closed the door and ran to the driver's seat.

"City General?"

"Yeah."

The ambulance barreled away, ripping his heart out as it left. He turned to the dojo and stepped inside on quaking legs. Shards of glass caught in the officers' flashlights. Each pane of glass and every light was shattered.

"Ufff!" Drew gasped as Tyler threw himself against his chest and clung to him. What happened to the chill skater kid? They both reeled from seeing Alex's injuries.

"Double D, I think she's toast."

Drew patted his back. "She's still breathing. The doctors will..." the next words of hope lodged in his chest. He couldn't lose her too. He held onto Tyler and shot up a prayer. He hadn't done that since he was a kid younger than Tyler.

Drew's gaze followed the beams of light as they scanned the room. The mats, walls, and even the ceiling were covered in blood splatter. *Please don't let all of it be hers.* Broken practice weapon lay on the floor. Holes were cut in the mats and punched into the walls. The glass was smashed on the case of the real weapons, and the wire cage inside was bent, but it hadn't given up its prizes.

"What the…"

Tyler followed Drew's gaze to the dozen or so switchblades stuck in the ceiling in the middle of the room. "She must'a jacked their blades."

"Yeah, but while the Pack loves their knives, they aren't opposed to guns."

"Looked like she got popped too." A rock song ringtone erupted from his pocket and Tyler jerked from Drew. "Mom?" Tyler pulled the phone a little from his ear as a scream and banging came from the phone. "Mom! Block the door!"

Drew snatched his arm as he raced to leave. "Tyler?"

"The Pack is bustin' in my place!"

Drew stormed outside with him. "The silver Fusion," he pointed. "Baxter, Weatherly, call back up, and come with us. The suspects that did this are now at—Tyler? What's your address?"

The kid had one foot in Drew's car as he shouted back. "5252 Oak Lane. Apartment 515."

The officers got in their patrol car and flipped on the lights and sirens.

Tyler couldn't sit still. "Step on it."

The call for backup came over the radio, and three more units responded.

"At least one of those officers will get there before we do, Tyler. We'll get to them. I promise."

Hatred boiled in Drew's veins. He wanted payback for what they did to Alex. He'd take it out on any Pack member that crossed his path.

Drew barely had the car stopped when Tyler bolted from it. Drew followed on his heels. They charged past the two officers wrestling a suspect to the ground. Tyler bowled down another Pack member on the third floor. Drew decked the gang member. He cuffed the kid to the banister before he could get his wits about him. The suspect's knuckles were raw. Blood covered his shirt. Drew drove his fist into him leaving him unconscious. Drew raised his foot to kick him too, but Tyler's shouts propelled him further down the hall.

Drew raced into the apartment. He seized a Pack member by the back of his shirt yanking him off Tyler's mother preventing her from being punched again. A roar exploded into the air. It came from Drew. He threw the man back against the wall. Pictures rattled as the thin wall shook. Rage and fear over Alex's condition spun Drew around. His fist landed in the gang member's ribs. Bones snapped. A whoosh of air burst from the target of his wrath followed by a groan.

The banger's blood splattered clothes acted like a red cape before a charging bull. Drew hit him over and over.

"Detective!"

Bang!

A patrol officer shoved Drew to the floor as a shot rang out. They drew their weapons and turned on the gunman. Pack leader, Bloodhound, fired again. Drew and the officer returned shots. The man dropped.

From flat on his back, Drew looked at Baxter. Both checked themselves and each other for wounds—but found none.

Drew popped to his feet—gun still drawn. "Tyler?"

"Yeah," the kid yelled back from down the hall. He appeared a minute later. "The rest skated."

Holstering his weapon, Drew noted the blood on Tyler's clothes, "Your siblings hurt?"

"Freaked, but okay."

"The blood?"

"Miss Alex's," He sat down next to his mom on the floor. She rubbed a welt on her face and brushed away tears.

"I'll call for an ambulance," Baxter said stepping over the body at the door. "Looks like that shot was meant for you, but hit his own man."

"Good riddance," Drew moved toward Tyler and his mom. "Paramedics are on their way, ma'am."

She crumpled into Tyler's arms.

Chapter 39

Chasing down paramedics for reports of injures. Tracking witness to their various locations to collect each statement. Filing all the aggravating reports to IA because he'd fired his gun in the line of duty. Completing yet more inane paperwork to justify the shooting and surrendering his gun due to an officer involved shooting. Securing a safe place for Tyler and his family for the night and all the subsequent paperwork that entailed. Finally Drew contacted an old friend to arrange for their permanent relocation.

Drew glanced at his watch again as he stepped through City General's ER doors. Nearly five a.m. He tried to stifle a yawn. "Excuse me." He flashed his badge to the nurse at the intake desk. "I'm looking for a patient brought in earlier tonight. Alexandria Wright. She was the victim of an attack."

"One moment, detective." The keys on her computer clicked fervently. She scanned the screen. Tapped some more. "You sure she was transported here and not to Mercy?"

"Paramedic—Chris?—tall guy, mid-twenties? He said they were bringing her to General."

"I can't find any record of her. Let me check…"

"Good night, Sally," a woman in scrubs said passing the desk on the other side of the glass.

"Night, Jean." Sally called before turning back to Drew. "I'm sorry, detective, but I don't have any record of an Alexandria Wright being admitted here."

Drew's lungs seized, and he gripped the counter to keep from falling. She couldn't be dead. They'd have that record. What had happened to her? And how had Alex worked so deeply into his heart?

"Did you say Alexandria Wright?"

Drew's gaze flew to Jean. "Yes, did she come through here tonight?"

The woman nodded and put up one finger. She opened the ER doors and joined him in the corner of the waiting room. "She came in terribly beaten, shot, we barely had her stabilized and were prepping her for surgery when four paramedics from some private firm came, flashed legal wavers, and scooped her up. They loaded her in a helicopter AMA —against medical advice—and took her to their facility. Sorry, detective, I wish I knew more. We have her clothes in the back, I think, if you need them for the investigation."

Drew nodded, his mind smothered by a blanket of dread. The nurse swiped her badge at the door, reentered the ER, and returned several minutes later. He took the sealed paper bag having her sign it before taking custody of the evidence and walked out of the hospital with her.

They parted ways near the parking lot. Drew stopped by the precinct and checked in the evidence before continuing home.

He dropped onto his couch and stared at the ceiling. Surely her people had her. They had to have medical knowledge from some other dimension that was far beyond this world. But if she needed it… he tried to swallow, but his mouth was as dry as the Sahara. Tongue glued to the back of his teeth, he could barely part his lips.

His eyes slid closed. Air leaked from his lungs until he sat deflated and limp. *Lord, save her.*

"Merritt!"

Drew focused on his partner.

"You still with me?"

Drew raked a hand over his head. He needed a haircut. It hadn't been this long since entering boot camp. "What were you saying?"

"The perp in the Johnson smash and grab is ready to be interviewed."

Drew nodded.

"Still no word I take it?"

"No, it's been weeks."

"We never could figure out who was paying her bills. You sure this shadow group has her?"

Drew grabbed a notepad and headed for interrogation. "I wish I knew."

Andersen came along side. "I've never seen you like this. This girl has had you twisted in knots since the beginning."

"She's something special." Drew managed a weak smile.

"I'm still trying to figure out if that is a good thing. You're whipped."

Drew slugged him the arm.

Four steps to the entrance of Alex's apartment, and Drew was convinced he'd climbed El Capitan in Yosemite again. A month. He forced the door open like he had lead weights strapped to his arms. All the surviving Pack members now sat in jail. With the evidence collected from their clothes, from Alex's studio, and their leader dead, most had taken pleas—even without Alex there to testify. Two were dead. Drew poked the elevator and listened to the hum as it approached. Still it had been a very long four weeks without word from her.

The fog that settled inside him the night of the attack, grew thicker each day. He replayed the events of the days after their date and before her attack again and again. If he had only…

The doors whooshed open. He couldn't step out. They slid closed. He poked the button, and they opened again. *Please be home.* He knocked softly on her door. No answer. He leaned his arm against the door and rested his forehead on it. *Please be alive. Please come back.*

A click sounded behind him. "You looking for Miss Alex?"

An elderly man stood bent over a cane in a doorway across the hall. His slacks were pulled up too high, and the long thin strands of hair did nothing to cover his age-spot dotted scalp.

"Yes, sir. Have you seen her?"

"Not in about a month." He shook his head, hand white on the cane. "She travels a lot for her job but never known her to be gone this long." His voice creaked like an old rocker.

Drew moved next to his door and used the wall to prop himself up. "Do you know who her employer is?"

"Can't say as she ever told me. Sure she'll be back any day."

"Then you haven't heard?"

The man raised one bushy gray eyebrow.

"Miss Alex was attacked by gang members in her studio last month."

"Oh my. That's terrible. A nice girl like that. It's so a body can't walk the streets anymore."

"I'm—" Drew sighed. How did he describe his relationship with Alex? Was there anything there to describe? "I'm a friend and the detective investigating the attack. Her company took her somewhere for treatment, but I was hoping she was home by now."

Again the old man shook his head. "Sorry, detective. I'd know if she was home. Been looking for her. Miss having our teas."

Drew forced a smile. He could see Alex sitting and keeping the old fellow company from time to time. He pushed off the wall and pulled a business card from his wallet. "I'm Drew, and I'd really appreciate it if you'd give me a call," he swallowed. "*when* she comes home." She would come home. She had to.

"Drew, I'm Jeremiah Thomas. I will let you know the minute I see her." He took the card, pushed it past his suspender, and slid it into his shirt pocket.

"Thank you, Mr. Thomas. Again, I appreciate it."

"I'll be praying she returns soon, young man."

"Me too."

Chapter 40

Alex rolled her head trying to work the kink out of her neck. She pulled up the strap from her sling and tucked her collar under it for more comfort. Not that it did much good. She turned at the next corner. The Conclave could have at least dropped her closer to home. Were they punishing her for getting beat to a pulp? She was supposed to help people, right? Well, she hadn't made any fans helping Tyler. He'd better still be all right. The detective would have looked after him—wouldn't he?

Alex sighed, worked at the knot, and fussed with the strap again. Her apartment building looked the same. What was the time differential between Celestial Fields and her home realm? She hugged herself and shivered. A puff of breath hung in the air. She climbed the four steps and entered the building. No one around. She slid a tile off the wall and retrieved her mailbox key.

She flipped through the bills. Only three of each—not that it mattered. The Conclave would have made sure they were paid on time. But surely more than a few months had passed here.

Returning the key, she stepped into the elevator and leaned back. She yanked at the strap again as the hum and vibration of the elevator told her it inched upward. The door whooshed open, and she pushed off the wall with some effort. She fumbled for her door key in the windowsill hide-away with her left hand. A few minutes later, her door at last clicked open. Home. Quiet. Cold. Empty.

"Alex, is that you, dear?"

She stifled the sigh and turned, forcing a kind smile to her face. "Hello, Mr. Thomas." She moved across the hall and stood shifting her weight between her feet.

"Well, if you aren't a sight for sore eyes, girl."

"Thank you. I missed you too."

"Are you all right? A detective came by looking for you a while back. Said you were beat up at work."

Drew's smiling face flashed through her thoughts, and her stomach fluttered. She stamped the memory down. She'd been gone a long time. The detective would have moved on by now. And it was for the best. "Yes, a gang I'd crossed came for payback. I'm getting better."

"That's good, dear. Nasty business these gangs. They are taking over the streets." Mr. Thomas' head shook.

"How have you been doing? Everything all right here?"

"Oh, can't complain—don't do me any good." He chuckled. He used his cane to point down the hall at the other apartments. "Wall Street Guy and Lawyer Lady are busy as ever, never see much of them. The place next to yours is still empty." Mr. Thomas caught her up on all the happenings of the fourth floor.

"Wow, thought someone would have snatched it up by now."

He shrugged. "It's only been on the market less than three months."

So it's November. She'd only been gone a little over two months.

"I'm hoping they find another quiet neighbor." Mr. Thomas drew her back into the conversation. "We don't need any party animals up here disturbing my nap."

Alex put her hand on his forearm and gave a little squeeze. "I think we have enough partiers up here too, Mr. Thomas. We wouldn't want anyone horning in on our fun."

He laughed louder, patting her hand. "Oh, you scamp. I have missed you, dear. You always make me laugh. I'm going to let you go though.

Need to sit a spell myself, and you look tired too. We'll catch up soon."

"That would be nice."

He disappeared back inside his place, and Alex returned the key to its hiding spot. She stood in her apartment and leaned on the closed door. She wanted to sit—or sleep, but she'd better take care of the dead food in the fridge first.

She pulled a trashcan close and started dropping spoiled things in it. She pulled a glass from the cupboard and filled it with water and drink mix.

Thud! Thud! Thud!

She jumped at the pounding on her door. Who could that be?

As she opened the door, Drew barreled into the room. She backed away from him, startled. Her heart stuck in her throat.

"Alex."

She tried to answer but sputtered.

"You know you shouldn't open your door without knowing who's on the other side. You need a peephole or at least a chain."

She cocked her head at him trying to make sense of what he was saying. "Chains are really easy to bust with the right leverage. And no one comes to my door anyway."

He stepped closer, and she continued to back up. Intensity radiated off him like a raging fire. "You *need* to be safe!"

She bumped into the small dining table, almost toppling the glass she'd left on it.

Drew closed the small gap between them. His gaze washed over her, landing on her injured arm. He brushed it above the sling with the tips of his fingers. "You all right?"

She nodded, trying to get her mouth to work. "Yeah," she managed.

His hand slid up her arm and brushed hair from her shoulder. His thumb slid along her jaw. Lightening fired through her nerves. His gaze met hers. His dilated pupils engulfed the amber of his eyes. His pulse throbbed in his neck. He smelled—tangy? Spicy? Aftershave maybe.

His head lowered.

Did he aim to kiss her? What would it feel like to have lips pressed to hers? His breath caressed her face. A hint of coffee. She couldn't feel her own body except where his hand still touched her searing the skin of her cheek. His breath puffed over her lips.

The song *Bad Boys* erupted in the silence. Alex jolted, upsetting the glass. She whirled to grab it before it shattered on the floor.

"What!"

She turned to see Drew's profile, his phone pressed to his ear.

"Yeah. Yeah! I heard you the first time. Don't get your boxers in a bunch. I'm on my way." He shoved the phone back in his pocket and brushed his hand over his buzz-cut. "Gotta go," despair dripped from his voice. He turned and smiled at her. "Glad you're home—safe."

Moving toward the door he spotted the trash. "I'll drop this down the shoot on the way out."

"You don't—"

"Take care of that arm." He inclined his head toward her injury. He started to pull the door closed behind him. "I'll bring back something from Daly's when my shift is over. Orange chicken?"

"You don't—"

His face lost its smile. His gaze bore into her. "I've missed you, Alex."

The air vacated the room. Her head spun. She nodded. Nothing else on her body worked.

His easy smile returned, and the door closed.

Alex slipped down into a chair and released the breath she hadn't realized was trapped in her lungs.

Chapter 41

Knock. Knock.

Alex stretched. Cradling her arm, she got up and went to the door.

"You really have to stop opening the door to just anyone." Drew moved past her to the table. He slid a grocery bag off his finger and continued to the kitchen.

"But I knew it was you." She tried to stretch the kink out of her neck as she followed him.

He set several bags on the floor near the fridge. "How could you possibly know that?"

She released a half huff, half sigh as she leaned on the counter. "You said you were returning when your shift ended." She pointed at the clock on the microwave. "It has to be after your shift and here you are."

"But anyone could come to your door."

"No one ever does—well except for Mr. Thomas." She watched him put soymilk, eggs, and turkey bacon in the refrigerator. "Is Bloodhound and his Pack still looking for me?" Her stomach clenched as spasms of remembered pain rippled through every muscle.

"No," he said, shaking his head as he continued to fill her refrigerator. "I got you a couple of cheeses though nothing fancy. It should hold you over until you feel like going out. Or you could give me a list, and I'll drop it off tomorrow."

She considered him as he stood and closed the fridge.

His hands went up in surrender. "I swear, I haven't been in here other than that one time. But I'm a cop, and I pay attention to details."

She smiled, and his hands lowered. "Thanks. This should do me for a while."

He held up the empty bags, his brows drawn together. She pointed under the sink. A moment later, he moved past her to the table. He pulled out one to-go container and froze. He glanced up at her and swallowed hard. "May I—ah—join you?"

"Please," she turned back to the kitchen and grabbed silverware.

"Where did...?" He went back to the kitchen. "What on earth?"

"What's the matter?"

"I can't find..." He left her front door open as he crossed the hall and waited for the elevator. The doors slid open, and Drew almost collided with Mr. Thomas. "Sorry, Mr. Thomas. Ahh, there they are." Drew waited for the older man to exit, then stepped in and came back out with a drink carrier holding two cups. With a triumphant smile, he hoisted them toward Alex who watched from her apartment doorway.

Mr. Thomas winked at her. "Now dear, if this young man gives you any grief, you give a shout, and I'll come runnin' and give him a wallopin'." He raised his cane and shook it in the air towards Drew.

Alex couldn't suppress the laugh that ended with the hated snort.

"I swear to be on my best behavior, sir."

Mr. Thomas waved him over. "You treat her like a lady, you hear, son?"

"Yes, sir. I will be a gentleman."

The elderly man patted him on the arm with a grin and turned toward his apartment.

"Mr. Thomas, we have plenty. You are welcome to join us," Drew said as he shot her a raised brow after the words were out of his mouth.

"Oh, no. I wouldn't think of intruding on you young folks. Enjoy your evening." He disappeared inside, and Drew rejoined her.

She put her hand on his arm.

He looked at it. There was something there—something growing between them. It wasn't merely her wishful thinking. He gave her all the signs of enjoying being with her.

"Thank you. That was very kind," she said

He nodded as she moved toward the table. She rubbed her arm. It was throbbing again.

"Sure. It was kind of me to invite *someone else* to your place without asking." His voice was husky. He looked up. "Where's the sling?"

She pointed to the couch. "The strap was cutting into my neck."

He sat the drinks in front of her. "I think the one on the right is your sickly-sweet sugar fest." He vanished down her hall.

"Where are you going?"

He returned a moment later with a hand towel, snatched up the sling, knelt in front of her chair, and replaced the sling using the towel as a buffer against the strap. "Better?"

"Yes, thank you."

"One more thing." He left again. This time he returned with a bolster off her bed.

"You really know my place well. How long were you here?"

"Maybe fifteen minutes. I really am sorry I invaded your privacy like that." He raised her arm gently, put the pillow on her thigh, and lowered the arm onto it. "There. How's that?"

She sighed. "Perfect. Thanks."

He stood with a goofy grin and started pulling out the containers and popping them open. He offered her chopsticks.

"No, thanks. I can't use those things even when I have a working right hand. And now it's hard enough with normal silverware to do anything with my left. I can handle a dozen different types of weapons, but two little sticks make me look like a bumbling idiot."

"Not possible." Drew vanished into the kitchen and returned with two glasses. "So, that one your swill?" He indicated the Styrofoam cup nearest her.

"My southern sweet tea, yes." He transferred the contents into the glass, and she took another deep sip, flooding her mouth with the cool delight.

Drew shook his head as he poured his carbonated green liquid into the other glass.

Alex wrinkled her nose. "You object to my tea when you drink that junk?"

"Are you sure there is tea in that? Thought it was liquid sugar." He chuckled as he sat.

"Yes, I'm sure there's tea." She tried to sound indignant, but her snort gave her away. Heat filled her cheeks, and she looked at her food.

"You have a great laugh."

Alex stared at him. He couldn't be serious.

"Truth." He folded his hands and looked at her with a raised brow.

"You want me to pray?"

"Don't you usually say grace over a meal?" He looked up, searching her face for the cause of her hesitance.

"Well, yeah…"

"Your home. You pray." He bowed his head again and waited.

"Heavenly Father, we thank You for this day,"

"Yes."

She hadn't expected Drew to speak, and it made her forget what she planned to say next. She stumbled over several words before picking up her train of thought again. "Bless this food to our bodies and bless our time together. Amen."

"Amen." The way he stared at her flooded her entire body with warmth. He handed her a fork and stabbed a piece of chicken with his own. Half way to his mouth he looked at her again. "I really am glad you're home, Alex."

Chapter 42

"So, the Pack," Drew turned to his meal and told her of the events in this realm between bites. "Tyler called me after finding you. He was so upset. I got to your studio as they were loading you in the ambulance." He stopped and looked at her for a long moment. "I don't know the last time I was that scared. You were hurt so badly… I didn't recognize you."

He shook off a shudder. How many nightmares had he had of her lying lifeless on that gurney? Her hand rested on his arm. His muscles relaxed under the warmth seeping into his skin.

"I'm all right."

"Thank God." He muttered, clearing his throat. "Yes, you are."

"The Pack?"

"Right. Tyler found me as the patrol officers on scene were checking out your place. What a mess. The only things they didn't smash were your swords. Apparently they couldn't get in the cage. Then Tyler got a call from his mother. The Pack had moved to her place looking for him."

Alex gasped, covered her mouth with her hand, and almost stabbed herself with her fork.

"They're fine. We, and a patrol units, headed over there, and they called for backup on the way. Patrol took down four of them outside. Bloodhound shot one of the pups, while trying to shoot me. Another officer and I took Bloodhound down." Drew took a drink of his soda.

"With your blood all over most every member of the gang, they'll be easy to convict, even without your testimony. I hear most are looking at taking pleas, but either way they'll be gone for a long time."

"And Tyler?"

"I have a friend from college. Danielle. She lives with her husband and kids. He's a pastor in Idaho. I sent Tyler and his family to her. Danielle called last week to say they were doing great. Tyler's fitting in at a good school, and his mom has a great job."

Alex's hand slipped into his. Soft, tender. She squeezed it. "Thank you, Drew." Tears pooled.

"I'd do anything for you."

Had he really said that? Her hand jerked from his like she'd gotten shocked. She looked down at her food but didn't continue eating. Say something. Don't ruin it.

"By the time I got to the hospital, your people had already whisked you away."

Silence.

"Did they take you to someplace with advance treatment?" Keep her talking. Don't let it end. There is something between us, something I've never experienced before.

She nodded, picked up her fork, and worked at her food again. "I was pretty bad. They said if they'd left me here I wouldn't have made it. Three gunshot wounds, close to half my bones broken, collapsed lung. It was bad. They put me in stasis for a while as they made repairs." She pointed to her injured arm. "This was shattered so badly they had to grow a new radius and ulna. Then they had to put the arm back together. Once they had me stabilized, I was under the doctors' care for a couple of months until things knit back together and strengthened. Then six months of rehab."

"I don't think I'll ever get used to that wonky time thing."

"Yeah, I figure I spent almost a year there. I was trying to figure out with all the time differentials exactly how old I am." She flashed a roguish grin at him. There it was again. The hope that she felt the way he did.

"Well, you gain some in some places but lose in others, so it probably all equals out in the end."

She tilted her head and nodded once. It was good to see her. He had to find a way to make this work. No matter what, Alex was meant for him and he for her. He knew it like he'd never known anything before.

"You're staring again." She smoothed her hair. "I must look a fright."

Drew glanced down at his food with a shake of his head. "No." Don't say too much. But say something. What? "It's really good to see you."

She yawned. "Thanks."

"You're tired." He stood and reached for her box. "You done? I can put the rest in the fridge for later."

She nodded as she covered another yawn. "Take yours home," she said stopping him from adding it to hers. "Please."

"All right, but I'm leaving dessert here." He popped open the brownie drowned in fudge.

"Yum."

He put it back in the bag and cleared the table. "You need anything else before I go?"

She looked at him for a long time. She wanted to ask something. The twitch in her jaw. She avoided eye contact. Shifted her weight between her feet. But she shook her head. "You have already been exceedingly kind, Drew. Thank you."

He moved closer.

She glanced up.

What did she really want? "You sure? I can—"

"No. Nothing. You have thought of everything."

He wanted to try to kiss her again. His weight shifted. She turned away, covering a giant yawn with the back of her hand. But there was something… a longing, he was sure of it. It couldn't be all in his head.

"Sorry."

"Don't be. You've been through a lot." He moved to the door, his leftovers dangled from his fingers. "I'll stop by tomorrow." His heart pounded.

Her glorious smile answered him.

He nearly jumped up and clicked his heels together. "See you tomorrow then." He knew it. There were feelings growing there, even if she didn't want to acknowledge them yet.

"Tomorrow. I'll save some of the brownie—if I can. Good night, Drew."

"Night, Alex." He did a jig down the stairs. It hadn't been much, but she'd said he could come back. He'd take it and work on keeping her hand next time. Something told him if this was going to work, he'd have to take it slow and convince Alex he was the one for her. He already knew she was the only one for him.

Chapter 43

True to his word, Drew stopped by the next day and the next. But he didn't try to kiss her again. Maybe she'd missed her chance. What was the matter with her? She'd never be allowed to have a relationship with a non-guardian. She needed to break things off with Drew. Whatever was between them would never be more than this. It wasn't fair to Drew.

But she couldn't give up the attention. She'd been alone for so long. She craved a little consistent human contact. Knowing who well-being mattered to someone fed an insatiable hunger in her soul.

She didn't have a lot of options. Every boy she'd grown up training with for the Conclave was either married or dead—mostly dead.

She really needed to stop seeing Drew. Even if the Conclave blessed their friendship, she'd most likely never live to see her thirtieth birthday.

Her phone whistled. She glanced at the text. "B there in 2 hrs 2 pick u up, B ready."

Her fingers hovered over the keypad. Tell him no—not now, not ever again. She ignored the orders piercing her thoughts. "Where r we going?"

"Surprise."

She couldn't suppress her smile. She really needed to end things, but what did he have planned? She had to know. But this would be the last time, she promised herself. "How am I supposed to be ready? Workout clothes? Ball gown? Kirtle?"

"???Kirtle??? Jeans. Nice but comfy."

"K"

She met him in front of her building dressed in jeans, a cowl-neck cable-knit sweater, and short boots. She pulled her jacket tighter as she moved from the building to his car. Heavy grey clouds sat on the rooftops. It smelled like rain. She opened the coat to get his approval as he held the door for her.

"Perfect."

She covered up and slipped into the seat. The heater was cranked to high. She tried to reach her fingers to the vents. The sling made it awkward.

"It's so cold, we might even see snow." He settled behind the wheel.

"When was the last time it snowed in Allen City?"

"I was still a kid. Not enough for school to close as I remember." He pulled into traffic.

"Where we going?"

He flashed a cheeky smile. "You'll see." Her heart fluttered. *Enjoy it now, Al, it will be the last time.*

They wound through downtown and out onto the freeway. About twenty minutes out, they took one of the off-ramps and were soon slipping between houses in a suburban neighborhood.

Houses. When was the last time she'd been in a house? Maybe when she moved out of hers into the apartment?

Drew pulled up to a two-story tan house with burgundy shutters and killed the engine. "We're here," he said stepping out of the car.

Well that was rather obvious. He held her door. "And here is?"

"Come on." The grin on his face could not have been any bigger without causing injury. He pulled a crockpot from a box in his trunk.

"Should I have brought something?"

"No, Molly is using hers for the cider and wanted mine for the dip."

171

Well, that cleared things up.

They moved to the front door, and Drew managed to poke the bell while holding the pot with both hands.

"Uncle Drew!" Three boys burst out and latched on to him with such force, Alex stepped back as he struggle to keep from slipping the contents.

"Hey, guys."

"Boys, let them get in the house before you maul him. Here, Merritt, let me take that." The man looked familiar. His light brown hair was longer than Drew's but neatly cut. He had a bit slenderer build too. "Come on in, Alex. Sorry for the rambunctious welcome."

Alex stepped past Drew as he worked to tickle the boys into releasing him. They squealed with laughter.

The man kept walking away from her, "Hang your coat on the hook. Molly's in here."

Drew stepped in behind her at last. He had one boy dangling by the ankles over his shoulder the other two younger ones each sat on a foot and wrapped themselves around his calves like legwarmers.

She stared at him as she eased her coat off.

"Oh, here let me help you," the man said coming back in the room.

"Alex, you remember my partner, Andersen."

"Eric," he stepped forward and gave her a quick hug. "Glad you could make it."

She was so startled she didn't know what to say. When was the last time anyone hugged her outside of the church greeters?

"And these minions are his boys, Landon, Dylan, and little Liam."

"I'm not little," one of the legwarmers said punching Drew in the knee.

Drew groaned.

"Take it easy on him, boys. He's got to protect your dad tomorrow." Eric motioned for her to follow him. They passed through the living room into a kitchen at least three times the size of hers. "Molly, this is Alex," Eric said. Drew's the crockpot on the counter under the window and pulled it in.

Squeals of laughter, grunts, and groans floated toward her leaving Alex fumbling for what to do and where to go. Drew never made it to the kitchen, but she had been brought in here. Her heart skittered, and her mind fluttered for a clear thought.

"It is so nice to meet you, Alex. I'd give you a hug but..." She lifted hands that were smeared with something she was moving from a mixing bowl to a casserole dish.

Alex's stomach was doing somersaults, and she was sure her knees were knocking together. What was going on here? "Can I do anything to help?"

"Oh, heavens no. I only have the dressing here to put in the oven and everything should be cooking. We'll eat in about an hour."

Molly washed her hands as Alex tried to figure out what to do. Trays of nuts, relish items, and cheese and crackers where arranged on the counter before her. Alex startled as something touched her hip and turned as pressure crossed her back to the opposite side. Drew's other arm came into view as he leaned around her and snatched an olive from one of the trays.

Molly swatted at him with the towel she'd used to dry her hands. "Out of here, you thief."

Drew was still touching her. Almost holding her. Bolts of energy exploded through her. She tried to swallow.

"Come now, admit it, Thanksgiving wouldn't be the same without me." Drew seized a pickle, winked at Alex, and escaped.

Thanksgiving? She was with a family for Thanksgiving dinner. She gripped the counter to keep from falling.

"That man is such a child," Molly said with a laugh. "Come, let's sit in the family room and talk where it's quiet." Molly waved her to follow.

The doorbell rang again. Eric called that he had it as they continued on their way out the back of the kitchen. "Sorry to say, we'll be outnumbered today. We're the only females. Eric invites all the single cops over for Thanksgiving every year. A handful take him up on the offer, but very seldom is there a female in the bunch."

Molly plopped down on a puffy denim couch and patted the seat beside her. Alex's heart raced like she was being chased by a giant lizard-like creature from one of the other realms. She couldn't do this. Send her on a mission anywhere with clearly defined objectives—no problem. But make small talk with a stranger? Her heat pounded. How'd she get into this mess? She eased onto the couch. *Breathe.*

Molly grinned. "When are you going to tame that man, and get him to put a ring on your finger?"

Chapter 44

Drew kept an eye on Alex throughout the day—when he wasn't either wrestling children, giving his fellow officers grief, or watching the game on TV. When he did see her, her smile looked forced and her color weak. Maybe it was too soon for a long day out like this.

She sat opposite him at the dining table but didn't eat much. The conversation kept her interest, and she laughed a little from time to time but not enough to snort. Alex only spoke to answer an inqiry. He raised a brow in question when her gaze locked with his. Something he couldn't read flashed in her eyes. She gave him a lopsided smile before returning her attention to her plate. He needed to do something.

The men started to head back to the game in the living room when they couldn't eat anymore. Alex stayed behind and started stacking plates.

"Oh, no you don't!" Molly said. "No one helps clean up. It's Thanksgiving. Go on." She ushered everyone out of the dining room.

Drew brushed Alex's arm. She jumped like she had when he sneaked a taste from the relish tray earlier. "You want to leave?"

Her eyes pleaded with him. Her head gave a little nod. But her words didn't agree. "I don't want you miss the game."

"My team's not playing. If you're tired…"

"You're having fun, and these are your friends. We can stay."

He slid his arm around her waist and pulled her a little closer as they walked back toward the living room with the others. He stopped near the doorway and called Andersen over. "We're gonna take off."

Alex tensed in his hold.

"Alex is still recovering and tired. I'm gonna take her home."

"So glad you felt up to making it." Andersen hugged her.

Molly came and embraced her as well. "Thank you so much for coming. You saved me an afternoon overwhelmed by testosterone."

Alex looked ill. Color drained from her face. She didn't say anything. She trembled.

Drew helped her on with her coat. "I'll get the crockpot later." He turned Alex to the door and led her out to the car where she dropped in the seat.

When he sat behind the wheel he glanced at her again.

"I'm sorry to spoil your fun," she whispered.

Drew turned the key. "I'm with the one who matters most." He meant it too. The more time he spent with her the more he was convinced she was the one. She seemed unsure, frightened. He'd waited his entire life to meet her. He could wait a little longer to win her affection.

Alex stared out the window as they wound out of the neighborhood. When they neared the freeway he reached over and took her hand. Her cold fingers startled him. "You all right?"

No reply.

"Alex?"

Her voice floated to him husky and edged with tears. "I'd forgotten what it was like."

"What what was like? A bunch of football screaming meatheads?"

Alex's head shook slightly. She didn't say anything for a few moments, and he squeezed her hand tighter.

"I'd forgotten what a family was like. And the holidays."

Drew gripped the wheel with his other hand.

"Mother was a Key. Always out on missions. Father was an Educator. They were never home at the same time. We rarely celebrated holidays with them both on the go so much. No one had time to decorate and, like I said, we rarely even shared a meal together." She cleared her throat, but the heaviness remained. "Mother died when I was… six? Seven? I'm not sure I remember anymore. When we lost her, Father had to go on missions. They didn't have any more Educators. He was the last."

She fell silent again, and Drew didn't know if she'd continue. He slowed the car wanting Alex to tell the rest of her tale.

When she began again, melancholy filled the car. "Ms. Sage, one of the few guardians to reach old age came. She couldn't go out in the field any longer, so she stayed with me when Father was away. At the age of twelve, I started going on missions with him. Nothing dangerous most of the time. Treaties, encouragements, general aid. Simple assignments." Her hand shook in his. "Father died when I was sixteen. Ms. Sage moved in to watch over me but, after only a couple of years, her health failed. I've been alone ever since."

What could he say? How could he comfort her? How could he fix this? His parents were gone now too, but they lived long enough to see him graduate the academy. And though he couldn't reach Brendon now, they still had a form of contact. Drew also had Andersen and his brothers in blue. He was not really alone—not like Alex.

Another tremor shook her body as he pulled up in front of her building. Alex slipped from his hand and started to exit the car before he could get to her door. He raced around the car and drew her into his arms and held her. Thankfully, because of the holiday, the traffic on the street was light. He didn't want to let her go. Drew wanted to squeeze her until all her broken pieces mended back together like her broken bones.

Alex stood rigid for a few moments. Then her forehead rested against his chest. Muscles relaxed, and she gripped his coat and clung to him. A cold blast of air hit. She released her grasp and stood beside him.

"Again, I'm sorry I spoiled your day." She moved away.

Drew reached for her, fingers sliding down her arm until their fingers caught. "You're not alone. Not any more."

A tremor. Eyes cast at the cement at their feet. A single nod.

"I can come…"

She shook her head and ambled up the steps into the building without a backwards glance.

He should have gone with her.

Chapter 45

Alex fought to stay asleep, but the memories Drew had unearthed smothered her, keeping deep rest at bay. She remained in her pajamas on Friday. Drew wouldn't be by. He and Andersen often volunteered to do crowd control for the biggest sales day of the year. She plopped on the couch and didn't move most of the day. The thought of food made her stomach turn sideways as she waded through memories of sitting on Mother's lap and lessons with Father. The melancholy of her spirit reflected in the dreary weather outside.

Late in the afternoon, she got a text. "How u doing?"

She responded with the obligatory single word: "Fine." She needed to break things off with Drew—not that she knew what they had. Nothing good could come from them getting closer, at least not for him. The Conclave didn't allow relations with outsiders—ever. No matter how much she needed Drew, the impossibility of it overshadowed all else.

Alex returned to bed early, trying to hide from her thoughts. Again, she forced her memories down and dead bolted them where they could never again see the light of day. It was the only way she could function. She begged sleep to come. Hide her. For oblivion to save her.

She'd finished a protein shake the next morning when a knock sounded at the door. Alex opened it to stare at an evergreen tree on her threshold. It pushed forward into her apartment as Drew's voice came from somewhere behind it.

"How am I going to get you to stop opening your door to every knock?"

"Stop knocking?" Her smile kissed her lips. She watched him lug the tree toward the dining table as she started to close the door bumping against something almost immediately.

"Hey, Alex. How're you feeling today?" Eric Andersen said as he passed her carrying a huge red tub.

"Okay," she said and almost closed the door again on someone else. A string of four more men filed into her tiny living room each carrying one or two tubs similar to Eric's. She recognized most of them from the dinner at Eric's home. They set their loads down and exited her apartment wishing her a Merry Christmas.

"Thanks," Drew called as the door closed behind them.

The tree stood propped in the corner. Drew and Eric folded the sides down on her dining table and shoved it aside. They worked together for a few minutes to get the tree straight in the stand before Eric flashed smile and left.

Drew stood beside her near the couch and looked at it for a minute. The scent of pine clung to him like sap. "A little to the right and it will be centered in the window." He moved the tree. Returning to her side, he checked it again. "Now for the lights." Turning to the tubs scattered in her living room, he started throwing off lids. "I really should label these things. Lights. Lights. Where are the dang—Ah-ha! Found them!"

He moved the tub closer to the tree and pulled out several bundled lengths. Drew plugged one strand into a switch, activated it with his foot, and started covering the tree.

"What are you doing?"

He stopped and looked at her—head cocked to the side. "Putting lights on the tree."

"But why?"

"Because you can't have a naked Christmas tree, Alex."

"And why do I *have* a Christmas tree?"

His boyish grin sobered, and he walked toward her. Alex shuddered as his hand brushed down her arm, and he laced their fingers together. Heat. When did the room get so warm? Why was it always so hard to remember to breathe when he was this close?

"It's time you had a good Christmas to remember." Though his voice was quiet, it still carried authority.

Her throat wouldn't work to swallow. Her tongue stone in her mouth. She nodded once, unable to even blink in order to break the grip of his consuming stare.

A bright smile filled his face, and he turned to resume work on the tree.

Freed. Eyes closed, she found her breath, and steadied herself against the side of the couch. She needed to sit, but the only spot available was the recliner in the corner, which she couldn't get to because of the tubs.

Gathering her erratic thoughts, she looked at him again. He was whistling a holiday tune. "What can I do to help?" Her voice cracked.

Drew shook his head. "Nothing yet. Got to get the lights just right…" The whistling started again as he pulled out a third strand and started winding it. If he kept it up, he was going he'd need over a dozen sets of lights to finish.

Alex grabbed the remote and flipped to a streaming music channel featuring holiday songs.

"Perfect." Drew flashed a smile.

"Want something to drink?"

He paused but didn't say anything.

"I have tea."

He wrinkled his nose.

"I can make it unsweetened."

He shook his head.

"Hot chocolate, cider, beer—"

"Beer?"

"Yes, I have a few beers in the house." A smile tugged at her lips. "Mr. Thomas likes one occasionally. Would you like one?"

"It's a little early for beer. Maybe later though. How about some cider? It fits the mood better."

In the kitchen, she pulled out the ingredients for a pot of homemade cider. She made one batch every winter, but this was the first time she'd ever had someone to share it with. Her stomach soured. She really needed to tell him to stop coming over.

Listening to him belt out Christmas carols in the other room, she couldn't bring herself to do it today. It would only make it harder later— but not today. Well, probably not until after the holidays when he collected all his decorations again. A big sigh deflated her, and she leaned over the counter. It would have to be said though.

Chapter 46

The tantalizing aroma of pizza filled Alex's apartment as she handed Drew ornaments. He teetered on the top of her stepstool making sure he left no branch unadorned. By the time he finished late in the afternoon, it looked like a department store window display had exploded in her apartment. From the Christmas towels in the kitchen and bathroom to the light-up hangings in every window. A nativity, endless strands of garland, enough candles to burn down the place, wreaths for hanging and centerpieces, a myriad of bows, lights beyond counting, and the tree overwhelming her dining area. All a bit nauseating.

Drew stacked the empty tubs in one of her supply rooms and came out to survey his handiwork. Arms crossed over his puffed-up chest and a satisfied smile on his face lifted some of the weight from her. He had worked hard all day—for her. To give her good memories.

Tears burned her eyes. She was being so unfair.

"You don't like it." He touched her arm again.

She swallowed hard. "No, it's not that. I don't know of anyone who has been more kind and thoughtful, Drew."

"But..."

She swiped at an escaping tear. "It's not right for me to let you continue. As much as I appreciate it, it's not fair to you." She turned away, unable to face him she stared at the bookshelves.

Drew came up behind her and enclosed her in his arms. "What are you talking about?"

Alex tried to pull free, but he held her fast. "You deserve someone who will be with you, for a lifetime."

"Okay."

Her muscles clenched. Tears fell. Her throat closed. She fought to say the words that must be said. "I'm already older than my mother, and nearly the age of my father when he…"

Drew's embrace tightened, and he pulled her back until she rested on his chest and the steady even beat of his heart pounded through her. "You're not going to die."

"Of course I will. Do you know how few guardians live to even reach thirty? We have a higher rate of people killed in the line of duty than most police departments."

He pressed his lips to the crown of her head, and his breath warmed her scalp setting her entire body on fire. "You will."

She fought harder to break from his hold, and he finally released her. Alex spun and planted her hand in the middle of his chest to keep him at arm's length. "You don't know that." Tears threatened to drown her.

A playful grin danced on his lips. "I do."

"This isn't a joke. The Conclave doesn't approval of relationships with outsiders. I'm going to die on some mission, and because you aren't a aurdian, you won't even get the knock on your door or the phone call to say, 'We're sorry to inform you…'"

His smile only grew. "Not gonna happen."

Her palm met his sternum with a resounding thump and she pushed him away. "It's a certainty!"

Drew reached out, grabbed her hand, and held it over his heart. The rhythm, strong and calm, pounded in contrast to the frantic beat ricocheting within her chest. "I know you aren't going to die because it would be cruel to have two people who need each other so much, not be given what they require most." He stepped closer, causing her arm to bend. His hand cradled her cheek. "Enough talk of doom." He spun her to face the tree. "This is the happiest time of year. And I want to share it with you, Alex Wright."

She struggled for a moment longer. Drew needed to understand. This was best for him. The warmth of his nearness worked to relax her muscles and steal her fight. She sagged into him, her head lulling onto his collarbone. His arms encircled her again. Warm. Strong. Protective. Her eyes closed. Logic fled. Hope struggled for life. *Please, let it last.* Even as the plea raced through her thoughts, she knew it could never be.

Chapter 47

The first Sunday of Advent revealed Alex's church nearly as decorated as her home. The pastor talked of God fulfilling His promises to Judah and Jerusalem living safe and secure. Sitting apart from the other families in her pew, Alex kept her head low. Let them think she prayed instead of seeing the truth of her tears. How long had it been since she'd heard God's voice? Had He ever spoken a promise over her life? Could it be Drew's promise? That she wouldn't die young?

The silence within nearly crushed her. Christmas carols and hymns of God's coming in great joy surrounded her, but for Alex, God remained silent. Maybe she had never heard Him. Was this a crisis of faith? Or did she ever really believe?

Lost in her wallowing, Alex startled as everyone stood for the final song. She slipped out before the pastor could make his way to the door to shake hands. Wind whipped her hair in her face and made her ears hurt. The hood of her jacket wouldn't stay up. Slap. A cold blast of wind hit her straight on and stole her breath.

Honk. "Hop in."

Drew pushed the passenger door of his car open for her.

She leaned over looking at him. "You still stalking me, detective?"

Color splashed his cheeks. He took a moment to check the mirrors for traffic. "Nope." He didn't convince her.

She slid into the seat struggling to get the door closed with her right arm still in the sling.

He started off. "I knew you'd be walking home. Weather's nasty. Thought I'd give you a lift."

"Thanks."

Drew passed her apartment. "How 'bout a peek at your studio and lunch at Daly's?"

She gave him a smirk. "Do I have a choice?" Oh, that boyish grin would be the end of her.

"Not really."

He parked near the restaurant, and they walked toward her business. "How bad is it?" She pulled her coat tighter around her.

"Looks great! A crew worked on it a couple weeks before you returned."

They passed the now double-paned windows, which now bore either an anti-glare coating or bullet proofing or something. At the door, Alex reached into the light fixture and fished out a key.

"You always keep that there?"

"I'm constantly popping in and out of places and leaving keys behind. I've started stashing them in hide-a-ways near every door I use. It has saved me a ton of aggravation." She pushed open the door before returning the key.

The fumes from the new paint made her eyes water and, mixed with the new rubber mats, her stomach lurch. Her breath stuttered to a near stop, and her eyes closed as the phantom voices from that evening overwhelmed her. Vile names shouted at her. Roars of anger. Pain. Unbearable pain. She had welcomed death—but it hadn't come.

Pressure tightened on her hand. "Alex? Alex, you still with me?"

She looked up at him. Concern pulled his brows close together. She dragged air back into her lungs.

"Bad memories?"

Alex nodded and turned from him before the tears started—again. When did she turn into such a weepy hot mess? She pulled from his hand and moved to the office. Everything was new here too. The glass panels on each side of the door were now shatterproof and the door stronger with a couple of deadbolts. If she saw trouble coming next time, she could lockdown in here, and call for help. *If* she saw it coming.

"Hey, can I get a quick lesson before dinner?"

Alex turned back to Drew. He had a practice sword in his hand, whipping the waster through the air with wild flourishes. That grin she'd grown to love filled his face as he took a wide stance, sword extended at full arm's length, other hand high over his head, and knees bent. Alex couldn't suppress a smile. "You have a fencer's stance, but you're holding a broadsword."

He stood straight, examining the wooden sword in his hand. "There's a difference?"

Now Alex laughed. "Huge!"

He moved it toward her ribs in a slow thrust. "Okay, show me what I need to know."

She slipped her jacket free of her good arm and from the shoulder of the other and pulled a matching waster from the wall. Alex had only begun to show him techniques for not allowing his sword tip to be pushed down when she felt it.

Drew pulled back from her, sword at his side. He looked around.

A doorway from another realm had opened. The sharp clip of high heels came from the locker rooms in the back. Awth, her case manager, stomped into the room. Her faint green hair pulled up into a sever bun on the top of her head. Drew stepped in front of Alex when the woman in clean crisp attire approached them. The psychedelic gingham pattern of her garments always made Alex dizzy.

Awth glared at him.

"It's okay, Drew. This is Awth. She's in charge of my after-action care."

Drew stepped aside as Awth turned her nose up further at him. Her narrowed gaze and disapproval shifted to Alex. "Why are you still wearing that?" Her nasal voice made Alex cringe.

"I was told to wear it for two weeks—"

"Which has long since passed with the time differential, Wright." She yanked the sling and the brace off, tossed them to the floor, and passed a hand-held scanner over her arm. "See. Healed. No sign of any deficit." Awth pulled a flash drive from her pocket and thrust it at Alex, harder than Drew had done with the sword. "Time to get back to work, Wright."

"You can't expect her to return already." Drew stepped forward. He used his interrogation tone on Awth. Not that it had any effect.

She glared at him but spoke to Alex, "The continued distraction of this AJ is interfering with your work, Wright. If it persists—"

Now Alex stepped between Drew and Awth, reaching her now unbound arm behind her, she rested her hand on his chest to restrain him. "I know my place, Awth. There is no problem here." She waved the drive. "I have my orders."

The woman harrumphed, shot Drew one final glare, and moved toward the front door. She retraced her steps back to the locker room, and the hum of an open portal stopped tickling Alex's skn.

"They can't seriously expect you to work mere weeks after you were nearly beaten to death."

Alex shivered. Her entire insides had dropped in temperature like she had spent the last hour in a deep freeze. "They can. And they have. This is what I do, Drew. This is what I tried to tell you. I have no sick days, vacation days, time off. I go when and where they need me."

"But—"

She shook her head moving to the door. "Thanks for the ride. I'm going to head home."

"Want some lunch?" He stayed close on her heels.

"I'm not hungry."

She locked up the studio, and Drew helped her on with her coat. He took both her hands in his. Warm. Strong. Reliable. "If you have to leave right away, you need to prepare. That means protein and that means eating. I'm not leaving your side until I know you've had a hearty meal."

He was right of course, but the thought of food repulsed her.

"Where are we going to get you ready?"

She raised her chin toward the diner with a deep sigh. Drew released one of her hands, and they started walking.

As he opened the resturant door, he asked, "What's an AJ?"

"An Average Joe."

"Oh. Guardians don't think too much of us little guys, do they?"

"Soon it won't matter. There won't be any of us left to look down our noses at anyone else."

Chapter 48

Alex held a cloche hat secure over her bob-cut black wig and lean into the wind. Her knee-length wool coat buttoned tight against the icy gust. Her T-straps clicked up the stairs as she stepped through an archway on Allen City's Second Street into Ekzaga, a realm reminiscent of the Roaring Twenties.

No wind here. The heat came up off the pavement in waves. She slipped both off the coat, and a cardigan, draping them over her arm. Alex tried to push up the long sleeves on her jumper without success. A car, sleek, low to the ground sped past, ruffling her pleated skirt. A blur of orange tires reminded Alex that all realms held a slight similarity to her world—but they weren't the same. A foghorn blast from another car stopped her before she crossed the street. She teetered on the sidewalk for a moment, drained by the transport. *Deep breath. No time to faint.* There was work to be done.

She waited for a break in traffic as she nibbled on a power bar, wrapped in a kerchief. Across the street and down the block, she spotted a sidewalk placard pointing to her destination. "Holy Roller Congregation. Meeting 3 pm." She checked her tiny gold watch. 3:20. She'd slip in and get a feel for what she needed to do.

The blast of spicy cigarette smoke almost propelled her back out of the room. The haze obscured her view and triggered a deep cough.

"The Lord is a God of vengeance. He punishes the children of the sinner to the third and fourth generation. We are His faithful children.

We must take vengeance on those evil doers who infest our city with their wickedness."

Alex's eyes burned and watered as they focused on the man bellowing at the front of the room. Sweat dripped down his face. A the preacher's waved his arms dramatically rings of sweat darkened the armpits of his light green suit jacket. His purple shirt tucked into the green suit slacks stretched near to tearing over his budging muscles.

"We will smite each and every one of them with God's holy wrath," he roared with a Bible thrust high into the air.

The smoke stirred, the men shuffling their weight between their feet, and muted conversation bantered between them.

A group of women sat on metal folding chairs with their heads bowed and handkerchiefs pressed to their mouths.

"Death to the sinners! An end to all lawlessness!"

"Vengeance is Mine, saith the Lord." The room became deathly still. All eyes turned on Alex.

"Women have no right to speak here," the leader spat and growled as he pointed her to the chairs.

The click of her T-strap heels echoed in punctuated pops as she moved further forward. "It is true God hates sin. But He loves the sinner, sir. He has not called us to mead out His justice, but to love our fellow man."

"Shut your mouth, woman," the leader bellowed.

"Did not Christ Himself answer and say unto them, 'I tell you that, if these should hold their peace, the stones would immediately cry out.' I must speak the truth as God has proclaimed it to me. We are to love our neighbor as ourselves. We are to be known by our love."

The men standing on either side of her started nodding their heads and murmuring agreement.

Emboldened by their support, Alex continued. "Christ came to seek and save that which was lost. And are not these sinners here in this city lost?"

More vocal agreement rang out.

"No one has ever come to a saving grace in Christ after threats and beatings over the head with the Holy Scriptures. God's love and care draws sinners to Him everyday. As the hands and feet of Christ, let us be His love. Let us meet a need. Food, clothing, a job—if you have one to offer. Minister to the widow and the orphan as the Bible instructs. When they know our love, they seek the Lord."

"We have baby clothes we can donate," a woman from the back whispered.

"I could use another man on the line at the factory."

"My Betty makes a mean casserole."

The congregation circled around and started planning. Alex sighed. Her weary shoulders sagged, as she slipped into a chair. It should be over. But no gateway opened.

"GET OUT!" the man in the green suit screamed. Alex jumped up so fast the back of her legs caught on the front of the seat bringing it up and folding the chair so it collapsed with a clang of a gong on the tile floor. She scurried toward the door with the other women. Some of the men stayed and tried to calm the man, but they soon joined the others on the sidewalk rubbing their reddened jaws.

A preacher that would strike his own flock was not one sent by the Lord. "I am sorry to have disrupted your meeting," Alex said.

"No ma'am, you were correct. We have all been looking for a place to worship, and we'd hoped this might be the place."

"The signs went up over a fortnight ago." One of the men took his wife's hand. "We were so desperate to hear the Word preached..."

"We knew what he spoke wasn't right."

"But when you spoke the truth, I knew it straight away. If I might be so bold, can I ask where you worship?"

Alex offered him a weak small. "Unfortunately, my home church is not within the city. But surely you can find a place that would meet your spiritual needs."

"We were thinking pure foolishness to listen to this man after that first meeting. Thank you for the reminder of how believers are supposed to behave."

"Are you new in town?" a woman beside her asked.

"I was walking along and saw the sign," she pointed to the placard behind the gentleman who'd thanked her. "Thought to pop in and get a bit of refreshing."

"Sorry, seems this church failed us all," another man muttered.

"I was supposed to be here." She pushed her lips up into a pleasant smile. "I better be on my way again. No rest for the weary and all. I'll leave you to your planning."

Their thank you's faded into the heat weighing the air and covering her skin in tickling droplets. She ambled down the street to a small ice cream salon. She could use a cool refreshing treat on the blistering hot day. Not recognizing any of the fanciful flavors, she picked a pretty pink one and sat staring out at the street. Why wasn't she going home yet?

Stepping from the cool interior of the ice cream salon, Alex slogged through the continuing oppressive heat even in early evening. Unfocused and aimless, she put one foot in front of the other.

A massive arm clamped around her waist, as a catcher's mitt of a hand covered her mouth before her startled yelp could escape. The arm encircling her waist was so tight she couldn't inhale. Dragged back into an alley, Alex went limp and allowed the movement. Getting her bearings, she forced her captor to drag her lifeless body and waited for the most opportune moment.

People passed the opening to the alley, but no one looked to see her plight. Harsh breaths rasped over her shoulder, heating her neck like she'd left the hairdryer pointed in the wrong spot. Sweat ran down her back soaking through her dress. She shuttered not knowing if it was her own or dripping off the man gasping behind her. His grip relaxed a fraction. She remained still, submissive. Another fraction and another.

Her left elbow slammed into her attacker's ribs, as her right heel landed on the top of his foot. A spasm raced through the arms locked around her. Spinning to her left, she smashed her right elbow into his temple.

He staggered back, and Alex saw her attacker—the church leader she'd confronted. He growled, his face becoming an alarming shade of red. Nlood seeped from the gash she'd opened above his eye. He lunged, but she sidestepped him with ease. His bulky muscles were no match for her agile speed. He whirled and came at her again, driving her deeper into the narrow space between the two buildings as she ducked and dodged one fist then the other. Each raging appendage narrowly missed, but the air in its wake buffeted her skin. Heaven help her if one should find its mark. It'd snap her head clean around.

She ducked his next blow waiting for his forearm to cross his body as it caught air. She moved in close, counter-acting his bigger size and superior strength and drove her fist into his liver.

As he jerked back from her attack his elbow caught her temple and spun her around.

You won't die. Drew's words whispered over her skin. Her step wobbled, and her shoulder banged into a large garbage bin further upsetting her balance. She tried to turn and face him. Dodge him. Pain exploded across her face like a semi plowed into her. Her arms flew out at her sides to keep from falling, Alex whirled around and lurched forward leaving her back exposed to her enemy. Puffs of light danced in her vision.

Agony. Head thrust forward. Falling.

Chapter 49

The slow pulsing throb in her head beckoned her back to consciousness. The ache in her cheek came next. Alex tried to lift her hand, but it wouldn't move. She cracking one eye open against the glaring light. Her arms were bound to the arms of a chair. She wiggled her legs and found them equally secure.

Letting her head hang, she prayed the nothingness would swallow her and never release her.

A vision filled her mind. Drew stood surrounded by blackness. "You won't die." She stared at him, too tired to respond or think much about him haunting her thoughts. His arms crossed. He straightened to his full height, and his gaze narrowed. "You will NOT die." The volume of his imagined voice echoed inside her aching skull making her cringe. Head pounding, she almost wished him away. But being alone sent bolts of despair racing up and down her quaking limbs.

The vision squared his shoulders, huffed in frustration, and tapped his foot in her mind's eye. "Alex Wright, you listen to me. Stop horsing around! I'm not telling you again." His authoritative words rattled in her head like some crazed echo chamber. She groaned, squinted, and lifted her gaze as slow as possible. The glare off the light sent needles of white-hot pain through her eye sockets pulsating directly into her skull.

"Well, the wicked wretch is awake." The snarling voice vibrated over her skin. A hand snaked to her throat as her chin was lifted to look again at the man who claimed to speak for God. Lips pulled back revealing a mouth full of teeth, drops of spittle sparkled at the corners. Rage flashed in his black eyes like lightning.

She gasped for a full breath around. Her thoughts swam in the haze he created.

"I will see the evil in this city ripped to shreds, and I will start with you." He clenched her neck and pushed her head back. Blackness bled into her vision.

Now! Drew's voice thundered in her head making her jerk back. Alex jerked from the man's sweaty grasp and threw herself and the chair to the floor landing hard on her shoulder. Her temple slammed into the floor adding to the pounding of her wounded head, nausea brought up the pink ice cream. It oozed from the side of her mouth as darkness closed in on her.

"What is going on…" a new, unfamiliar voice trailed off as she floated in a sea of pain. Angry words of others in the room clattered around her, disjointed and incomprehensible.

She floated for a moment then her head lulled forward as her chair righted. Struggling to pry her eyes open again, electricity buzzed over her skin. *Now the doorway home opens. It couldn't have done that a couple of hours ago?* Hands worked to free her bindings. Faces of the congregation came into focus. Wide-eyed women stared at her, their gaze flicking to the man they almost made their leader. He still raged. He thrashed against the four men who bound his arms behind him.

Free from the chair, her arms were lifted to drape over others' shoulders, and someone pulled her to her feet. Her gelatin legs would not support her, but the two men on either side helped Alex out of the meeting hall's back room and out into the setting sun. Lowered to the top step at the entrance, she sat with her elbows braced on knees and her head in her hands. A cool towel pressed on her throbbing head.

What Alex could only describe as a paddy wagon rolled up and parked in front of the steps. A police officer opened the back end. He smiled at her. Blinking several times to clear her vision of Drew in a long, dark officer's jacket with gleaming gold buttons down the front, Alex finally saw the shorter man before her.

The would-be church leader spit venom as they wrestled him out of the building and into the vehicle. The remaining congregation turned their attention to her.

"Let us take you to the hospital, ma'am," one man offered.

"Yes, you poor dear. That is quite a lump you have on your head," the woman placed her hand on Alex's shoulder.

"I have a car we can use," another man said.

Alex forced a smile. "Thank you, but I think I will be heading home now."

"We thought you said you weren't from the city?" someone asked.

"The place I'm heading isn't far." She pushed to her feet, swaying as her temperamental stomach rolled like a ship in an ill wind. "I should be there quick enough." *Please let the door on the other end be close to my apartment this time.* Finding strength in her legs, she slowly wobbled down the last two steps and headed toward the ice cream salon. In the same alley where she had been attacked, she lurched through the hidden gateway she could feel on her skin. She stepped into her own world. The chill wind licked at her exposed flesh. Great! Only six blocks from home—in December. She braced her hand against the building and started walking.

Chapter 50

Alex headed down her hall, pulling a baggy sweatshirt over her head on the way to her front door. The relentless knocking rattled the entire wall again echoing the drumbeat in her head. "Keep your shirt on," she grumbled.

"You didn't call when you got back. You promised." Drew stomped into her apartment without an invitation.

"It was next on my list. I've only been home five minutes and haven't found—" She spun away from him as he closed the door, and a wave of dizziness crashed over her. Grasping for the back of the couch before she fell, Drew's protective arm wrapped around her as he pulled her back against his steady frame. She drew strength from his solid safety and leaned into him.

Air hissed between his teeth, and in the next heartbeat, she found herself cradled in his arms. He walked past the couch and into the hall. His eyes straight ahead focused on her bedroom, Alex fought to swallow the lump in her throat as heat coursed through her body. Opening her mouth, no words of protest escaped before he made a quick turn into the bathroom and sat her on the edge of the claw-foot tub. Her feet inside the empty bath, he removed the wig dropping it in the tub and placed his hands on either side of her head and gently probed her wound with his thumbs.

"Tell me what happened." Detective mood took over as he ordered her to report. "You've got a lump the size of a softball, a gash longer than my finger, and blood splattered all over the back of your shirt."

She winced as he pulled her hair aside to get a better look. Her shoulders slumped, and she fought not to slide into the tub fully. "I love this sweatshirt. Now I'll have to throw it away."

Drew kept one hand on her shoulder to steady her as he stretched to the sink and wet a washcloth. Wringing it out over the tub, he worked to clean the wound as she told him the whole story. Once clean, he found her superglue and closed the gash. Lifting her back in his arms, he turned toward her bedroom.

His phone rang on his hip.

"The couch is fine," she blurted, her body tense. "Besides, it sounds like you're needed."

He considered her, his brows drawn together, mouth pulled in a deep scowl.

"Really, a little TV, the comfy couch next to the warm fire. It'll be perfect."

Turning, he moved back down the hall as Alex let her cheek lay against his collarbone. His steps slowed, and his grip tightened. The steady strong beat of his heart lulled her. Nearly asleep before he sat her down, she roused as he released her and pulled the blanket from the back of the couch. Poking the gas fireplace on, he vanished for a few moments and returned with a protein drink and cheese. The *Bad Boys* ringtone blared from his hip again.

"You better get that."

He reached for his phone. "I'll tell Andersen I'm staying—"

A raised hand stopped him. "You go do your job. I'm going to eat this and take a much needed nap."

Again with the scowl and furrowed brows.

Marking an X over her heart with her finger she said, "I swear I won't move from this spot until—"

"I get back."

There was that cop tone again. She didn't have the energy to argue with his order and only nodded.

"You promise?"

"I'll only get up if I have to pee," she vowed, annoyance coloring her words. Oh, that deadly smirk sent her heart ricocheting around her ribs. He stood in her doorway. "I'll swing by Daly's." The phone interrupted him. He ignored it again. "Orange chicken?"

"I'm in the mood for their pot roast."

"You got it, babe." He winked and closed the door. The last word reverberated through her as if her entire body suffered an internal earthquake.

Chapter 51

Drew went out of his way, as he usually did, to swing by Alex's apartment on his way home. Still no lights on. He slammed his fist into the steering wheel and headed toward home. She'd come home with a gash in her head and been back out on Guardian business within a few days. This was the third day for her latest business trip, and already his nerves were on edge.

Flinging his keys into the dish by the door and locking away his gun, he grabbed an apple from the bowl on the table as he made his way to his bedroom. His tiny one-room apartment was dark and lifeless compared to Alex's. He shook his head as he held the fruit between his teeth while he slid out of his shirt tossing it on the chair. No, everything was lifeless without Alex.

He kicked off his shoes and jerked off his socks. In his flannel bottoms, he dropped back on his bed and stared up at the ceiling. The rest of the apple pinched between his fingers.

It had only been a matter of months since Alex had gone from hated suspect to… what? Friend? Definitely. Girlfriend? "Please." He whispered a hope-filled prayer. No, he wanted more.

His breaths grew shallow. Heart pounded. Heat raced through his veins. His eyes closed and he let the dream slip in again. The one he had pushed away for days. Alex, dressed in white, walking toward him where he stood at the front of the church. Halfway up the aisle, she vanished.

His heart slammed into his ribcage with enough force to roll him to

his side and curl him into a fetal position. The apple dropped to the floor
with a thud. "Blasted guardians." No, he didn't hate them. Alex was one
of them. He hated that *he* wasn't one of them.

"Your girl still out of town?" Andersen slapped him on the shoulder
as they entered the elevator. "She can't call from these business trips of
hers, or she won't take your calls?" He winked as he pushed the button
to the squad floor.

"Personal calls aren't allowed when she's working. She should be
back soon."

"She'd better be. I'm tired of working with a love-struck partner."
Andersen elbowed him in the ribs as the doors slid open. "You got it
bad, bro."

"Don't I know it."

In the middle of a call to verify a suspect's alibi, energy shivered over
Drew's skin. Like a thousand centipedes crawling all over him. He
brushed down his arms to rid them of the sensation. Alex was back, or
at least a doorway was open for her imminent return. He hung up the
phone not even sure he got the answer he needed. "I'm gonna take an
early lunch." He grabbed his jacket off the back of the chair as his
partner eyed him.

"Say hi to Alex for me," he said with a smirk.

Drew's fingers drummed on the steering wheel as he snaked through
traffic towards her apartment. "She better be uninjured this time or
heads are gonna roll."

He took the stairs two at a time and rounded the corner the moment
Alex stepped off the elevator.

"Drew!" She stepped back from him startled. "How do you know
when I get back?" Her eyes scanned the walls and ceiling. "Do you have
cameras here or something?"

"Something." He couldn't keep the smile from his lips. Oh, the woman had spun a web around his heart. His eyes raked over her from head to toe looking for any injury, limp, or wince. She wore an odd puke-purple shapeless wide-legged jumper like an obnoxious polyester version of something out of the seventies.

She moved to the windowsill and retrieved her hidden key. He'd have to remember that. "You can stop staring. I'm fine." She brushed past him to her door.

Every nerve in his body quaked as he kept himself planted in the hall so he didn't seize her about the waist and kiss her soundly. A groan whispered over his lips, and she looked up at him as she returned the key.

Her features pinched as she stared up at him. "You all right?"

His hand raised, and he caressed her cheek. She leaned into the touch sending his pulse into an erratic rhythm. Shifting his weight forward to the balls of his feet he leaned. She raised her lips to meet his.

His phone blared at his waist, and Alex pulled away.

"You're going to get fired if they catch you ditching work so often." She turned and entered her apartment, longing in her eyes, and disappointment on her lips. "Go back to work, Drew. I'll see you later."

Drew put the phone to his ear as the door closed. "What?" He screamed into his phone, turned, to the stairs, and pounded down them.

Chapter 52

A week later Alex shrugged off her heavy coat as her gas fireplace flared to life and chased the chill from her apartment. She passed the Christmas tree as she went to hang the coat up. The lights twinkled, visions of her walk home from the studio flooded her mind. Jolly St. Nick ringing his bell near a kettle swinging in the stiff wind. Children bundled against the cold, pointing mitten-covered fingers at toys in window displays. The nativity in front of the church. Would this be the Christmas joy finally extended to her lonely heart? The next week would reveal her answer, but if Drew had his way—

Thump, thump, thump.

She tossed the coat over the couch and headed back toward the door.

Thump, thump, thump.

"For heaven's sake, keep your shirt on." She jerked the door open, and Drew plowed past her. The book he used to communicate with Brendon open on his arm.

"We've got to go back. Right away. They're in trouble. We have to do something." His frantic words tumbled from his mouth as he whirled toward her.

"Drew I can't go anywhere unless it's approved."

"But I need you. Honestly, Alex, I don't understand you. I'm trying so hard, and at times I think you want a relationship with me, and at others you pull away, and I'm not even sure you want me as a friend.

Now, I need your help."

"As usual, you aren't listening to me. I didn't say I wouldn't help. I have to ask permission. The doors are are't open for me to come and go as I please. And you know the Conclave won't approve of our relationship, no matter how much I want it."

Drew stalked around her tiny living room, before he whirled on her and talked slowly back toward her. He only stopped when he stood inches from her again. "So you do want to be with me?"

"It doesn't matter. It's not allowed." She crossed her arms and tapped her foot. She wouldn't admit how much he meant to her—even to herself. This was for the best. Break it off now before either of them got more hurt.

He thrust the book at her. "Alex forget the rotten Conclave. Will you look at this and help me? We'll discuss *them* later." He put his finger on the blank page. "It's right here?" That cop tone. She really hated it.

"I can't read it."

"Why won't you help? Brendon's in trouble!" He slammed the book closed. "They all are. We have to do something and you won't even—"

Alex slapped her hand over his mouth. The skin, hot and smooth under her touch, sent a shiver through her. Her thoughts leaked out of her head as she brushed her thumb along his lips. He kissed her hand, startling her back to the moment. She swallowed her heart. It took a couple of times before she could form words. Her hand slipped to her side, chilled by the lack of his touch. "I didn't say I wouldn't. I said I can't. The page is blank, Drew. There is nothing for me to read."

"What?" He opened it and pointed again. "There? You don't see any writing?" She looked up to see she make sure she was still in her living room and not behind an interrogation table at the precinct.

Drew was rattled. What could have gone so wrong? Best to put her irritation aside and get to the bottom of it, though she doubted the Conclave would let her get involved again. She moved toward the couch.

Tucking her foot beneath her, she patted the seat beside her. "Maybe it's because I made it. Or it was the other-worldly tech. I don't know. Now, tell me what's going on. We'll see if we can figure something out."

Drew dropped beside her, book in his lap, and knee pressed against hers. Heat flooded her body washing away all else for the moment.

"Alex? Alex, are you listening?"

She pulled her gaze from their point of contact. "Sorry, you were saying?"

"Brendon says Vilnund is under attack, or soon will be. They are hugely outnumbered. Kolena, is expecting. Brendon doesn't want to leave her. There has to be something this blasted Conclave of yours can do. They can't have put Brendon there only to let him get wiped out less than a year later."

"I will send a message right away." She placed her hand on his arm. "They probably already know, but I'll make sure of it." She went to her bedroom, signed on to the secure site, and sent the urgent information. She bit her lip as she signed off. Even if they knew, and allowed her to return, what aid could she render in a battle with three to one odds?

She turned to see Drew leaning alongside the doorframe of her room. "It's sent." She stood and moved toward him. His arms opened to welcomed her into his embrace. She hesitated. "Even if they allow a third trip there, Drew, they won't let you go back. And I don't know what I can do."

He closed the distance and wrapped his arms around her. The chill fled. The trembling stopped. She rested her cheek on his chest and drowned in the sound of his heartbeat. "Thank you for doing all that you can. If you go, I know you'll find a way to save them."

"How?"

A kiss pressed to the top of her head. "Because you've saved me, babe."

Chapter 53

Drew took time off. Dressed in the medieval clothes from Brendon, he waited near Alex's building. He pulled the heavy trench coat around him to ward off the chill. A couple of hours ago, Drew sensed the gateway's opening, so he took a taxi to her place in hopes of following her through again. Over sixty hours passed since Alex sent the Conclave the message for help. If his calculations were correct, that meant a week had passed in Vilnund. Too long when danger was so near. He knew he wasn't allowed to go, but this was family and the Conclave could…

The lights clicked off in Alex's apartment. Drew pulled back to the shadows and out of the wind. Her long cloak covered her outfit, but as the wind whipped it, Drew could see she wore something different than their earlier trip. The sleeves of her blouse were tight on her forearms. The full leather vest covered everything important, and pants covered her legs until they disappeared into her tall boots. Her bag dangled from her fingers.

Following her for a block and a half, he realized she was going to the same spot where he caught up to her the first time they went. Cutting through several alleys at a run, he got their first. His skin buzzed the nearer he got to the open gateway. He put his hand in but nothing happened. He could sense it, but not open it. Alex was the Key.

As she appeared at the corner, Drew stepped out of sight. The modern trench coat of his world slid off his shoulders, exposing him to the frigid air. A few feet. A couple more steps. He watched Alex approach, head down, leaning into the wind. As her toe crossed the threshold of the invisible gate, his arm slid over her waist and pushed his chest into her back.

The breath-stealing blast, disorientation, Drew's lungs burned. The bright warm sun in the middle of the low valley left him squeezing his eyes closed and unsettled.

When all other movement stopped, Alex jerked from his grasp and whirled. "By all the saints, what are you doing here, Drew?"

Hands braced on his knees, waiting for the nausea to pass, he raised one corner of his mouth. "I came to attend m'lady."

Her hands flew to her hips, and she scowled.

He cringed as he straightened. He hadn't missed that expression focused on him. Bowing deep at the waist he said quietly, "Your humble servant, Andrew, is at your service, Lady Alexandria."

When he stood straight once more, her arms crossed and her scowl remained. "The Conclave is not going to like this."

He threw out his arms and turned a complete turn for her inspection. "Appropriately attired, no mystical gadgets, I remember my place quietly in your wake, m'lady." He bowed again.

The corner of her mouth quirked, and she cleared her throat as she fought to control her lips.

He moved toward her on slow steps, judging her reaction. She didn't move. He reached forward, put his hands on her shoulders and slid his hands downward. Her arms relaxed as he took her hands in his and held them tight. "Are you hale, m'lady?"

The smile blossomed, and she leaned into him. The tip of her tongue wet her lips, welcoming him. With a husky voice she responded, "Aye."

A jingling caused her to turn her head before he could claim her lips. She pulled from him and dropped her bag to the ground. Pushing her cape back over her shoulders she pulled her long braid free and started to roll it at the base of her skull. "Riders are coming," she gasped, eyes on the hill that led toward the palace.

She pulled a bobby pin from a loop of fabric at her waist. A long strip of cloth unwound covering a little of the linen pants she wore. They were similar to his breeches only darker and a little looser in the fit. She placed the pin in her hair and she pulled another from her waist releasing another strip. Before the horses crested the hill, her hair was secured, and she wore a skirt over her pants and boots, this one all in separate panels that ended above her ankles.

"Interesting skirt," he said lifting two short swords and her dagger from her bag.

She wound a belt around her waist, "A fighting skirt of my own design." Alex drew the longer blade as a lone man appeared over the rise with two rider-less horses in tow. The weapon returned to the sheath, and she glanced up, brows twisting as she considered him. "It seems your brother knew we were here as well."

"I didn't tell him anything. There wasn't time. I barely had enough time to call in my absence, dress, and get across town before you left."

"And how did you know?"

Drew swallowed and inclined his head toward the approaching rider. "Time to leave, m'lady." He leaned in to whisper. "I'll explain later, babe."

Again, the wide-eyed look that made him want to pull her into his arms, and never let her go, filled her face. He managed to step away, as the rider drew to a stop.

"Laird Brendon sends greetings, m'lady." The soldier tossed her a set of reins.

Alex moved to the horse's left and raised her leg for the stirrup.

Drew dropped to one knee, cupped her foot, and boosted her into the saddle.

"We appreciate his kindness," she said.

"War's in the air, m'lady. He did not wish ye out here unprotected. A few soldiers wait over the rise to escort ye to him."

"'Tis why we have returned. To lend aid where we might."

Handing the other reins to Drew, the man continued. "Glad the lairds will be to hear of it, m'lady.

Drew moved to the left side of his horse, gripped the front and rear of his saddle and pulled himself up. He caught Alex staring at him. Her lower lip clamped between her teeth. Seated, he locked his feet in the stirrups and straightened. The horse beneath him shifted its weight and a nervous flitter, like butterflies, skimmed through his belly. But the creature didn't rear and dump him on his backside like the spiteful beast at camp when he was a kid, so he relaxed his shoulders and gave her a nod.

They put their heels to their mounts and joined the soldiers for a less than comfortable ride back to the palace.

The fields they passed lay void of activity this time. Guards lined the wall, and they had to wait for the portcullis to be raised to enter. War and fear definitely weighted the air.

Chapter 54

Alex passed the reins of her horse to the squire as a second portcullis at the inner gate slammed back into place. The vibrations echoed from the souls of her feet, rattled her teeth, and further set her nerves on edge. Drew being here was bad. The Conclave would have something to say about it.

She turned to him, and what irritation remained melted like dew in the morning sun. He dismounted on wobbly legs, shook them out while clinging to the animal, handed over the reins to the stable hand, and moved in behind her. She handed him her blades as they briskly crossed the ward and entered the hall.

Lairds Eldridge and Brendon closed the distance as she curtsied. Drew had taken a knee behind her and remained there as the two men greeted her with a kiss on both cheeks.

"Lady Alexandria, I can't believe ye came at such a desperate time," Eldridge said.

"I heard of yer need and came to lend aid where I might."

The lairds glanced at one another. Laird Eldridge spoke again. "Unless ye've brought us another thousand or so fighting men, I fear yer trip has been in vain."

"And now ye may be trapped here with us until the end," Brendon frowned.

"Forgive me for being so bold, but I might know where soldiers can be found."

Laird Eldridge shifted his weight to his heels and considered her with one brow arched high.

"I have consulted me wise advisers, and they believe there is a clan to the north that is also at risk, but when yer forces are combined would tip the odds in yer favor, m'laird."

"Really? Who?" Hope lit Brendon face.

Eldridge glared at her, lifted his arms and firmly crossed them.

"The Sinclair clan, my laird."

"No!" Eldridge spat.

"But—"

The slap of Laird Eldridge's fist into his palm cut Brendon off. "I won't have it. Thieves, cut-throats, murderers. The entire lot of them. Let the vermin die for their sins. I'll not come to their aid."

Alex glanced at Brendon as his shoulders slumped once more. She hadn't expected Eldridge to jump at the chance of making his northern neighbors allies, but she thought he might consider the idea. She put her hands on her hips. As they would say in her world, time for some tough love. "Forgive me, my laird, but when exactly was the last time ye had any dealings with the Sinclair clan?"

Eldridge blanched, his arms dropping to his sides. "I think they stole livestock from my father's father."

"So no contact in two generations, and ye would cut off any chance of them coming to *yer aid* to save *yer* family. I hear tell yer daughter is in the family way. Do ye not wish to see yer grandchild, my laird? Not to mention yer own wee son growing into a man."

"Only ye could get away with speaking to me so bold, my lady." He raked his hands through his hair. "And what makes ye think those heathen Sinclairs will be willing to make treaty with us?"

"That is what I do, m'laird. I broker peace between peoples. It is something in which the good Lord has gifted me. Let me go to the Sinclairs and see if they will meet with ye at a treaty table. Neither of ye can stand alone. But together, ye might each return unscathed, to yer beds and yer wives."

"I can't spare men to escort ye."

Drew rose to his feet and stepped between her and the laird. Alex sucked in a breath as panic coursed through her. Drew remained silent however, gaze cast at Eldridge's boots, but his shoulders were squared. His stance imposing.

Laird Eldridge's glare raked over him. "Ye wish to speak?"

"'Tis me honor and me duty to protect *m'lady*, m'laird. I shall be accompanying her."

The steel in his words, the conviction flooding them, and the possession of the way he claimed her as his alone, rocked through her. She swayed on her feet from the power, as if in the wake of a mighty explosion.

Eldridge put his hand on Drew's shoulder. "Well said, friend." Turning to Brendon he added, "See this man suited and armed before they leave, and find two men willing to journey with them."

"I'll gladly go, sir," Brendon offered.

"Nay, m'laird," Alex said. "Yer place is with Lady Kolena. One knight to add safety and one fast rider to bring ye word of our success is all we require."

"Ye are overly confident this frivolous venture will succeed."

"I have spent the last handful of days in prayer. God goes before us. He will not fail."

Laird Eldridge inclined his head toward her. "Then ye will leave at first light, and I wish ye Godspeed, my lady."

Chapter 55

Drew followed Brendon down the same hallway they traversed to his whipping the first time he visited. Before opening the door into the yard, Brendon turned and embraced him. "Thanks for coming."

Surprised by his brother's open affection, Drew thumped him on the back. "I couldn't leave you hanging."

Brendon released him and studied him for a moment. "Has she been training you? You can protect her?"

"I had barely starting to get a lesson with the sword a few weeks ago."

Brendon's fist slammed into his shoulder knocking him off balance. Stepping back to steady himself Drew rubbed at his arm. Brendon's words ground between his locked jaw in a harsh whisper of mixed modern and old world verbage. "Fie man, you are going to get yourself killed, and her too. Why are ye here anyway if ye can nay lift a finger to help."

Drew pushed in until he was nose to nose with his brother. "I've served in the military, and walked the beat as a cop. I know how to handle myself when the going gets tough. And," he narrowed his eyes, "I'll die before I let anything happen to her."

Brendon pulled back, his eyes wide, mouth hanging open. "You and Alex? When you left I thought she surely hated you. I mean the breaking into her place and spying on her. Now, I didn't see this coming. Ye haven't written about her either." He turned on his heel and stepped out of the dark hall into the blazing sun. They walked to the armory, where Drew was given mail and a broadsword. After securing the volunteers who would be traveling with them, Brendon led him to a hidden corner of the bailey.

Pulling his sword, he pointed it at his brother. "Ye've about fourteen hours before ye leave. I aim to instruct ye everything I can in that time so ye can keep yer promise to her."

Drew pulled his blade, and the lessons began.

Brendon had whisked Drew away before Alex had a chance to talk him out of coming with her. Not that it would have done any good. He'd found a way to Vilnund; he'd find a way to fight at her side. His words still echoed in her ears, filling her with hope and something more she couldn't yet put her finger on. She was glad he was here. She needed him.

"M'lady."

She turned to the young man crossing the hall.

He bowed, "I am Gregor, Laird Eldridge's squire m'lady. I will be riding with ye on the morrow. Laird Brendon sent me to gather what we need for our journey and to ask ye to go to the armory for mail. He wishes ye as protected as might be on this mission."

"Lead the way Gregor, and I will give ye the list as we go."

He bowed again and waved out his hand for her to precede him.

Supplies were gathered and everything at the ready for the coming journey. Alex sat at the high table beside Lady Selby and Laird Eldridge. There were no murmurers this night. No musicians to lighten the weight of the room. Though the farmers and their families now dined at the laird's boards, the room had no life as though someone had let the helium out of a balloon and left it flat on the floor.

The oppression weighed on her. "M'laird, might I say a word to your people?"

Eldridge looked up from pushing his food around his plate and nodded.

Alex stood and moved to the edge of the dais in front of the high table. "Men and women of Clan MacDougan, hear me. The Lord fights for ye. And where the Lord is, there is peace. The Christ said, 'Peace I leave with ye, My peace I give unto ye: not as the world giveth, give I unto ye. Let not yer heart be troubled, neither let it be afraid.' I go on the morrow to seek treaty that ye might stand against the enemy coming to yer gates. But know this, whether or not aid be found in a treaty with men, God fights for His people. Our God does not look at the strength of our enemy, nor our allies, nor even our own hands. He looks only to Himself, and He will not fail ye."

As if air had been breathed back into that balloon she imagined, the weight lifted from the hall. People smiled and talked with one another. And they started eating the food before them.

Lady Selby stood as Alex took her seat. "Our chapel has newly been finished and, though there is not yet a priest to lead us, I ask all who are able to meet with me each morn to pray for our lands, our families, and God's victory."

The room came alive with fists pounding on tables. Eldridge looked past his wife to Alex. "Thank ye, my lady. We were in sore need of uplifting."

"Look to God, my friend. He alone is the author and finisher of yer faith."

He lifted his tankard to her and then to his lip in a long drink.

Her gaze swept out over the people gathered. *Lord, don't make a liar out of me. Save Your people, please.*

Chapter 56

Alex rose from a fitful sleep long before first light. Drew's pallet in the outer chamber hadn't been slept in, and he wasn't at the breaking of the fast. He and his brother were still nowhere in sight by the time she went to the stables to meet her escorts. Four horses stood saddled and ready. A knight in full mail stepped from the shadows with Gregor at his heel. They both bowed. "Sir Hugo, at your service, my lady."

She curtsied. "Greetings, sir. Glad I am to have yer strong arm."

Mail rattled as Drew and Brendon approached from her other side. The detective now wore tall boots, leather breeches, and a long mail hauberk over his padded gambeson. There was a broadsword belted at his waist. His coif pulled up over his head kept much of his face in shadow in the minimal morning light.

Alex's pulse ticked up a beat—well several beats. Her knight in shining armor, or mail in this case, come to protect her. She stared at him.

"I swear no harm will come to ye, m'lady."

Her heart did a summersault, her breathing took a vacation, and her thoughts addled. He was… gorgeous. But it was more than mere looks. He embodied the dream she could never have. Tears stung her eyes, and burned her throat.

"M'lady?"

She waved him off and turned before he saw the tears escaping. "Aye, Andrew. Let us be about it."

He stepped behind her and lifted her coif to cover her head. She winced with a sharp intake of air. "M'lady?" His whisper raked over her raw nerves.

"My hair is caught," she managed to stammer through her tight throat. The two of them worked until the large knot of her braided hair was free of the weight of the mail, then he boosted her into the saddle. She slid on leather gloves and turned her mount to the gate.

Laird Eldridge blocked their path. He raised his hand and bowed his head. "Lord, we send these few out in Yer care. We ask Ye grant them the favor of Yer strong hand to see them safely to their destination and their mission well accomplished. Amen."

Drew's strong *amen* on her left drowned out her own reply. She glanced at him, but he looked straight ahead. He hadn't looked so serious and determined since she was a suspect. The narrowed gaze and set of his jaw made him look like a chiseled statue in his armor.

Hugo called for both portcullises to be raised and the outer gate opened as Eldridge and Brendon wished them Godspeed. The first rays of light kissed the eastern horizon as they turned north and kicked their horses to a canter.

Alex became lost inside herself. Trees zipped by in an blur. Weighed down by more than her borrowed mail, her thoughts turned to the gallant man riding beside her. He looked more comfortable in the saddle than he had mere hours ago. He represented everything she needed and all she wanted. But the Conclave would never allow Alex to entangle her life, even in friendship, with one not their own. He was a distraction; Awth had warned. Anything that detracted from her demands as a guardian had to be eliminated.

There would be no sweet Christmas memories. This mission had to be their last—everything. No more dinners, visits, or calls. She had no choice but to cut things off. If she didn't, the Conclave would without hesitation or kindness.

Every cell in her body ached at the mere thought of the loss to come. Body trembling, heart tearing in two, she doubled over the horse's neck and silenced the sob shredding her insides. She mistook the shriek of the band of highwaymen bursting from the tree line as her own cry of pain. Alex sat blinking as the three men of her guard surrounded her, swords drawn, shouting orders to one another. Blades clanged against the assault long before she gathered her wits and drew her own weapons.

Alex locked her knees around her horse and drew her swords. As she moved to push back one of the eight attackers, Drew shifted his horse between her and the man. Her leg became pinned between their two mounts. Gripping her blades in her left hand, she slapped his horse on the rump to get free.

Drew shot her a glare as his horse fought to decide which command it would follow. Gregor moved forward on her right giving her more room to maneuver, and she surged into the gap charging at the man she had tried to address before Drew interfered.

Drew's broadsword and mailed hand shot out blocking a blow aimed at her. His fist caught her in the mouth. The metallic spray of blood danced across her tongue, and her leg once again became pinned.

Elbowing Drew in the shoulder, she drove him away. "I have this one. Concentrate on those two!" She leapt from her saddle and charged at the man before her. Ducking under the neck of his horse and a swing of his long sword, she came up on his left side driving a sword into his thigh.

"Alex… Andria!" Drew bellowed her shortened name, and tried to correct it, then tried again. "Alexandria, m'lady!"

Blocking the backwards swing of her attacker's blade with the sword in her left hand, she jerked her right blade free. The man roared and tried to whirl his horse to trample her. With another slash of her blade, the man bent low over the side of his horse. Alex grabbed him by the back of the neck and yanked him to the ground. Blades in both hands again she sunk them into his back before he could rise.

Drew moved towards her as she looked up. "Get on your horse!"

"On your right!"

They both yelled at one another at the same time. Drew spun, and raised his sword to block the blow aimed at his unprotected jugular. Again Alex ducked around a horse and confronted the second man directly in front of Drew. They both engaged their enemy. The one Alex challenged kept turning his horse to face her. Keeping his thighs out of her reach, as he tried to trample her.

She made a shallow cut across the horse's front, but only enough to make it fight against its master's orders to move toward her.

"Hugo!" Drew ordered. "Get the lady back in her saddle."

"Leave me be and address yer own foe," she shot back. A quick dodge and weave and Alex stood on the attacker's side. She came up driving a sword into the man's chest. He dropped, and the horse darted away.

Chapter 57

"What in heaven's name is the matter with you?" Drew leapt down beside her and stood shouting in her face as the dead attackers lay around them.

She met him toe-to-toe. "Me? As I recall, I am the master of the sword, and ye're a *servant*. What were *ye* thinking?"

"We shall go scout a little ahead. See if any further surprises await us." Hugo called Gregor and the two left at a trot.

Drew threw his sword on the ground and jerked off his gloves. "You're bleeding." He reached for her face, concern swirling in his eyes.

She shoved his hand away. "Aye, by your own hand."

He staggered back a step. His voice broke. "Me? I did…"

"Aye," Alex cut off part of one of the fallen men's shirts and used it to wipe her blades clean. "In one of your wild blocks." Her blades back on her hips, she handed the rag to him.

Drew ignored it and stepped closer, his thumb brushing at the cut in her lip. "Forgive me, m'lady."

She tried to pull away, but he grasped her face between his hands.

"Alex, you scared me to death."

Her hands pulled at his wrists trying to get him to release her. In one swift thrust, she slammed the heel of her hand into his sternum and her elbows thrust up under his forearms breaking his grip. She stepped back —fists on her hips. "I have trained for situations like this. I can take care of myself and have for years."

"But you don't have to do everything alone any more. Alex, I lo—"

Her hand flew over his mouth, stopping the words she couldn't bear to hear, yet wanting to hear them above all else. "Don't!"

He jerked his head back, but she kept pushed on him.

"Don't say it. This… us… we can never be."

His eyes squinted, brows pulled together as if she was speaking an alien language.

"I am what I am, Drew. We are not allowed relationships with outsiders. There is nothing to be gained by pursuing this any longer." Eyes burned and throat choked, she stepped away from him. "This ends now. As it should have ended weeks ago." She turned her back to him. "You deserve better—someone you can share a life—a very long life with, Drew. Someone who can cherish you in all ways. Not someone who will die soon."

"Tell me you don't love me." He stood right behind her, his hands on her hips. His breath against her neck brought more tears. "You can't lie. You're too good for that. Thou shall not bear false witness."

"It matters not at all what I want, or what I feel. The Conclave will never allow it."

Hugo and Gregor rode back toward them, and Alex moved to her horse. They gave a hard look, them glanced at one another. No doubt Eldridge would hear of the odd behavior with her servant. Nothing to do about that now.

Drew's hands—strong, secure, tender—encircled her waist. His voice so low only she could hear. "This is not over between us. I will find a way, even if I have to take on every single member of this Conclave in hand-to-hand combat. I won't give you up." With a less than gentle toss, she landed in the saddle again. Drew collected his sword and mounted his horse. A single look passed between them. His flickered with hope, love, and a steely determination.

If only it could be that easy.

The sun ducked toward its hidden home as an inn came into view. They tethered their horses out front and slipped inside. Footfalls echoed off floorboards. The few patrons peered over their tankards in silence. A rather man who was neither short nor tall, fat nor skill, stood behind the bar at the opposite end of the room.

Drew remained close to Alex. He had heard what she said—and what she didn't say—but they belonged together. During his training with Brendon, Drew had confessed his love for Alex. There was a compulsion driving him toward her. He couldn't breathe or think clearly when she wasn't near. Here, beside her, life made sense—no matter what crazy dimension they were in. Brendon had said he felt the same when he wanted to come and meet Kolena. Nothing would have kept him from coming to her.

"Have you any rooms to lend, my good man?" Hugo asked.

"Mayhaps."

"One room," Drew said, his voice firm.

The owner's glance swept over them, lingering on Alex for a moment, continued, and came back to her.

"Two." Alex glared at him narrowed eyes. She turned back to the inn keep. "Please. We come from the MacDougan on our way north."

The man nodded, wiped his hands, and stepped out from behind the bar. "Three sables per room. Five if any of ye be wantin' to cleanse the road off ye." He stopped in the middle of the narrow corridor lined with doors on either side. "All these here rooms are yers to choose from, exceptin' that one there, and this one 'ere." He pointed to two rooms kitty-corner from one another.

"We'll take the two next to one another on the backside," Drew said.

"We'll take the two at the end of the hall," Hugo said at the same moment.

Drew looked at the knight and quickly lowered his gazed. "Sir, there is a door which I assume leads outside. There is not time for warning or defense should someone enter through it."

"But if the inn is attacked, it would serve as an easy exit and not have us locked in the middle of a stone dwelling with no escape."

"These rooms are better to defend from, sir." Both Drew's volume and head rose slightly.

"And those lead to freedom."

The owner put out his hand for payments while Drew continued to try to convince the stubborn. Backwards-thinking man. After all, how many safe houses had Hugo ever secured? How many people had he ever protected?

Coins jingled, "I'll take a bath, if you don't mind." Alex pointed to a room not at the end of the corridor and not in the middle. She didn't favor either man's opinion. "We also have horses that need to be stabled and fed."

"Two more of them coins, and me boy will see to 'em."

Two more coins dropped into his hand, and he ambled back down the hall. "Food's hot if yer hungry."

Alex skirted the men still vying for their way and opened the door to the room she had selected. Drew moved to follow. She planted her hand firm on his chest. "No."

"'Tis my duty to see to yer safety, m'lady."

"Not in this wee room. There be no windows, so I'll not be snatched." She leaned closer, her words tight, low, and void of the medieval drawl. "And I can darn-well take care of myself. Knock it off." She pushed him back and closed the door in his face.

Gregor held the door to the right of Alex's room open. The one closer to the exit. "There are two beds in here. I can sleep on the floor."

Drew spun, crossed his arms, and thumped back against the wall beside her door. "I shall stand guard."

Gregor shrugged, Hugo inclined his head, and they disappeared inside.

Drew grit his teeth. He should walk in her room and make a sweep of it, but he reconsidered. He worked to loosen his shoulders and rolled his head to relax his neck. A smirk tugged at his lips. She'd run him through if he walked in on her.

Chapter 58

Alex cracked the door to a soft knock. "Water for yer bath, m'lady," a scrawny lad said. She nodded widened the entry and he dragged the bucket in that nearly out-weighed his small frame. She noted the shadow at her door.

"What are you doing now?" Her arms akimbo once again, standing in the hall.

"Guarding you."

"You haven't slept since we arrived. Not even sure you've eaten more then the tack in the saddle."

His head turned to face her, though it still lolled against the stones behind him. "I'll see you safe before I waste time eating or sleeping." His gaze devoured her and filled her at the same time.

The lad left to refill his bucket, and Alex stepped toward him. She slugged him in the arm.

"Owwww!" He rose off the wall and rubbed at the spot.

"If you can't stop one feeble woman's punch, how do you aim to protect her? You know full well, lack of sleep dulls the reflexes and causes you to miss things."

The boy returned and slipped past them.

Drew's hand brushed her cheek. "I'll see you protected no matter the circumstances."

She smacked at his hand. "Stubborn, irritating, bull-headed... aww!" She threw up her hands as the lad retreated down the corridor. Alex made to follow. "If you aren't going to help the poor boy, find something useful to do. I'm going to grab something to eat."

She only made it a step before his arm encircled her waist and he pulled her back to his chest. "I am doing the most important work I have ever done in my life." His words washed over her neck and shoulder with the power of a raging waterfall. "I am taking care of you."

A tremor shook her, and he tightened his grip. She fought to swallow the hope struggling to take root and the heat filling her entire body.

The boy passed and neither of them moved. The lad dared a look and a smirk as he left.

Drew turned her to face him and then he returned his arm around her, his other hand cradled her head, and he pushed her to the wall where he'd been standing. "I told you earlier, we aren't finished. I really don't care what the rules are or what your *Conclave* has to say. We belong together."

Alex's legs trembled. Drew's hold was the only thing keeping her off the floor. She shook her head, strangled by her need for him. "You don't understand," she choked.

His gaze narrowed, lit by a fierceness that matched his warrior outfit. "You're right, I don't understand how you can fight what you know to be true to keep following a bunch of backwards thinking elders who needlessly put you in harms way at every turn. I will protect you."

Alex opened her mouth, but no retort came. He hovered so near. His lips only a breath from hers. The door beside them opened, and he released her as Hugo stepped out, she was back in her room before he could stop her. She allowed the boy in with another bucket then closed the door when he left.

"We go to get something to eat, coming?" she heard Hugo ask Drew through the closed door.

"I'll stay at me post, but the lady spoke of her hunger. Mayhaps ye could bring her a plate?"

"Aye, and I'll relieve ye so ye can eat when I'm done."

Alex secured the door, shed her clothes and snuck into the welcome warmth. But it did nothing to cover the hope Drew stirred in her.

Phantom sensations of Drew touching her face and holding her, kept any deep sleep at bay. The man promised things he could never deliver. Too many others had tried to join their lives with AJ's and failed. There was no hope for them.

Giving up, she rose, dressed, and secured her blades over her hips. Her meal from last night rolled in her stomach. She wouldn't be stopping to repeat that mistake this morning. Hand resting on the latch, she took a steadying breath. A day or two more, that is all they would have together. She had to make him give up on her dreams.

No—*his* dreams. He had to get this foolhardy notion out of his head.

Of course the man waited outside. "Did ye sleep well, m'lady?"

"Did you sleep at all?" *Don't stop, don't engage him.*

"Aye, both Hugo and Gregor took a shift at yer door." He walked in step beside her. He was too close.

"We should be on our way, why don't you get them—"

"They see to the horses now. I was about to knock on your door when you opened it." His hand brushed hers, fingers searching to lace with hers.

"Stop!" She jerked away.

Drew pulled her to a stop before they entered the main room and held her by both shoulders. "Oh, Alexandria Wright, I know ye well, m'lady. Ye have it in yer head," he tapped his index finger on her temple and let the medieval burr roll, "we are nay meant to be. Plan to shrug me aside with a wee cold shoulder." Now he was mixing his English and

Scottish accents. A smile pulled at her lips. "Hoping me resolve will slip, lass? But ye know me not, m'lady." His lips brushed her ear as he whispered. "I can be every bit as stubborn in my pursuit as you are in your denying it, babe." He pressed his lips to her neck below her ear.

The corridor spun. Another feather soft kiss brushed lower on her neck. A tiny moan eased from her.

He straightened. The smile so large on his face it was a wonder it didn't cause injury. "Aye, m'lady, trust me and you'll be receivin' more of the same." Heat seared her cheeks as he looped her arm in his and led her from the inn.

Too addled by his kisses to do more than be led around like a pup on a leash, she went where he took her. As they neared the stable his arm slipped from hers, and he stepped back to follow in her wake. Drew had sent her thoughts and senses into such a tumult she nearly collided with Gregor as he exited with two of their horses.

The squire apologized, but Alex's brain and mouth were still too muddled to connect to coherent thought. Drew's hands were soon embracing her again, and she sat atop her mount before she understood what he intended. They continued on their journey, as Alex's neck warmed under Drew's heated stare.

Chapter 59

They rode in silence for much of the day. The country to the north lay more open than MacDougan territory. They passed a burned out village late in the afternoon. Later as the sun reached low on the horizon, they approached the castle perched on a high knoll, the dark waters of an expansive loch at its back.

"The Sinclair standard," Hugo pointed to the battlements.

A rattle of mail and weapons shattered the air. It didn't come from the castle they approached but from the valley stretching before it to their left. Kicking their mounts to speed, they raced to the protection of the walls.

"We seek entry in the name of treaty with Laird Sinclair," Alex shouted at the wall with a fleeting glance over her shoulder. The men with her all turned to face the threat though it was far off yet.

"Let spies in our gates at a time like this? Ye be daft!"

"We travel with a woman. We are not part of the war band!" Drew said.

"Ye think us so addled-headed as to believe—"

"My name is Lady Alexandria, Guardian of the Truth, Servant of the Most High. I come to the righteous Laird Sinclair on mission of forging a treaty of arms with the honorable Laird MacDougan. Open the blasted doors before we are run aground!" She hadn't intended to lay out her entire mission from the foot of the massive gate. But the band behind them was charging their way. Still more than a mile off but coming fast.

Discussion fluttered atop the wall like the pennants flapping in the breeze. "Drop your weapons."

Alex yanked her swords and her dagger free and dropped them in the dirt. The men did the same, as the drawbridge's chains creaked and moaned in the effort of to lower. Further rattling proved the portcullis also rose.

Alex spun her horse around and urged it several feet from the lowering entrance. When she was assured the beast could clear the leap, she spurred it ahead. She sprang onto the drawbridge before it reached the ground, ducked under the half raised spiked barrier beyond, and hurtled into the bailey. Drew entered last as a Sinclair squire darted out and collected their weapons before the bridge and gates were secured again.

Alex ignored the bows and swords pointed at her, as she leapt from her saddle and raced to the top of the battlements. She skirted the startled men who stood between her and her destination. Those she passed muttered of her boldness to move about with such authority and their uncertainty of whether they should seize her. She moved to the center above the gate she'd ridden through.

"M'lady!" Tension bit at Drew's call from where he remained below.

"What is the meanin' of all this uproar and entrance at this crucial hour?" A deep voice with a rich Scottish burr filled the entire bailey.

"We come from Laird MacDougan—" Hugo had started to explain. The stomach turning sound of a nasty loogie cut him off. That, and a few expletives.

"M'laird?" the man standing atop the wall beside her called, his voice rattled with indecision.

As the Sinclair laird stomped up toward the battlements, Alex snatched up a bow and quiver resting against the wall near her. The soldiers nearest her took a step back, but she kept her gaze trained on the approaching threat.

Soon the big man in red plaid towered over her. He snorted. "Think ye can take down an army with yer one wee bow, lass?"

"'Tis not the entire army but only a small attack band to test yer defenses. And if I can bring down any, will ye hear us under band of truce at yer boards, laird?"

A boisterous laugh erupted. "Ye have a wager, lass. Prick any one of them vermin with an arrow, and I assure ye a right pleasant discourse with me da."

Alex nodded. She drew half a dozen arrows from the quiver propped against the wall in front of her. She hooked five under the last two fingers of her left hand and notched the sixth.

The junior laird laughed all the harder.

Drew soon appeared on her other side. She caught his one raised brow from her quick sideways glance and smiled at them both.

The approaching band of whooping bare-chested men was now about four hundred yards away. She'd shot over two football fields before, which meant they were still too far. They slowed. "Come on," she whispered. She needed to prove herself to get the meeting.

"Looks like ye be out of luck, lass. It'll be off to the dungeons till I decide what to do with ye and yer men."

Letting her arms relax, Alex drew in a huge breath, shot the laird a glance, and shrieked at the top of her lungs. Her cry caused a few of the womenfolk within the Sinclair walls to do the same. It had the desired effect for the band picked up speed again.

Weapon raised, she drew back, and earned a grunt of approval from Junior. Another few yards, and they would be within her range, but they were slowing again. *Lord, I could use a little help here.*

They continued forward. A little more draw on the bow, the arrow pointed high to the sky to cover the distance. And she released. Within fifteen seconds she sent all six arrows to flight and reached for another set.

Five men fell. Six if you count the stagger of Junior that accompanied another curse.

Drew's chest on her other side looked three times fuller, and his chin higher.

After her next volley where she brought down another three men, the Sinclair defenders snatched up their bows. Matching her trajectory, they managed to leave a couple dozen dead on the field, though the Sinclairs couldn't match her quick draw technique.

The enemy turned and pulled back out of range.

Alex spun, thrusting the bow at Junior. "I shall be enjoying me cup of welcome and me meeting now, sir."

Chapter 60

The junior laird looked her over, slack-jawed for a moment, before waving out a hand for her to head back to the bailey. Drew on her heels, she collected Hugo and Gregor as they wound through the crowded city to the keep inside the inner wall.

"How many have been displaced?" she asked as they walked.

Junior scanned those huddled in any open place. "Two villages have made it here; the losses were great."

"We passed one between here and the inn at Moors Hill," Hugo said.

"Aye, ye must be meanin' Grigsai. It fell three days ago." Junior bounded up the keep's stairs and pushed open the heavy oak doors. "I'm surprised ye made it here without meetin' our friends out there."

The hall had fewer windows than Eldridge's. The torches did little to light the small space. Alex and her men walked toward the center as Junior barked orders that sent servants scattering.

"Ye may wait here. I'll fetch me da. He's not in good health, so it may take a moment. Eat and refresh yerselves."

Maids brought them bread, cheese, and ale. Alex filled a tankard, but Drew snatched it before she could take a drink. After a deep gulp that he finished by wiping his mouth with his sleeve, he held it out of her reach.

"'Tis not poisoned," he said passing it to her.

"Well of course not. 'Tis a cup of friendship. No honorable Vilnundian would dare use it for murder."

Hugo took it from her next and drank deep. "A true cup of greeting is shared with the host."

"Oh, by all that is holy, the two of you, stand down. The Lord has gone before us. We are safely at journey's end, and all is well."

Drew and Hugo exchanged glances over her head.

Alex snatched the tankard back and, at last, quenched her thirst. Refilling it, she passed it to Gregor before waiting on a bench.

Junior returned supporting a man who appeared to have once been nearly as tall as his son, but age and battles left him bent and crooked. The little white hair left on his head wisped out in all directions.

Alex stood and curtsied low. Her men took a knee around her. "Laird Sinclair, greetings."

The old man harrumphed as he lowered into his tall-backed chair on the dais. "Niall, allowed ye in me hall, woman, but nay will I make bonds with the MacDougan." He spat on the rushes.

Alex rose, arms held before her in a relaxed clasp. "The MacDougan said as much. The Sinclairs could only be trusted to lop their own noses from their face rather than see reason."

Hugo stifled a sputter beside her.

Senior tried to stand, a boney bent finger pointed in the air. "Why that murdering, good for nothing. I've a mind to ride out and wallop him but good." He dropped back fully in his chair with a puff of air.

She glanced at her men. "Strange, but he said the same of ye."

"No Sinclair has fouled themselves with the likes of a MacDougan—"

"Aye, for how long, laird? One generation? Two? Mayhaps more? Neither of ye are keen on the other. But neither have any of yer people harmed one another since the time of yer father's father. Might it be time, as a raiding band camps at yer front gate, to consider the men ye were told about may, in fact, be the men wishing to stand with ye to rid yer land of this common enemy."

"MacDougan's can nay be trusted."

Alex sighed. "The enemy of my enemy be me friend."

The two men seated above stared at her. The younger, Niall, rubbed his red-tinted beard thoughtfully.

"Neither ye nor the MacDougans have the men, stouthearted as they may be, to defeat this enemy alone. But if ye be unwilling to talk reason, preferring to be gossipmonger instead, we shall leave as soon as safety allows."

Drew gripped her elbow. She knew insulting the laird in his home came with risks. Drew's previous whipping was reminder enough.

"Lass." Senior's finger waved at her again.

"Da," Niall rested his hand on his father's arm. "They have come far in dangerous times to present us with a possibility of seeing another winter. This be not a matter that can be decided in haste on old tales. Ye need to discuss it with the clan, Da."

The laird's wagging finger came to rest on the chair.

"And Da, remember. She is not a MacDougan. She wears no plaid and says she is a Guardian—a servant of the Most High."

"A thing easily claimed and near impossible to prove," the laird snorted.

Alex pulled the skeleton key amulet from around her neck. Swirling tendrils of dark metal encased the bright blue stone. She held it in her hand and approached the Sinclair lairds. "As ye took me dagger, Laird Niall, would ye be so kind as to prick me finger?"

She offer her hand. After a nod from the senior laird, Niall did as she requested. She let a drop of her blood touch the stone, and she held it out for the lairds to see as the blue stone glowed red, then green, and finally purple before becoming inert and blue once more.

The lairds exchanged glances as she returned the amulet to her neck."

"Niall, show our guests to rooms and assemble the clan elders."

"Aye, Da."

Chapter 61

"That was a pretty cool trick." Drew slipped out of the darkness coming to stand beside her atop the battlements. The last of the waning moon danced on his skin, giving him an ethereal appearance.

On this bit of wall, they were alone. She didn't bother with the medieval verbiage. "The same bit of technology that worked to create the books you and Brendon use to communicate. But the changing colors will happen anytime the stone is exposed to blood."

"So, they know about guardians here?"

"Many of realms have legends about a secret or mythic group that once helped people. I took a chance that the title would mean something to them."

"I'm glad it worked." He leaned back on the outer fortifications beside her. "You should relax and rest. Old Rodric Sinclair told us the clan agreed to send his son to meet with Eldridge. Niall seems inclined to sign an ally pact."

Alex rubbed at her arms. "I can't sleep."

Drew came and wrapped his arms around her, but she pushed him off. "I'm not cold. Something's bothering me."

"What?"

Her arms jerked rigid at her sides, fists clenched. "I don't know."

"Okay…" Drew walked beside her as she continued along the battlements with only a sliver of moon lighting their way. "If this is about us—"

"Hush."

"I know you don't—"

She clamped her hand over his mouth again. "Shut up! Listen." She moved to look out over the darkness surrounding the castle, and closed her eyes. The rustle of Drew's mail followed, then he stilled. Scraping. She was sure of it. A muffled clink of metal to stone, so faint she wasn't sure it came from somewhere other than her own rattled thoughts.

No it was definitely there, below her near the wall.

Her eyes flew open and her head snapped around. She raced the couple feet to the nearest guard. "I need jars of oil, tar, pitch. Anything ye have that is liquid and will burn. The hotter the better. Bring it as quickly and quietly as ye can."

The guard stared at her.

"Go man. Hurry before the castle falls to yer enemy."

The guard still looked confused, but he moved all the same.

She spun back and ran square into Drew. "I need a bow and quiver, a length of old cloth, and a lit torch."

"I'm not—"

She planted her hand on his chest. "Everything we have done thus far may have been for nothing if you don't get me what I need. Now!"

He finally turned.

Alex paced and prayed for everyone to hurry.

"Ye may be a Guardian, lass, but ye can nay go ordering me men about." Niall stomped up next to her as several guards returned their arms laden with jars. She seized two and turned to the darkness below her.

"By the saints, what are ye doin,' woman?" Niall yelled.

"Hush, laird."

Drew joined them a moment later with the items she requested,

Gregor and Hugo on his heels.

"Point the light there," she told Drew. "But don't ye drop that torch." She tossed her first jar near the wall and threw the other one farther out so they landed a few feet apart. The pottery shattered allowing its contents to ooze over the ground. "Take the remaining jars and smash them in between those two."

Niall, took hold of her arm. "I'll not waste good oil till ye tell me what ye're doin.'"

Drew pushed him aside breaking his hold and grabbed two more jars sending them crashing over the wall. "The lady is saving yer castle, laird."

She tore a bit of cloth and secured it behind the tip of an arrow. Notching it in the bow, she lit the rag with the torch Gregor now held, and sent it into the oil soaked ground below. Hugo did likewise, and soon the ground near the wall leapt high with flame.

Everyone atop the battlements waited for a few still heartbeats. Then muffled screams floated up to them.

"The ruddy vermin were undermining our wall!" Niall choked. "I hope they cook like the rats they are."

"Some will escape," Alex told him. "Any way to get down there and cut them off?"

He turned to her with a smile, "Aye, there's a wee slough gate out to the loch." He moved toward the stairs, and she started to follow.

Drew gripped her arm.

She glanced up at him and jerked free. "Ye want to protect me?"

"Aye."

"Then watch my back." She ran to catch up with the laird. They fed single file into a tunnel with Alex and her men sandwiched between handfuls of Sinclairs. As they spilled out into the night, a few were left to guard the gate while the rest raced toward the coughing and sputtering near the dying flames.

Swords drawn, she leapt into the fray. The bare chests were easy to distinguish from the white shirts draped in plaid. Those dying on the ground were mercifully run through before the defenders turned to the cluster springing from the trees to defend their fallen men.

As Alex slashed her way into the mêlée, Drew's firm presence literally pressed to her back. It only lasted a moment before he eased from her enough to allow them both to move.

Metal clanged rending the stillness of the night. The enemy howled a fearsome war cry. Men grunted. Others moaned their last breath. The sharp tang of blood filled the air. She gripped her swords because of the slickness covering them.

Drew grunted and went down on one knee behind her. "Stay down," she ordered. Swinging wide over his head she opened the throat of the man facing him.

Drew brought up his sword back under his arm, running the man through at her back. They stood staring at one another for a moment before each charged men running at the other's back.

The noises faded, clinging only to the mist hovering over the loch. She braced herself breathing hard will she leaned into Drew's back. His forced breaths and thundering heartbeat echoing her own.

Niall materialized beside them. "A few escaped, but the rest were killed." He nodded to them. "Me thanks."

Alex eased her weight off Drew's support and looked to the sky. "Dawn's still a few hours off."

Niall smiled. "Aye, sent twenty men to roust the rest of the vermin from their sleep." The distant clash of battle filtered through the trees. "Come, me friends. Let us prepare the victory meal for them. They won't take long." He waved them forward as he returned to the slough gate.

Chapter 62

In the murky, flickering light of the hall, Niall's band, Alex, and her men washed and saw to their wounded. She tugged Drew's tunic free of his sword belt exposing the gash over his right hip. She pulled the shirt over his head and threw it on his mail she'd already helped him remove. His arm draped over her shoulder, he tried to sit still as her fingers probed the slash. He winced as she pulled it open looking for debris and then brushed the oozing blood aside.

"A few stitches and a little poultice will hold you for now," she told him. But her touch was setting his skin on fire. A tiny moan slipped past his clinched teeth.

"Sorry. I'm hurting you." She took the clean cloth from the bucket on the table beside him and slid it over the wound.

"I'll be fine," he croaked. "Blade slipped under the mail shirt. It's not deep." He wanted to reassure her. She was already trying to get rid of him. He didn't want to consider what she might do if he was seriously wounded. He leaned forward for only her to hear. "Not as bad as a gunshot." He glanced down at a round scar above his collarbone.

Alex's gaze followed, and she brushed the old wound with a feather-light touch sending a shudder skipping down his spine.

He gripped the table he sat on. It took all his will not to tighten his arms around her and kiss her lips now held in a sad curve.

"M'lady," Gregor bowed pulling her attention away. "Laird Niall says the enemy has been routed. I seek permission to leave at once to carry word back to m'laird of the meeting."

Alex faced the squire as Drew's arm still sat perched on her shoulder. "But the hour?"

"Sun will be up well before I reach the inn. When we stayed, I made arrangement for a fresh mount to await me. I shall ride in the MacDougan gates before the sun has fully set, m'lady."

Her brows crinkled a bit, and she chewed on her lower lip. Drew's heart fluttered at her familiar signs of worry.

Niall approached from behind her laying a hand on her shoulder.

Drew's fluttering heart, and his warming thoughts jerked. Again he gripped the table. He must stay put.

"The healer will be over in a moment."

"Thank ye," Alex said absently. "Were many of yer men hurt?"

"Nay, a bad gash in a thigh was the worst of it. Most fared as well as yer guard here."

She nodded, her gaze brushing the cut low on his side again.

"M'lady?" Gregor said.

"My squire wishes to make haste to the MacDougan."

"If he leaves now, we can meet at the inn at Moor's Hill the following evening afore any more of the enemy returns." Niall said. "I am sending one of me own with him."

"Gregor can be trusted—"

Niall held up his hand cutting her off, then waved over a young man near Gregor's age though much shorter. "'Tis not a matter of trust, but safety, my lady." He stepped away. "See to yer man, I will see these two on their way."

Alex stared after them without moving.

"See even he knows I'm your man," Drew whispered.

She spun; knocked his arm from her shoulder and thumped him in the sternum with the tip of her finger. "Hush you."

He smiled and brushed the fresh blood from the cut he had made in her lip yesterday. She'd reopened it fretting over Gregor's return trip. Their eyes locked for only a moment. Her gaze held him with a mixture of sorrow, hope, and longing.

The healer greeted them, and she stepped away lowering her head. She moved to a bucket of water and washed the blood from her hands and face. Her shoulders and head hung. Her steps were heavy.

If he could hold her in his arms, it would be all right. A sharp poke of the healers needle made a curse leap from his lips. "A little warning there, doc."

The healer looked at him, brows arched high.

Chapter 63

Alex mounted her horse. Her emotions churned in a hurricane of epic proportions. She let them swirl not catching a single train of thought for more than a moment. Drew had protected her. She should have died, surrounded as they were, but he had been there. Steady. Strong. And hurt. If she hadn't brought him along… but of course she hadn't; he came of his own. Did as he pleased. Stayed close beside her.

The open line of flesh. The streak of dripping blood. True, it had been a shallow cut, but no antibiotics would be found here. Her insides did an odd dance again. The injury lay far well below an enticing sprinkle of curly hair over his chest that begged her fingers to explore. The two images fought. He would have given his life for her. She shuddered.

He didn't belong here. This wasn't his fight. Not that he would have agreed. His brother lived here with his wife and their coming child. A niece or nephew for him. And she was here.

"M'lady?"

She turned to look Drew in the face. He had one brow arched high reminding her of some handsome actor, whose name she couldn't remember. But he was famous for that same stare.

His hand stretched out to her, offering a biscuit and jerky. "Ye hale?"

Alex nodded and nibbled but didn't taste. The tumult in her head overrode every other sensation.

Drew said they belonged together, and she felt it too. But *they* would never allow it. Her heart convulsed, threatening to tear in two.

Alex blinked, and the inn stood before them. The sun hung low on the horizon. Niall and his men dismounted. Drew stood beside her mount, his features pinched tight together. Alex shook herself and dismounted. Eldridge's horse and another sat rider-less out front.

One of the last to enter, Alex stepped between the two lairds as they glared at one another. A hand on each man's chest, she spoke first so neither man could end the talks before they began.

"There will be no speaking of treaty this night. We eat and sleep so you might come to the treaty table level headed and ready to speak with civil tongues on the morrow. Are we agreed?"

Both men nodded.

"Will ye eat together?"

"Nay." They spoke as one man.

"Laird Eldridge of the MacDougan, when did ye set out this morn?"

"An hour before first light."

"As ye have traveled the longer, ye choose where ye and yer men will eat. Near the door, or near the rooms."

"Door."

"Laird Niall of the Sinclair, ye choose where ye and yer men sleep. Near the hall or near the rear exit."

"Exit."

Both men continued to stare the other one down. Alex crossed her arms and tapped her foot. They moved to opposite corners of the room and plopped on benches. Each with his back to his foe, both trying to prove they did not fear the other. Alex rolled her neck and shoulders to shake free the tension, and she went to the owner. Their rooms secured, servants soon brought food to the tables. They each invited her to dine with them, but Alex yanked a table into the aisle of the room and sat, being mindful to keep equal distance between both to show neither favoritism. When they retired to their rooms, she again took the one in the middle. This night, she didn't go to her bed but to her knees, for she intended to pray for the treaty talks in the morning. But Alex couldn't keep a clear line of thought in her head. With her folded hands on the edge of the bed, she leaned her head against them. *Lord, help.*

Chapter 64

After the breaking of the fast in the morning, Niall and Eldridge met her at the table in the center of the room. Each man sat, unarmed, at opposite ends. One of their own guards and one of the other man's guards stood behind them.

Alex stood between them facing the door. Drew served as her shadow a few feet behind her. "Will ye bow yer heads in prayer, lairds?

"Heavenly Father, we come before Ye. Fill this inn with Yer deep peace. Knit hearts and minds to Yer will alone. May Ye receive all the glory and honor in all that is said and done this day, and in the union forged between these two honorable, God-fearing houses. Amen."

"Amen."

"I have but one rule, then I will leave ye to discuss the matters that threaten yer land, yer families, and yer lives. Ye may *only* discuss past events which ye have personal knowledge of seeing or experiencing. There will be no mention of sheep stolen two score years before ye were born. Or boats scuttled in the time of yer father's father. If ye know of an ill or bear a grievance because ye witnessed it, then the matter may be aired. Is this term agreeable?"

Neither man spoke. Alex slammed her fist on the table rattling the candles almost out of their holders. "Lairds, are we in agreement?"

"Aye," they said in unison.

"Very well." She pulled two rolled parchments from her bag.

Light flooded the dark room as the door banged open. The guards sprang to their feet, blades drawn. Drew shouldered in front of her, his blade half out of its sheath.

The man standing akimbo in the doorway remained completely in shadow. She couldn't tell if he was friend or foe, but she could see he didn't have a weapon drawn.

"A Sinclair sitting at board with a MacDougan. I didn't believe me man when he told the tale. Had to come bear witness to the oddity meself."

"Jon," Niall rose and reached out his hand in friendship, pulling the man into the candlelight of the room. Lean, but muscled, Jon did not look as old as his wavy white hair claimed him to be. Niall turned to her and Eldridge. "Jon, Laird of the Murray clan. Ye know the MacDougan. And this is Lady Alexandria of the Guardians who arranged this talk."

Jon bowed to her and extended his hand to Eldridge. The MacDougan laird rose and took the man's forearm in friendship.

The alliance forgotten, Niall asked, "How is yer lovely wife, Sharon?"

"Well, other than frettin' over this threat now burnin' our crops and villages. Took out one of our holdings night before." Jon turned to Alex, then glanced at both men. "Is any clan welcome at this table?"

Both lairds nodded, and Jon waved in three other men wearing enough variations of plaids to make Alex dizzy.

Jon introduced them. "Paden of the Banff, Lydell of the Cockburn, and Duff of the Kinnaird clan."

"Welcome lairds," Alex curtsied, and grabbed four more scrolls from her bag as the men arranged themselves at the table. As she set out the two inkpots and handful of quills, a shiver raced up her arms. Her head rose and she noted Drew's head raised a moment later. Their eyes met and he shuddered slightly as though he were chilled. Did he know when a gateway opened? But how? He inclined his head. Their time was up. These would be their last moments together. Unless God intervened.

Chapter 65

Drew continued to fret over Alex's withdrawn behavior. Since the fight against those who tried to undermine the Sinclair wall, she had slipped within herself. She avoided him. And other than the directions, well orders really, to the lairds now gathered at the table in front of her, she'd stopped talking. It seemed her gaze didn't focus on what lay directly in front of her. She seemed lost.

She moved to the back of the inn and sat. He couldn't tell if she listened to the men's discussion or if she'd floated away again. He set a bowl of steaming stew in front of her. The savory flavors made his stomach growl, but it took her a moment to even notice the mouthwatering meal. She pushed it away.

He leaned to whisper. "You need to prepare for travel."

A hollow glance met his, but she picked up the wooden spoon and sipped at the meal, eating about half before she lost interest.

He sat beside her on the bench, but faced opposite her, his back to the men she monitored. He wanted to talk with her, but she rose, propelled into action.

"It's time." She strolled away. Closing the door on their future as surely as she closed the door of the inn.

"Sir Hugo, m'lady needs to return to her various responsibilities." Drew handed the knight the sword and armor Brendon had given him and the mail Alex had worn. "Will ye see these returned to Laird Brendon?" He wouldn't get to say good-bye to his brother this time.

That bothered him almost as bad as Alex's distance.

Hugo looked at the items without a word but nodded. Drew stepped out of the dark, near windowless inn into the blaring light of midday. His hand rose to shield his eyes, causing him to squint. *Where are you? You set the boundaries, believing our growing relationship an impossible dream. Would you leave me behind? No, you're scared, not cruel.*

Eyes adjusting, he spotted her at last about a dozen feet down the road heading toward MacDougan territory. Her arms hugged tight around her, shoulders rigid, her head low.

Drew almost reached her.

"Hold!"

They both turned to see Eldridge hurrying toward them.

"Lady Alexandria, ye come and gather six lairds at one table. Ye propose peace and action for the common good. Then ye slink away before the job is complete?" He reached out and took her hands.

She pushed a smile to her lips. Did the laird see it as forced as Drew did? "This was never about me. Ye merely needed an introduction. The clans will be stronger now. Ye all have matters well in hand, and I will praise the Lord with ye when I hear reports of His victory through yer alliance against this invading army."

Eldridge kissed both her cheeks causing a hint of a blush to wash over them. "Well, nonetheless, we give ye our heart-felt thanks, my lady."

He released her, and his hand extended toward Drew. He stifled the shock reverberating through his chest and clasped the man's forearm. "Sir Andrew, yer brother will mourn yer going without farewell, but ye're always welcome at our hearth."

Drew and Alex exchanged glances.

Eldridge laughed and slapped Drew on the shoulder while he still held his arm in a fearsome grasp. "I noted how he trained with ye, and yer own behavior toward yer lady. I questioned Brendon at length until he finally confessed ye were kin. The confusion at yer first arrival on finding him quite by accident living with me family, and me hot temper caused ye a beating I sore regret."

"Think nothing of it, laird."

Eldridge slapped his shoulder again. Drew smarted at the bruise that would certainly form under the man's thumping. "Ye take care of yer lady, and we shall see ye when me grandchild is born." The laird at last released him and turned back to join the others who waved and bowed, and called their thanks before returning to their talks.

When Drew turned around, Alex had already ambled a few feet ahead of him, steps heavy and head hanging. He tried to take her hand, but she refused hugging herself tight once more.

Down the road, she turned from the road and headed into the woods. Two bent trees crossed each other four feet above their heads forming an arch. The hairs on his arms stood on end, and his skin buzzed.

He stopped beside her. "Are you prepared? You haven't eaten much in the last few days."

She didn't answer, but seemed to stare at the space between the trees. She stopped. What would happen if she wasn't ready? Brendon said something about his first journey here almost killing her. He remembered Alex had collapsed in the grass and how her hands shook. He stepped behind her wrapping her in his arms. "Together."

Every muscle in her body turned to stone. She resisted leaning against him. Then, like a rubber band pulled too tight, her tension snapped. She melted back into him. Her head lulled and tucked under his chin. Her arms uncrossed, and her hands clung to his. A stuttered breath skipped through her as though she suppressed tears. "One last time," she whispered, and they stepped forward as one.

Cold blasted his face whipping tears from his eyes. Lungs burned for air. Too long. He pushed forward. Something was wrong.

Chapter 66

Drew landed on his hands and knees and sucked in air. He dragged great drafts into his aching lungs while his palms stung at slapping the smooth surface. His knees ached. "Alex?" he wheezed. The ground was slick and cool under him. He glanced around. Huge stone columns rose high overhead. This wasn't home. Not Allen City. Not Hope Park.

"Alex?" louder, steadier this time. He couldn't see her in the dim light. Flames from a few torches glanced off the polished surfaces and skittered around the room casting dancing shadows. He pushed back onto his heels, breaths coming easier. "Alex!"

His call only bounced back at him. He stood on legs filled with gelatin. "Alex!" Stumbling to a column, he leaned on it drawing strength from the marble until he could stand on his own. "Alex! Where are you?"

"Not 'ere." The voice came out of the dark, scratchy and worn.

"Who's there?"

"Just an Average Joe."

Drew followed the creaking voice to a man slumped at the base of the wall. A slim shaft of light from an open door a good thirty feet away revealed a man in filthy rags. Homeless. Out on the streets too long.

Drew stood over him. "Where's Alex?"

"I told ya, not 'ere."

Were those rags once a suit? Maybe a zoot suit, long jacket, and baggy slacks. "What have you done with her?"

"Her?"

"Aye. Yes, Alex. Alexandria. Lady Alexandria. Guardian—"

"Oh, she's one of *them*." The last word spit from his mouth. "This is all *their* doing." His words disintegrated into a muddled mix of curses and accusations toward some unseen oppressor.

"Now you've gone and done it," another voice said.

Drew turned to another man in rags worse than the first man's. "Where's Alex?"

"As ol' Henry told you, the guardian isn't here, boy." The toothless man came into the light. "They have her with them."

"Them who?" Drew clenched his fists fighting the urge to seize the man and shake him senseless.

"The elders. The *Conclave*. They say they are giving her a choice." A bitter laugh skipped past his cracked lips. "Ain't allowed but to choose one option though."

Summoning his best cop tone, Drew barked. "Explain."

"You're like us, merely average. Not one of them almighty *Guardians*. The elders frown on fraternizing with the likes of us. But your guardian, your Alex, broke the cardinal rule if she took you with her into their world. Now she has to decide. Give up her birthright, who she is. Never step into another world—ordinary, plain, without a purpose or support —and she'll get to keep you. Or she continues to do as she's told, and you get stuck here with us."

"No choice. No choice. Won't allow it," Henry babbled.

"He's right. They say it's a choice, but in all the years I've been here, ain't seen no one get to return to their life in the dimension of their birth."

"There's more of you here?"

"Here? A few. Most accept they ain't ever goin' home again and try to make some kind of life for themselves here." The man shuffled toward the open door and Drew followed. Stepping out into rays of sun glistening off a silver sea, he squinted. Houses with half-round tiles in greens, yellows, and blues topped whitewashed walls. It reminded Drew of an odd mixture of Greek and Roman architecture. "Most move there. They find people to share their lives with. They're given all the food they want and everything they need. Everything except havin' children and being able to go home." He turned to enter the building again but paused. "A few of us remain here as our protest of what they've done. They make sure we get somethin' to eat, but nothin' more."

"Where's Alex? Where have they taken her to make this decision?" Given the choice, she'd beg to be let go. He believed she wanted out. Both her fear of dying young and her growing feelings for him would push her to give it all up. But though lording over her would fight her.

"Why?"

"I need to know."

The man shrugged and waddled past him, the few remaining strips of his shirt fluttering in the breeze. They walked to the end of the building and turned away from the sea. A field stretched out in front of them, and as they walked, a rise came into view on the far side about two football fields away. Perched atop it stood a building much like the one he'd exited—a structure that looked like the Parthenon in Athens.

The man pointed. "If they haven't made her decision for her, she's up there being lectured about her duty."

Drew jogged down the stairs and out onto the field.

"Where do you think you're goin'?"

Drew threw a smile over his shoulder. "To get my girl."

The man said something else, but it was lost as Drew picked up speed and ran.

His legs started to cramp before he reached the rise. They usually only did that after he'd run a couple of miles full out. It hadn't looked that far when he started. Portal travel must have a weakening effect on him as well.

He ignored the pain and started to climb. He had to get to her before they sent her away. The sun beat against his back as anger radiated up from his gut. Saying a guardian as a choice but only allowing one outcome, became another matter he needed to discuss with this Conclave. They were going to get his thoughts shot from both barrels as it were.

Pulling himself up onto the top of the bluff, Drew stomped toward the building. A list of his grievances echoed in his head. No opening lay on the side he approached near the middle of the structure, and no road to indicate which way to go. He turned right. The sun, which had stood directly overhead when he started, now appeared to touch the water on the horizon. *Surely it hasn't taken me that long. Maybe this was one of those short day worlds.*

The end of the building had no opening either. Drew started running down the long length of the temple on the backside, past its many columns until he came to the other end. Huge metal doors four times his height blocked his path. Drew stared as he caught his breath.

On the other side of this barricade, the Conclave must be pressuring Alex to leave him behind. He had to get to her. Stomping up the steps, he pictured the biggest suspect he'd ever taken down. Planting his hand on each door, he shoved with all his strength, anger, and worry over what might be happening to Alex.

The doors moved with ease, swinging open to reveal Alex crumpled on the floor before a long marble judge's bench which held seven ancient individuals in purple robes.

"STOP!"

Chapter 67

The boom of the doors hitting the walls, and the shout captured everyone's attention. Alex sat up as Drew stomped toward her. The smooth leather of his boots slapped the floor as the distance closed. Her aching heart had seized in her chest. *He came for me.* He brushed a hand over her head as he stopped one step in front of her.

"Stop what you are doing right now," he ordered the Conclave.

The elders glared at him. Some fell silent, eye wide and mouths agape. Others' color darkened as their gaze narrowed on him. Wilton, the Conclave leader, stood pointing a finger. "You do not belong here. Guards—"

"You can call your guards. Call the whole dang planet for all I care. But you will not treat Alex this way. Demanding she give up everything and deny who she is or else."

Wilton raised his hand higher, his mouth open to bellow an order.

Drew cut him off before the first word flew. "You are all a bunch of morons! You have this huge calling. Saving every world for God, but you treat your people like dung. Who in their right mind would want a job with no breaks, the threat of death at every turn, and a mandate to never have a life or a love? Terrified to have children knowing you'll never live long enough to raise them while dooming them to the same future. You sit up there and manipulate her into staying by threatening her with cutting her off from who she is. How dare you!"

Drew's voice boomed off the marble walls and filled the council chamber and Alex. He came for her. And in his best cop voice, he was giving the revered Conclave a dressing down. They stared at him, but no one stopped him. *Could there be hope for us yet?*

"You cannot continue to treat your people as expendable and expect your organization to grow. The evidence is in your own shrinking numbers. You cannot take who she is away from her, and you cannot continue to ask so much of her—of any of them. She is excellent at what she does, and your efforts would fail without her."

"But she took you with her. This is forbidden." Wilton glared at Drew.

"She didn't take me anywhere. I forced myself into two of her missions. The first to find my brother—who *you* agreed could go with her to make a new life for himself—and the next to help him save his world. You can't fault her in that. I gave her no choice."

"Yet you demand we give her the choice you did not," Mathis, another elder, said.

Yet Anna, one more elder, added, "You know too much to return to your world—"

"There is nothing there for me." Drew turned and smiled down at Alex.

Air burst from her lungs, and her ears filled with the shattering of her heart. Drew didn't want her. He was here to throw her away. Wilton said something. The pain tearing apart her insides kept her from hearing. Drew stepped forward shouting back. Hands gripped her arms and hauled her to her feet. They dragged her toward a gateway. Bellows echoed off the chamber wall. The guards tossed her through the gate.

Alex landed on her hands and knees in the hallway of her apartment. She crumpled to the floor and wailed. She had known from the beginning, Drew Merritt would cause her nothing but pain. But this agony was beyond imagining. He had said that there was nothing here for him. She was nothing to him. He didn't fight to stay with her. He

convinced them to keep her, and he abandoned her. She wasn't worth
fighting for after all. *He never loved me!*

Drew hadn't saved her. He doomed her to life alone.

Tears long since dried up. Soul empty and hollow. Alex struggled to
her feet. She stripped off her medieval clothes and threw them in the
spare room. Whether she cried on the floor for hours or days she didn't
know—and didn't care. She stumbled to her room, dressed in old sweats,
and turned to the computer. She signed into the Guardian message
board. Typed: "I'm done!" Then she ripped the special modem from the
wall with its fingerprint scanner. Alex hurled up the window, breaking
one of Drew's Christmas decorations, and tossed all three items into the
alley below.

The scattering of the priceless technology echoed the sound her
heart made at Drew's betrayal. She slammed the window closed and
pulled down every decoration. She piled them haphazardly into the tubs
he had left in one of the rooms and tossed them and the tree out the
window.

Her apartment cleansed of anything that reminded her of him and
his empty promises, she curled in bed. Covers drawn over her head to
block out the worlds, life, hope, everything. She vowed never to get up
again. *This will be where they'll find my body. If anyone ever cares to come looking.*

Chapter 68

Her end didn't come. Alex was forced to get out of bed to succumb to her cravings. It betrayed her as *he* had. She pulled a large trash bag from beneath the sink and filled it with all the protein-laden food inhabiting her refrigerator, cupboards, and drawers. No more. Never again.

She dragged the bulging bag to the trash shoot. It took her several attempts followed by grunts before her burning muscles hefted the load and sent it careening down to the bin in the basement. As she went back to her apartment, she rolled her shoulders, then grabbed her phone. Plopping on the couch, she scrolled through local restaurants that delivered.

Not Daly's. Couldn't order pizza either. Both came with too many memories. They often had Chinese at Daly's, so that was out. Too bad the ice cream parlor didn't deliver any of its myriad of flavors. She could eat a whole carton at this point. Maybe a grocery store order? They would bring multiple orders of ice cream—and toppings.

The phone slipped to her lap as she sighed. Nothing sounded good. She wasn't hungry. *Grrrr.* She put her hand on her disagreeing stomach. Barbeque? There was a rib and wings place around the corner.

With the end of her career of disguises, maybe it was time to cut off her flowing locks. She'd only managed to comb out her tangled hair before her meat and sides arrived thirty minutes later. She tipped the delivery guy and dropped the food on her table. Drew had moved it last time he came and it still sat pushed aside to make room for the Christmas tree.

A tear splashed on her hand. How could he? He promised her the world, a real holiday, friendship, laughter. Love. Her head dropped to rest on her hands and sobs racked her body again. *There's nothing there for me.* The food grew cold as her tears ran hot.

Alex drew back the covers. Her room was dark, only lit by a shaft of pale moonlight. The hunger gnawing a hole through her pushed her to her feet. She lumbered to the kitchen without turning on any lights. Wincing from the glare inside the fridge, she jerked out the food she'd ordered earlier and pulled a couple of ribs from the untouched contents. She ate at the counter and dropped the bones in the sink. After washing her hands and face, she plodded back to bed and buried herself. If only it were with dirt and not cloth.

A few days of hiding in sleep from her pain passed before Alex managed to get up, shower, and head to her studio. The key was still in its spot. The lights came on. Phone blinked with messages. *So the Conclave was still paying the bills. They hasn't cut me off—yet.*

She poked a button. "Hi. I'd like to sign up for some classes to start the new year getting in better shape. What are the hours you offer kick boxing?" The woman left her name and number.

"Hey. Is this the place where you can get sword fighting lessons?"

"Do you offer water aerobics?"

The messages continued as Alex booted up her computer. She checked the date—the third of January. Well, at least the holidays were over for everyone. She replayed the messages taking notes to contact each caller. She blew her nose and started again. It took several attempts to get all the information. She would take the list home and call later.

Alex turned off the computer and turned out the lights. She pulled the door of the office closed.

"Excuse me."

Alex jumped, her heart lodging in her throat for a moment.

"Sorry. I didn't mean to startle you." The woman in flaming pink yoga pants and animal print top bounced with excitement. "Are you open? My friend and I saw the lights on." She pointed to another woman in purple and black zebra-striped yoga pants and bright yellow shirt. They both smiled wide enough to show gleaming teeth. They were entirely too cheery. "We were hoping to get a little workout before heading home."

Home. That sounded good. Sleep would be better. "What type of program are you looking for?" The words leapt from her lips before she could stop them.

The two women glanced at each other and giggled. "Something fun and hardcore."

"There is boxing, kickboxing, Jiu-Jitsu, or Karate."

The women listened to a sampling of the different disciplines Alex had mentioned and settled on kickboxing. They learned some basics over the next forty-five minutes, their annoying giggled grating on Alex's already raw nerves. They promised to return three nights a week. It would give Alex something to focus on other than *him*—if she could tolerate their cheerfulness.

After they left, she crossed the street and buried her head in her jacket to avoid the sight of *their* restaurant. Trudging up the stairs she bumped into Mr. Thomas as he waited for the elevator in their hallway.

"Are you all right, dear?"

She nodded.

"Where is that nice officer friend of yours?"

Tears pooled blurring her vision thus smoothing the old man's wrinkles.

"He won't be around anymore."

He stroked her arm, causing the treacherous tears to escape. "I'm meeting my son for dinner, but let's talk tomorrow."

The doors whooshed open, and he was gone before she could decline. She'd have to go to the studio early to avoid him. Maybe she could find a new place to hide. She could move to a new apartment now. Nothing held her here either. Why couldn't she make the tears stop?

The elevator dinged behind her as she entered her apartment, the doors sliding opening once more.

"Al!"

Chapter 69

Her old childhood friend, Conner, stomped across the hall and thrust a file at her. "I don't know what's going on between you and the Conclave, but I'm not your messenger boy. I have a new wife I hardly see. We can't both be taking up your slack and running errands for that crotchety old group too." He spun on his heal and headed toward the elevator. "Turn your computer back on." He stepped through a gateway and was gone.

Alex stepped into her apartment and threw the file on the counter with no intention of reading it. She took the last of the ribs from the carton. As she headed to the living room, the name on the file in large purple letters caught her attention. Raiter, a world controlled by women. More advanced than Earth except for its harsh discrimination against men.

She left the file and dropped on the couch clicking on her small TV. Maybe it was time to upgrade to a big flat screen. The books behind the screen mocked her. All that training and research wasted. It didn't matter anymore. She should strip the shelves and throw it all in the alley with *his* Christmas junk.

An obnoxious sitcom flashed on the screen. Happy families with stupid problems. She flipped the channel. News. No. Another flip and a crime drama with detectives leaning over a bloody body. Absolutely not! Off.

Bed, there was only freedom in sleep—unless Drew visited her dreams. A new modem and finger scanner sat on her desk. Those meddlesome elders weren't going to let her go. And they'd resorted to breaking into her house to make their point. She belonged to them. The purple light flashed. She threw her shirt over the light and crawled into bed. But the Raiter file wouldn't let her sleep. Should a whole population suffer because she wanted to quit? What of Conner? He had said he and his wife had been picking up her assignments. There was too much to do as it was. It wasn't fair to add her burden to their heavy load. She tossed and turned for half the night. No. Even at the end of her rope she couldn't and wouldn't dump make someone else carry more because she wanted to give it all up.

She got up and scanned the file. Civil war coming. Train men to fight.

Her answer stared at her from the page. Train them to fight, and join them on the front line. I'm doomed to die on the job no matter what. Now is as good a time as any.

Chapter 70

Alex, now dressed in a foam green latex onesie, stepped through a gate. Personal aircraft hummed overhead as she hopped on the public electric train to the capital. For an advanced society, their cities were not cold angular steel buildings. An array of colors and twisting curved buildings zipped past as she glided to the heart of the city. Metal ornate carvings graced the windows and doorways, and glass in them came in every color.

The colors and style of the garments of the citizens contrasted with the beauty of the architecture. Almost everyone wore the same unisex garment she did. With rare exceptions for top officials all were the same pale green. Though hair came in the same shades as at home, all the women wore long braids, and men bore short military buzz cuts.

Alex stepped onto the platform and into a lift that slid her down the sidewalk to a round rose-colored building.

Three women in white onesies greeted her inside. She handed the document the Conclave had provided to one of them, giving her an audience with Grand Empress.

She waited in the royal reception area, staring at the elaborate mosaic floor for a few minutes. The Empress entered from beyond the dais dressed in an orange onesie with a flowing skirt that only went three-fourths of the way around her waist, to allow for free movement of her legs. She scanned Alex's electronic document shimmering on a paper-thin reader.

Here in this world, she would go by the name Ax. It wouldn't clearly be marked as a male or female name. Sometimes it was challenging to remember to answer to all the many variations of her name.

Alex waited to be acknowledged before saluting. Arms crossed over her chest one hand formed a fist and the other rested flat against her shoulder. Then her arms came down straight and swung behind her. She stood in a lunge and dipped her head.

The empress sat, again looking over her documents. "Greetings."

Alex rose, arms resting behind her.

"Ax, you've been sent here to assist in the preparations for the coming battle."

"Agreed."

"What can you do that the entire ministry of war and defense could not?"

"I have been instructed to train your men."

Springing from her chair, the empress tossed the reader aside. "Have you lost your gravity boots? Train the men to fight?"

"I can assure you, I am well grounded, Empress."

She paced the dais, her skirt swirling around her when she turned. "I know what I have read in the Holy Text that has recently been discovered, but this can't be done. You are cracked and venting oxygen. You ask too much in leaping to militarizing our tenius as our first step to righting some many wrongs." She shook her head but continued to pace and mutter mostly to herself. "Men with weapons. What will the people say? Can they even learn such skills?"

"I am well sealed. Who would fight harder for their freedom and rights than the ones earning such privileges?"

"The Board of Mothers would never agree."

"Then put me to the test. Give me two-fists of men from your own household for ten rotations. Let us demonstrate what can be done. Either the council will be impressed, and you will have men to train others, or the council will refuse their deployment, and you have lost nothing but their service in your dwelling for a short time." Alex watched her continued pacing hoping a month would be enough to prepare the men for a mock battle demonstration.

"Shouldn't the best and most able be selected? Perhaps a contest held to assure you train the elite?"

"A contest would alert your adversary to your plans. They could counter with their own regiment of men or, more likely, sabotage your effort thus proving men should have no rights at all. And if I only to train those most likely to be successful, how can you persuade the Board of Mothers my techniques will hold air?"

The empress sat drumming her fingers on her throne. "If we can find an accord, what would you require?"

Alex listed her few needs; a private, enclosed space to conduct the training out of sight from surveillance, non-lethal practice weapons, and a group of average men.

The empress asked the AI for the time. "You will be provided a sleeping unit for moon hours. Come to me again with the sun, and I shall give you my answer." The empress disappeared the way she had come. A small boy, about twelve, approached Alex.

He did not speak but waved for her to follow. Never looking at her, he led her through the serpentine corridors to a door that looked exactly like all the others. It slid open without a sound, and the boy bowed as she entered. No window and no furniture other than a bed somewhere between a twin and full size. One blanket covered it.

"Helper?"

"Yes, Ax." The AI did not have the mechanical sound of the few voice-activated devices of Earth, but it also didn't sound like a real woman.

"Where might I find something to eat?"

"What sustenance do you require?"

"Something to eat and drink."

The computer recited a short list of selections that meant nothing to Alex. "How about something that would provide strength and energy with a sweet drink."

A chime sounded, and her door opened a moment later. The same boy offered her a tray holding a plate with a dark orange mound on it and a glass of red liquid.

"Thank you."

The tray nearly fell from the lads grasp.

She poked at the goop, finally trying it. It wasn't terrible, but it wasn't Chinese food either. The drink was more pleasing though not sweet tea. Maybe if the empress agreed to allow her to stay she could train the computer to make her favorite libation.

Having nothing else to do, she climbed in bed. "Helper, wake me in enough time to return to the empress at the first sun hour."

"Affirmative."

The lights dimmed, but Alex couldn't sleep. If the Empress refused, could she go back home to face her solitary life? Could she still join the fight here and manage to get assigned to the frontlines. *All my life I have feared an early death. Now it can't come fast enough.*

Chapter 71

Alex stood before ten men of various ages and builds. After their meeting this morning, the empress had arranged their covert arrival, in the last of the moon hours, to an empty basement, in a little used government building, near the edge of the capital city. A portion of the space had been set aside for sleeping mats and two long tables stood nearby for eating. Two young boys were there to wait on them.

The men stood at attention with arms crossed ready to salute but stared at the floor. From her positions at the top of the three steps near the entrance, all Alex could see was the crown of their heads.

"Gentlemen," she refused to refer to them as Tenius, as she found it demeaning. "my name is Ax, and you have been specially selected for a very unusual endeavor. It will require things of you which will shatter all your norms and suck the air from all you have ever done."

A few shifted the weight between their feet, but none moved.

"Let us begin with instructions from the Grand Empress.

"Helper, replay the empress' message for those gathered."

"Affirmed."

"Tenius, you were selected for an unprecedented opportunity. The fate of our sphere could be anchored in what you do here. You are commanded, by your Grand Empress, to breathe the air of Ax."

The men gave a silent salute as the image dissolved.

"Then let us begin. My first breath is for you to stand tall with your arms at your sides and look at me."

The men hesitated, the boys complied first then the ten. Alex descended the stairs near the entrance to their level and walked the length of their line. She made eye contact with each one pausing until they connected with her. She smiled.

"I am going to tell you a secret. I have friends who are tenius—men. I work alongside them as equals all the time." Her heart ached as *he* flooded her memories.

A strangled gasp sent a few men into coughing fits.

"Your empress and some of the Board of Mothers have come to realize that they need you. Not as slaves, but as helpers. They know that not everyone inhabiting this sphere will agree with elevating the men— the weak, to stand beside the women as their equivalent, but we are going to prove them wrong. We have exactly ten rotations from this sun hour to make you warriors and ready to fight side-by-side with the women for your freedom."

The oldest serving boy said, "Great One, you mean to say I don't have to serve people and never talk anymore?"

The men closest to him gasped and tried to silence the lad. But Alex got down on her knees and looked the boy in the eyes. "That is exactly what I am hoping for. What would you like to do if you were free to do anything?"

"Drive a hover transport."

She stood and ran her hand playfully over his head. "Keep that in mind as you learn to fight like a soldier in the next rotations."

"Great One, I get to train too?"

"Only if you never, ever, call me Great One again. And that goes for everyone. The only way to suck the air from my enclosure is to address me by any name other than Ax."

Now the men buzzed. "But it is forbidden," one man stammered.

"Must I replay the digital of the empress? Did she not direct you to, 'to breathe the air of Ax?'"

A few heads nodded slowly.

"My next breath then is for you to repeat after me. 'Good sun hour to you, Ax.'"

The men glanced at one another, and in a timid whisper repeated her greeting.

"Well, unimpressive, but at least we have begun. Next I will know all your names."

There were awkward glances between them.

"I don't have a name, Ax," the lad said.

"What? What do the women call you?"

"Tenius… and you."

Ax went to the beginning of the line of men starting with the two younger boys. "When I come to you, tell me a name you prefer to be called. If you cannot think of one I shall assign you a name."

No one dared suggest their own names, so she did. To the precocious lad, she gave the name Peter. The other younger boy, she called John, and to the men she gave the names: Nathaniel, James, Andrew, Jude, Matthew, Philip, Simon, Luke, Paul, and Thomas.

"For my next breath, I will ask you to remind me of your new name until each becomes clean air for all of us. Now that you're named and we are introduced as equals, let us begin."

They spent the remainder of the day stretching and working on cardio exercises with a break for midday sustenance. Their fear made them tentative. But with only a month, she didn't have time to waste coddling them or waiting for them to relax. This would be as challenging for them emotionally as it would be physically.

That night, Alex curled on her mat near the boys and praying God would make a breakthrough. Soon.

Chapter 72

Almost a week passed before Alex's soldiers-in-training relaxed enough to speak during meals. Another week before true banter started. Stretches, strength training, and basic hand-to-hand tactics were practiced without resistance, though they would only spar with each other. When she handed them their mock weapons, however, they would not touch them.

"I know we are to join the warriors in the battle, but it is forbidden," Matthew said.

Luke nodded his head. "The penalty is death, if ever we take up weapons for any reason."

Alex spent much of the day trying to convince them, but they could not overcome the restrictions ingrained into them since their first breath. She sat against the far wall of the training area as the men went to eat.

Thomas, a man near her age, took a knee in front of her. His mournful eyes reminded her of Drew. "Don't be mad, Ax."

She stared at her hands. "I'm not angry, Thomas. I'm… sad. I know I can't make you want freedom. It's hard to imagine something you have never had or even dared dream of, but without your help, and others like you, your sphere will continue to disrespect men for generations if it survives the coming attack."

"But this is the way it is supposed to be." Luke said as he sat beside Thomas.

Alex's head snapped up. "Says who?"

"The Creator," they both said together.

She leapt to her feet. "Helper."

"Yes, Ax," the computerized voice responded.

"Do you have access to the first book of the Holy Text?"

"The Beginning? Yes."

"Good. Recite from the second episode starting at unit five until unit seven."

"At the time the Creator made Terra and Heaven, before any grasses or shrubs had sprouted from the ground, the Creator formed man out of dirt from the ground and blew into his nostrils the breath of life. The man came alive—a living soul," the flat computerized voice droned.

All the men returned from the meal tables and sat around her listening to the computer read. Alex made eye contact with each one. "Who did the Creator make first?"

"The *man*." Their words seeped into the room with a reverent awe.

Alex nodded. "Helper, continue with unit fifteen."

"The Creator took the man and set him down in the Garden to work the ground and keep it in order."

"And now units eighteen through twenty-two." Alex watched as the men listened.

"The Creator said, 'It's not good for the man to be alone; I'll make him a helper, a companion.' The man named the cattle, named the birds of the air, named the wild animals; but he didn't find a suitable companion.

"The Creator put the man into a deep sleep. As he slept he removed one of his ribs and replaced it with flesh. The Creator then used the rib that he had taken from the man to make the helpmate and presented her to the man."

The men jabbered between themselves in excited utterances most of which Alex couldn't understand as they talked over each other.

"Is this true? The Creator made men first and women were to help us?"

"Is the Helper allowed to lie?" Alex said.

"No, I am not," the mechanical voice declared.

Alex gave her next command watching the men, now hungry for truth, lean forward. "Helper read, Paul's letter to the gathering at Ephesus, episode five unit twenty-three."

"The male provides leadership to his life-mate female the way the Sacrifice does to His flock."

The room erupted. "We are made to be the leaders?"

"Affirmative, that was the schematic of the Creator, but I think it will take a while to become truth here." Alex stood as she explained. "Women are not to be trampled upon or treated as you have been treated. The Creator made you equals. But there were roles to be fulfilled, and it has gone off course here on Raiter. The empress has recently excavated ruins containing the Holy Text. She has been studying them, and the Creator has moved in her heart to put right what has gone so far off course. Many have not agreed with her. Thus, even now, civil war begins to tear your sphere apart."

Matthew, Luke, and Simon marched to the far end of the open practice area. Their footfalls soft on the matted floor. Hanging on the wall—like in her studio, were racks of mock weapons. They snatched them up and moved to the middle of the floor.

Simon, the oldest among them, spoke to the others. "It is time. Time to right the course, breathe the Holy Text, and join those who would do the same—regardless of their chromosome. I will not allow one more of my offspring to be created without my permission. I will stand for the right the Creator has given me. I will raise my offspring to breathe the Creator's breath."

"Huzzah!" the other men shouted.

Alex laughed. It seemed to be a universal shouted cheer, for it was in the history of her own world, in the medieval world of Vilnund, and even here in the futuristic world of Raiter.

"Ax," Luke caught her attention. "In the rotations we have remaining, you will train us to use these weapons—and how to read, for we want to know the Holy Text ourselves?"

"Acceptable. Let's eat, and we can begin with the letters." Alex knew there wouldn't be enough time to teach them to read in the time they had left to train, or before she was allowed to die in battle as she wished, or if the Conclave forcible recalled her. But she could at least lay the foundation.

Chapter 73

The Board of Mothers sat around a U-shaped table with the empress standing in the open center. The harsh jutting angles of the formations of the walls made the room look like it was constructed of shards of glass. The stark white, unadorned surfaces created a glare in the artificial light. A few weak shafts of light came from a couple of long narrow windows at one side, but they added little to soften the room. Even the tight monochromatic onesie uniforms of the women, and their severe hair styles that keep their coifs pinned to their heads, were harsh. The curved table looked out of place.

The empress took to each woman. "Mothers, we have discussed the Holy Text. The restoration of our men is vital to our continued breathing."

"The men ruled us once. Our mothers', mothers', mothers, told the tale of the abuse and abasement at the hands of men. We have stripped them of their power, but we do not inflict harm on them. We do not kill the unborn boys, or sacrifice them as they did girls in their time," one silver-haired mother said.

Another across from her spoke next. "To force them to servitude and deny them even a name. Is this not equally wrong?"

Alex listened from the corner as the council discussed all men's freedom and her twelve served silently. They slipped between the woman unnoticed to fill their drinks, remove plates and napkins, or place filled trays of nutrient blocks.

She pushed off the wall, brushed Simon's arm, and whispered. "Be on your guard." She slipped from the council chamber and out into the street. Their discussions were getting them nowhere. The board needed a demonstration. The final week of the men's training, she had taken them out on street surveillance. It taught them to blend in, act decisively, and disappear as quickly. Her time in during their on-the-job training had taught her where the opposition lurked. It was time to show the Mothers what their men were capable of.

Stepping into the dark gaming room, Alex sat at the bar and ordered a drink.

"I haven't seen you here before," a redhead in a grey onesie eyed her.

Alex nodded. "I can't take it at home any more. Mother talks of bringing the tenius she used to spawn me into our house to live. Can you imagine the horror of living with one of them? I will be laughed out of university."

"We agree. Something has to be done."

Alex leaned in as though she were sharing some covert information. "I heard the empress meets with the Board of Mothers even now to convince them to ratify the liberation of all tenius."

The redhead turned to her friends, and they invited Alex to a gaming table. It looked something like pool but with lasers and holographic balls that exploded if they were touched. Getting a beam to crisscross the table as many times as possible without blowing anything up was the goal. It was all about the angles, but Alex sucked at math. Even Tyler had been smart enough to go to Drew for math help.

She watched while listening to the women's anger grow. Then she leaned near the table. "I know a way into the council chamber."

The room fell silent for an instant, then four imaginary pool balls exploded as the woman with the laser jerked around to stare Alex.

"And how would you know something like that? You're not any older than I am." A skinny woman moved toward Alex.

"My aunt worked for one of the Mothers when I was younger. I'd go and visit her after morning courses. And when she was distracted, I'd explore."

Every activity in the room stopped as the dozen or so occupants backed her into the corner. "Tell us what you know." The redhead closed the distance.

Alex' gaze held but remained unwavering. "Do you want to waste time talking or are you ready to stop this madness? The Board of Mothers will dismiss for another fist-full of rotations in a few sun hours."

They talked, or rather shouted, amongst themselves before coming to some kind of agreement. "Lead the way," the skinny one ordered.

Chapter 74

By the time Alex returned to the council building with her small band of challengers, it had grown to a couple dozen. The women sent messages over their communication devices or pulled in others they passed. The group drew too much attention. The odds were already two-to-one for her men. Maybe this hadn't been such a great idea.

As they hid near her access point waiting for the patrol to finish its sweep, she considered her options. Should she continue with her plan to let the enemy in the door in order to prove her men worthy of an actual fight? Maybe she should come up with some excuse why only some, or maybe none, of this challenging mob could enter now. Would it be better to put off the showdown to another time? Perhaps Alex simply needed to go home.

Her stomach soured making her nauseated. She couldn't face her empty life there again. Alex closed her eyes still hoping the wave would pass before she puked. Her legs trembled and sweat dripped down her face. Even here, playing warrior-trainer in the future, she hadn't escaped Drew. He was in Peter's laughter and Thomas's eyes, Simon's kindness, and Luke's quick temper. She would never be free of the man.

Maybe she should lead the women in and stand in the way. A laser pistol to the heart or head could be an acceptable solution.

One patrol disappeared on the far side of the building, as another materialized from the rear. Now or never. She darted past a metal sculpture and through the access point Helper had shown her a few days ago. The group from the bar, and a handful of additional women, made it in the door before Alex acted as though she'd been jostled and *accidently* kicked the stopper holding the barrier open. It sprang closed, nearly slamming on a few fingers, locking them out. These were better odds.

"What's your damage?" The redhead's harsh whisper buffeted her face.

"Tripped." Alex squeezed past her to lead the way.

"Open it!"

"I can't. It sealed and will set off an alarm now." Alex kept moving.

They slipped from room to room, level to level, avoiding cameras and sensors. This futuristic government building was easier to break into than most any building on earth. But then, if you kept your only threat in such abject servitude, what did you have to worry about?

She stopped outside the council chamber. The redhead nodded. Alex reached for the door, but the woman charged ahead of her.

Alex stumbled aside as the combatants flooded the room.

Lasers whizzed.

Thomas barked an order.

Women screamed.

When she entered, she watched a few of her men pull the mothers to safety while Simon and Luke guarded the empress. Peter smashed a pistol out of one attacker's hand with a serving tray, while Mathew used his tray to slap another attacker across the face and bean a third on the head. She dropped unconscious to the floor.

As the first wave of attacking women were disarmed and wrestled to the floor, the men snatched up their weapons, stopping the rest with only minor injuries. The redhead charged to the door to escape. Alex thrust her foot in the woman's belly and kicked her back to Thomas's waiting hands.

The skinny woman escaped the fray with the men and now held a mother around the throat with a pistol to her head.

The men didn't look to Alex for direction. They acted decisively like she'd trained them. Somehow that only added to Alex's ill mood. They didn't need her. If she finished here, the wretched Conclave would send her home.

"You—you have trained the tenius," the skinny woman holding the mother captive gasped. "How could you?"

"It is time for this cruelty to end, daughter." The empress rose from behind her guard and spoke to the captor. "We have talked of this for years. I will not wait another moment in unproductive conversation. The men will be freed at once. You have the choice to accept the change or die here."

"Like a man has the skill to kill me."

"This boy is the best marksman I have seen in quite some time." Alex put her hand on young John's shoulder. "But I would never put that burden on one so young. And the first death in this fight will not be attributed to a man." She took the pistol from the boy's hand and leveled it on the woman. "I have never missed." Alex waited for heartbeat. "Surrender."

The attacker narrowed her gaze, her elbow rising slightly as the barrel of her weapon pressed firmly against the mother's head.

Alex read the signs of her eminent attack against the mother and fired first. The beam flashed through the attacker's hand that held the pistol and into her face. The captor dropped, and the room became as quiet as a tomb.

Alex's skin hummed. A gateway opened. The Conclave controlled her still. No! She didn't want to go back. She couldn't face that life again. Why couldn't that pistol have been pointed at her head?

Chapter 75

Alex wouldn't think about the open gateway and her impending journey home. In a single breath the council room went from pin drop silent to roared shouts.

"Who are you?" A mother pointed at Alex.

The mother who'd been held captive crossed her arms. "Explain yourself, Empress."

The other mothers continued to shout over one another.

"How dare you arm these men without our permission?"

"But they saved us."

"That isn't the point."

"Silence!" The empress slammed both fists on the table. "Yes, I agreed to see if the men could be trained. As you are all still alive to protest the situation, I would have to say their effort hold air." She pointed her finger at Alex. "I did not plan, ask for, or even dream of a trial by gamma ray."

Alex narrowed her gaze. "Your words had no gravity. The men needed a chance to prove themselves in a real situation."

"You brought those wild women here?" The mother who had been held with a pistol to the head charged her.

Matthew and Nathaniel stepped between them.

"Tenius, how dare you challenge me."

"My name is Matthew."

"I am Nathaniel, and you will not harm Ax."

The mother staggered back, hand to her chest gasping. "N-n-names!"

"Elite Guard, sound off," Alex called with a smile.

"John."

"Peter."

"Matthew."

"Andrew."

"Luke."

"Paul."

"Nathaniel."

"James."

"Jude."

"Philip."

"Thomas."

"Simon."

Each stood at attention and gave a military salute with their right hand over their brow. "We are the Mighty Men. The first Special Forces Operational Detachment." The voices rang out as one.

"They have proven themselves quick and decisive in their action. Not one of the attackers was killed, because of their skill, save the one I put down, and none of you were harmed. They are not only trained, they have proven themselves—from the youngest to the eldest—to be exemplary warriors." Alex inclined her head toward the empress.

The room hushed again as the mothers took their seats. The regular guard finally burst into the room.

"You're a bit late," Alex said under her breath. Her stomach knotted. She'd killed someone to prove her boys were ready. She'd brought the women here knowing what could happen—what would most likely happen. If Alex hadn't brought her in the building, the skinny woman lying on the floor would still be alive. Was this the thing that would cause the Conclave to cut her lose? She'd done the unthinkable.

"Empress?" the captain said.

"Remove the prisoners. Hold them in suspension until I have time to set their trial. And remove the body."

"Do you want her to go to the examiner?" The captain moved to the lone dead body and glanced up to the empress.

"No. There will be no investigation."

"Yes, Empress."

As the combatants were escorted from the room, Alex moved out of the way. Cold bit at her skin. The wild rush of air stole her breath. The pressure crushed her bones and ate away at her fleeing strength as she fell through a gate. She landed on her rump in Hope Park.

She yanked up a clump of grass and roared. "I hate you!"

Left without her travel bag, she was forced to walk the four blocks home in her spandex onesie drawing odd stares from all she passed. And her despair grew.

Chapter 76

Alex stomped home, head down to avoid more of the smirks and disgusted stares she'd already seen. She must look like some dominatrix on the prowl. Her face was so hot she could light tinder with it. She sprinted up the stairs to the entrance to her building and nearly collided with a utility worker. Too embarrassed to apologize, she hurried on.

The elevator dinged its arrival as she put her foot on the first step of the interior stairwell. She changed her mind to race up the stairs and turned to hop inside instead. Before she could enter, she bumped into a man in overalls. They had been white at one time. Now they were splattered with every job he'd ever done.

"Pardon."

"Sorry."

They exchanged places, and the doors closed. But as luck would have it, Mr. Thomas awaited the elevator when the doors opened on her floor.

"There you are, Alex dear. I have been awful worried about you." His gaze ran the length of her and one brow rose, but he didn't comment on her attire.

"Been working out of town."

"Well, probably for the best." Hammering came from the vacant apartment. "Looks like we're getting new neighbors. Must have completely remodeled that entire unit while you were gone. Making racket at all hours of the day and night. Haven't heard so much commotion since before you moved in." He glared and shook his cane at the men entering and exiting the unit. "Why I have half a mind to go down there…"

She patted his arm. "If they have been here for three months, they should be done soon."

"They had better be. And the new tenant better be more considerate." He stepped into the elevator. "We need to sit and chat a spell, dear." The doors closed before she could answer.

A sharp whistle, and a wink from the workers pulled a growl up her throat. She shot a sharp glare back and turned away. They disappeared into the other unit, and she snatched her key from the sill hide-away. Safe inside her apartment, she collapsed against the door and slid to the floor. Here she was again. Alone. Seeing all the places he had stood and remembering every conversation. Tears stung her eyes. *Lord, I simply can't do this any more.*

She fled to the studio the next morning not long after the sawing and banging started next door. Mr. Thomas was right, the noise grated—and she'd only suffered with it for a few hours yesterday afternoon and a short time this morning. Not that she had noticed through her tears.

The studio was quiet. There were a few angry voicemails concerning her extended closure. She contacted everyone she could and offered free sessions to make up for the inconvenience if they were still interested. She would be here as long as her slave masters kept the lights on.

Coming and going to the studio, she avoided Daly's and any other place she had been with Drew. The church bells rang out as she turned the corner on the way home. She'd been avoiding that place too. How many times had she been told that God specially chose her for an amazing purpose? She wanted to be un-chosen—immediately. This wasn't a life. There were no blessings in running herself into the ground to die alone.

The ring of the bells faded in the wind, like her hope.

When she arrived home, all was quiet. The apartment down the dark hall had the door closed. Well, at least that was over. She wondered about the new tenant for a moment. But it probably didn't matter. If she continued to refuse to acknowledge the Conclave's summons, she would be out on her ear soon enough. She hoped.

She left her apartment dark. Grabbing a pint of mint chip from the freezer, she climbed into bed. Nothing better to do.

She barely had her oversized sweatshirt pulled over her head the next morning before someone started banging on her door.

"Take a chill-pill, geez." She yanked open the door and stared at—him.

Chapter 77

Drew stood outside her door with a huge grin as though he had stood there only yesterday and the last months of pain and agony had never happened. "Hello gorgeous. What am I going to do to get you to stop opening this door without checking to see who's on the other side first?"

"How—" Words wouldn't form since her heart lodged in her throat. She couldn't stop shaking. "You escaped?" He looked the same. Short buzz-cut. Soft eyes caressed her skin filling her with emotions and feelings she wanted to bury. There were changes though. A close-trimmed beard now hugged his jaw. Oh, how she'd missed that cheeky grin.

"No." He stepped toward her, and she backed away. His head tipped, and the smile faded a little. "I didn't escape. They sent me back. After the dressing down I gave those old farts, they knew they had to change their ways." He walked toward her with slow purposeful steps, but she attempted to keep her distance as she backed away.

"Conclave doesn't change," her words were hoarse and strangled. Was it possible he looked better than before? More toned? His arms bulged with muscles beneath the short sleeves of his dark polo, and the outline of sculpted abs showed through the thin fabric. His skin, now a deep honey color, looked good enough to eat. She shook away her longing thoughts. This man had destroyed her. She couldn't go there again.

"You were there. You heard what I said."

Oh, she had heard. The knife he had left in her heart twisted again. *Don't fall for him. Don't let him in again.*

He stopped. His brows pulled together. "The Conclave—those old coots—agreed with me. They couldn't continue to send out their people all alone. I've been recruited." He reached for her, and she jerked away.

Recruited? He'd become a guardian? It couldn't be. Impossible. *Don't let him get to you.* "You're not a—you're only an—"

"Turns out I'm not as average as they wanted to believe. Brendon and I have a great-grandmother who was a guardian. The bloodline isn't strong enough to open the gates, but that's how I can sense them." He started forward again.

"But you don't believe…" *Stop!* She threw her hands out in front of her to be block his continued advance.

He pulled up. "Careful. I don't need another thump in the sternum."

How could he possibly be back—be a part of her life? She couldn't accept that her dreams might actually come true after all.

His smile grew sheepish. "I have a confession. Since we came back from Vilnund the first time, I've been attending church."

Her hip caught on the billowed arm of the couch she'd been using for support as she inched away from him. The obstruction sent her off balance, and she nearly fell. Drew tried to catch her, but she pulled away from him walking backwards along the end of her couch toward the hall.

He was lying. This was all some trick. This couldn't really be happening. She grew bolder as the anger bubbled to the surface. "No, you didn't. I never saw you."

"I'd wait for you to enter and sit in the very back. I slipped out during the last song before you could see me."

She stared at him.

"I needed to know what was different about you—and Brendon. He had changed so much. I didn't want you to think I was there because of you. I accepted Christ before we met for my birthday. I simply never brought it up. I didn't want you to think I was saying I'd become a believer merely so you'd go out with me. Then after a while it didn't seem to matter."

Her heel bunched the area rug in front of the couch, and she fell back landing on the trunk she used as a coffee table. Again, he reached for her, but she stood and pulled away. He had an answer for every objection. But this couldn't be real. Her shattered mind had to be playing a cruel joke on her.

"I thought you would be happier to see me. I mean they said they told you I was coming."

She continued to back away from him as she slipped between the couch and the trunk. She shook her head. "No one said anything."

"They sent you an email on the secure line. They prepared the apartment next door. I'm going to be your guard."

"I threw all the Conclave tech out the window—twice."

Now he stopped. "Why'd you do a thing like that?"

"I couldn't..." The tears cut her off.

He took another step.

"You said—"

"I said what?" He waited, searching her face.

"You said you didn't want me." There, she'd said it, giving voice to the words that crushed her heart.

"I never—!"

"Your exact words were, 'There's *nothing* there for me.' That's what you told the Conclave when they said you were to remain with them. I was *nothing* to you. You let them haul me to a gate and toss me through like trash down a chute."

He closed his eyes until they squeezed tight together. His head tipped to the side. How did his every move make her want to leap into his arms? Then he was still.

"Do you deny it?"

Nothing. One heart beat. Two. His eyes popped open, and they shone with delight. "I may have used those very words, but you didn't hear them at all."

"I heard you loud and clear, you—you—"

He stepped forward, and she banged into the bookcase at the end of her room. Trapped by the TV on one side and the lamp on the other, she had nowhere else to go. Drew closed the gap between them. "As I stood on that planet in front of the Conclave, I could say there was *nothing* for me to go back to *here*. No family. I didn't need my job. But I didn't abandon you." His hand reached up to caress her cheek.

Tender, real. His touch was a balm to her battered spirit. The longing she fought to deny sprang up like a tidal wave. She tried to slap his hand away, but he was faster and grasped her hand. His nose almost touched hers. The warmth of his body so near hers seeped over her skin.

"I couldn't abandon you when you sat right beside me. There was nothing left back here on earth, because you were there *with* me. And that is all I wanted."

That's all he wanted? I'm all he wanted? She relaxed against the books and stared at him. His other hand slid around to the small of her back. "When that Conclave leader, Wilson, ordered you returned, I charged at him and told him there would be a war if he did anything to keep us apart. By the time I realized they had already sent you back, I almost took his head off. They restrained me, and when I could finally calm down enough to hear them, they told me about my great-grandmother. They had no intention of separating us; they wanted me to train so I could come join you."

Join me? It isn't a dream? This is really happening? Drew held her. He wanted her.

His forehead pressed to hers. "There has not been a moment in the last year of training that I have not thought about you, Alex Wright. I love you."

His lips pressed to hers. Soft, gentle. He held her his arms, and they were going to be together. She released all doubt and let her arms encircle his neck. She pressed in for a deeper kiss. He answered with a passion that curled her toes.

He released her lips, and his forehead again pressed to hers as he stared into her eyes. "So, where are we off to first?"

Glossary

Bailey - the courtyard itself inside the defensive wall surrounding an outer court of a castle.

Boards – long picnic style tables with bench for serving many a meal in the laird's hall

Broadsword – a sword having a straight, broad, flat blade

Bairn – another term for a child (Scottish)

Canter - an easy gallop.

Coif – *armor* - a covering for the head and neck, made of leather, padded cloth, or mail.

Crenel – any of the open spaces between the merlons of a battlement

Crenelated – referring to the top edge of a castle battlement wall with the even alternating tall and open scetions

Doublet – a close-fitting outer garment, with or without sleeves and sometimes having a short skirt, worn by men in the Renaissance

Duster – a long, light overgarment, worn especially in the early days of open automobiles to protect the clothing from dust.

Gambeson – a quilted garment worn under mail armor

Hauberk – a long defensive shirt, usually of mail, extending to the knees.

Jonessing – *slang* an intense desire; craving specifically for illicit drugs

Keep – the innermost central tower of a medieval castle

Larder – a room or place where food is kept; pantry.

Lying in – a period at nearing the end of pregnancy of being in childbed; confinement

Merlon – (in a battlement) the solid part between two crenels

Pace – old measurement of distance about 3 feet

Portcullis - (especially in medieval castles) a strong grating, as of iron, made to slide along vertical grooves at the sides of a gateway of a fortified place and let down to prevent passage

Rushes – In medieval Europe, loose (or woven into mats) rushes would be strewn on the floors in dwelling for cleanliness and insulation. They were often sprinkled with herbs.

Stouthearted - brave and resolute; dauntless.

Waster – a wooden practice sword

Zoot Suit – a man's suit with baggy, tight-cuffed, sometimes high-waisted trousers and an oversized jacket with exaggeratedly broad, padded shoulders and wide lapels, often worn with suspenders and a long watch chain and first popularized in the early 1940s.

About the Author

Michelle Janene (Murray) is a teacher by day and writes Christian fantasy and historical fiction in all her free time. She lives in Northern California with two crazy dogs and the characters of her imagination.

If you enjoyed *Guardians of Truth* please review it on your favorite site.

You can connect with Michelle on:
Facebook: Turret Writing or Strong Tower Press
Twitter: @MichelleJaneneM
Pinterest: www.pinterest.com/michellejanene
Goodreads: Michelle Janene
StrongTowerPress.com
TurretWriting.com

Other Books

Check out these books also by Michelle

Mission: Mistaken Identity

The Changed Heart Series:
God's Rebel
Rebel's Son
Hidden Rebel

Seer of Windmere

Barbarian Hero